# Gone Crazy

## by

## Terry Korth Fischer

*Rory Naysmith Mysteries, Book Three*

Cover Art by *The Wild Rose Press, Inc.*

The Wild Rose Press, Inc.
PO Box 708
Adams Basin, NY 14410-0708
Visit us at www.thewildrosepress.com

Publishing History
First Edition, 2024
Trade Paperback ISBN 978-1-5092-5597-9
Digital ISBN 978-1-5092-5598-6


Published in the United States of America

## Dedication

For my family, and the wonderful crazy friends I call family. You fill my heart with joy.

Chapter One

The wind caught Detective Rory Naysmith's fedora as he stepped off the curb. He made a grab for the brim, and the biting cold slithered down his collar. Man, he wished someone would plop him down in Key West.

Snow dust swirled in the Winterset Police Department parking lot and the barren trees along the tarmac edge were black silhouettes against a gray sky. Another gloomy February morning, the season not half over. Yup, call him crazy. The Florida Keys, seventeen-hundred miles south and more than a twenty-four-hour drive, might as well be on the other side of the world. Still, today, he'd prefer sunshine and warm breezes to the Midwest winter. That, and a meaty case. With crime controlled, his daily tasks bordered on the mundane. Which was good for a small Midwest town, but not for a seasoned detective with an itchy need to detect.

Rory entered the station from the back, the closest door to his office at the rear and surveyed the open vestibule that served the public and the hallway leading to the city offices. February popped up awfully soon after Christmas. He swiped the fedora from his head, rubbed his balding pate, and sighed. Confound it, February meant another gift-giving holiday. He was too old to spend time worrying about presents. Particularly, picking out gifts for women. He unlocked his door, switched on the light, and entered.

When he first took the position with WPD, he wasn't sure he'd ever adapt to working in a small town, but he had. The setup was different from the Omaha precinct where he'd work prior to becoming the only detective for WPD's eleven-officer squad. Because Winterset was the county seat, it was convenient to have law enforcement and civil services housed in one compact downtown compound. The police chief also served as the city planner and the town's civic offices were housed down the hall from the chief's office.

" 'Morning, Mister Detective. Decide to grace us with your presence?" The voice of the department's civilian dispatcher, Sunny Gomez, came through the wall speaker and filled his office.

Rory hung his hat next to the door and over the CCTV camera pointed directly at the desk, then settled his coat and scarf on the hook behind the door. "Good morning to you."

"Chief Mansfield has been checkin'." The glee in her voice detectable even through the public address system.

"I'd expect no less." It was too early in the morning for Sunny. He unlocked his desk drawer and removed the binder containing the Tom Hutchinson investigation. "I suppose he is looking for my report."

" 'Course. He's been off all weekend. He'll expect to read it so he can fill the mayor in over their breakfast."

"I've had two days off, too."

"If you want my opinion, and I know you do, I'd toot it and boot it."

Rory sat, opened the binder, frowned. There wasn't much to report. Did Chief Mansfield think he was super-human? He couldn't invent developments. Six days ago, the Hutchinson Hardware store had been burglarized. Entering through a door in the back, the power tool aisle had been stripped clean. Luckily, no one was injured during the crime which happened in the early hours after midnight, but the store had lost all its electrical hand tools. Fingerprints were numerous, too many to eliminate those belonging to customers and staff and isolate the perpetrator. Tire marks in the alley by the back door indicated a trailer was used to move the equipment on to new homes. With no way to hunt down the burglar, and unless he was caught red-handed, Rory was at an impasse. No witnesses, and unfortunately, no surveillance cameras outside the back door or in the tool aisle. It became a wait and see game, hoping the criminal incriminated himself. Or herself? Rory had learned to keep an open mind. He wondered if the night patrol had any news. They had been tasked with running a drive-by and keeping an extra vigilant eye on the hardware store.

"Sunny?"

She didn't respond.

Knowing the patrol's log would be with the day sergeant, he opened the door to dispatch and stepped in. Sunny Gomez sat in an L-shaped workspace with three over-sized monitors. In a blue shirt and jeans, her dark hair tumbled around her head in riotous curls. Large heart shaped earrings dangled from her ears. When the phone rang, she held up a ruby lacquered nail, gesturing for him to wait while she took the call.

Rory crossed to the day sergeant's desk. Powell wasn't there, but the in-basket which normally contained the printed patrol logs sat on the corner. The detective rifled through. Nothing interesting. He took a seat and glanced at the monitors over the pass-through window that separated the dispatch office from the public access vestibule. He still felt that the window's bulletproof glass, complete with money pass-through, made the station look more like a bank than a law-enforcement facility. Under the monitors, Sunny had tacked a lacy heart streamer. Cupid cutouts were taped around the window.

"Roger that," Sunny said slamming down the phone. "Chief is on the way. Looking forward to his short stack and cuppa with the mayor." She swung around to face him. Rather—the set of pulsating red lips pinned to her chest faced him. "You ready?"

"As I'll ever be." Rory stood. "I don't suppose Powell filed the patrol logs from last night. Where is he anyway?"

"In the file room."

Rory grimaced.

"Have you decided on a Valentine's Day gift for your sweetie?" Sunny beamed a smile in his direction. "Esther don't need no chocolates this year."

"What's wrong with candy?"

"You had a whole weekend to pick out a gift. Don't tell me you squandered the time."

"And that would be your business because…?"

"Us girls got to stick together. Don't be getting her a vacuum cleaner either. It's about time you presented her with something personal." She studied him through squinted eyes. If her intent was to make him feel uncomfortable it worked.

"What do you suggest? I could do a nice dinner in the city and a dozen roses."

"That's a cop out." She grinned. "No pun intended. Esther deserves more, and you know it."

Yeah, he knew it. But wondered what the right thing was. They'd been seeing each other for a year but he knew Esther would hate the sweetheart and sentimental route as much as he did. Maybe a nice evening out. A place they hadn't been, maybe a fancy restaurant in Omaha.

"Officer Thacker's got himself a girlfriend." Sunny's grin lit her face. It was plain that she wanted to gloat, thinking she knew more than Rory did.

For the past year, Clarence Thacker had been his roommate in the apartment above the old Hillard Department Store. What had started out as a convenience while Rory recovered from ankle surgery grew into a full-fledged friendship. Thacker, a rookie when Rory arrived in Winterset, had progressed from street guide, to detecting assistant, to policeman during that time. Although there was a twenty-five-year gap in their ages, they had formed a bond. His and Thacker's schedules differed, allowing them their personal time to themselves. Apparently, too much time. Rory had no idea the younger man was dating.

He scratched his forehead trying to decide if the news was good or bad. "You sure about that?"

" 'Course I'm sure. I ain't blind to love like some old geezer I know."

"Huh? Who are you calling old?"

The door connecting the police department to the city offices opened; Sergeant Richard Powell stepped in. He cleared his throat, ran a finger around his starched collar, and gave Rory an accusing scowl. Without greeting, he crossed to the duty desk and turned abruptly to face Rory.

The first thing Rory noticed was the bold red bow

tie. Then he spotted the disapproving expression. " 'Morning, sergeant."

"You had best warn Thacker about that girl," Powell said.

"He can make his own decisions." Did everyone except him know about Thacker and his friend? And what was wrong with the girl anyway? Powell would take too much pleasure in Rory's ignorance of the situation. He wasn't going to give him the satisfaction. "Thacker is a grown man. He does as he pleases."

Powell harrumphed. Rory frowned.

"Chief's here…" Sunny sang out.

Rory glanced at the surveillance monitors. The screen displayed Mansfield's office and showed the chief hanging his coat on the rack, then moving to his desk. The detective went to face the inevitable.

In his early fifties, Bryce Mansfield, had thick gray hair, deep, hooded eyes, and a chiseled jaw. From behind a large mahogany desk, he jutted his chin and roared, "Naysmith, I need that update."

"There's nothing new to tell you, sir."

"Don't give me that. I need concrete headway to take to Mayor Becker." He crossed his arms as his frown deepened. "I'm not going empty handed."

"The mayor will understand that the theft is unsolved. If it could be, I would have done it already."

"You're not getting insolent; are you?" The glare from his hooded eyes bore into Rory's.

"Our best hope is another break-in," Rory said calmly. "This time drawing attention during the act, or at least in a location with working surveillance cameras. The power tools taken from Hutchinsons didn't have serial numbers, therefore, there's no way to recognize

6

them once they're sold or fenced. I've talked to all the pawn shops in town. They'll keep an eye out and will let me know if anyone is trying to move them."

"I can't carry excuses to the mayor."

"You won't need to if you distract him with an update on his pet project, Janus Chances. That'll keep him happy."

"Ahhh, Janus Chances." The chief rubbed a finger under his chin. "That does seem to be moving along nicely."

"With several prominent citizens offering to employ the parolees from county jail," Rory grumbled. "Beats me why they're coughing up jobs that will fulfill community service obligations. But it's taken off. All thanks to our mayor."

Mansfield relaxed his shoulders and picked up a report from the in-box. "Here is the latest—"

"Spare me the details." Taking convicted criminals and placing them in the hardworking, trusting citizens' homes begged for trouble. Rory agreed they deserved a break, had served their time, but the proximity to the worldly goods and big hearts in town worried him.

Behind him the wall-mounted monitor that displayed the patrol car video downloads must have started up. From his position he couldn't see it, but Mansfield's attention was immediately drawn to the screen. The chief sat forward and picked up a remote-control device. "Damn thing is still a nuisance," he said, pressing the button on the remote. "It's Thacker arriving for duty. Or is he ending his shift? I can't keep it straight."

"Should be ending his shift," Rory said turning to view the monitor. It was black. "Thacker wasn't home when I left this morning." He stood, crossed to the door, and paused. "I don't want to overstep my bounds, but can I ask if you plan to give your wife a gift for Valentine's Day?"

Mansfield looked surprised. Rory cringed. Oops. Too personal? He decided against sharing his insecurities with his old police academy classmate.

Mansfield surprised him by answering. "We don't usually exchange gifts. Heck, Betty and I've been married for over two decades. Not that our devotion to each other has waned, but there's no need to exchange gifts to prove our love for one another. It's not like you and Esther." Rory felt his face flush. Mansfield continued, "And it's not like Thacker and that new gal." He shook his head, a sly smile on his lips. "Young love."

So, Chief Mansfield knew Thacker had a new girl, too. Rory *was* the last to know.

"I'll tell you what"—Mansfield slid his middle drawer open and reached in—"I have two tickets to the Literary Awards Banquet. Betty is keen to go, but I'm really not a poetry fan. You know what I mean?" He held them out to Rory. "Take Esther to the shindig. She will thank you. Gals eat that written love sonnet, sappy poetry stuff up. It will soften the blow when you don't give her the gift she wants."

"What do you mean?" Had Esther shared her expectations with Betty? He wasn't so hot at reading subtle female signs. He excelled at solving crimes and failed at understanding most women—unless they were criminals. He did know he enjoyed Esther's company. A feeling, he hoped, she reciprocated. Esther wasn't a frilly girl, and they weren't teenagers.

After thanking Mansfield, Rory tucked the tickets in

his pocket and went back to his office hoping to find Thacker there; he wasn't. Rory fingered the tickets, then pulled them out. Across the top the words Winterset Literary Guild Award Banquet were printed, and below, Old Orchard Restaurant. In smaller lettering he read the time, tomorrow evening at seven.

Rory picked up the phone and called Esther. It went to voicemail, and he left a message.

By the time she returned his call, he'd forgotten all about Key West and soft spring breezes.

Chapter Two

Rory parked the city issue sedan on the street and walked around the house to Esther's back door. Laugh lines crinkled at the corners of her eyes as he stepped into the homey kitchen. In his opinion, Esther radiated health and had a substantial look which he called handsome. Both led to his amazement that she had never married.

At fifty-two, gray had begun to lighten her thick auburn hair. Tonight, Esther wore attractive dark slacks, and a sweater topped with a pearl necklace. He noticed her low-heeled shoes. The fact that she was six feet tall might intimidate a lesser man, but it didn't bother him.

"How fancy do you think this award ceremony will be?" she asked. "I opted for comfortable over fashionable."

"You look stunning."

She lifted one brow. "So, you approve?"

"Naturally. We aren't the ones being honored."

"I spent some time looking into the affair." She handed him her wool coat. As he helped her into the garment, she said, "There are three poets reading: Phoebe Sheehan, a retired librarian; Lillie Anderson, an English professor at the community college; and Perry Benson, a local boy. I didn't find much on him. There is almost too much info on Professor Anderson. I've done taxes for Phoebe Sheehan the last two years, although I wouldn't call her a friend and was surprised to discover she is a poet."

Excitement brought a flush to her face. "The write-up in the Gazette says each poet has a poem featured by the literary magazine, *Sandhill Whispers*. It's not so much an award ceremony as it is to celebrate local talent promoted by the Winterset Literary Guild. Plus, Adeline Yost, the Nebraska State Poet, is presenting. I love her work."

He nodded, taking her by the elbow and escorting her to the car as she chattered. "I read there is a local movement to appoint a Winterset Poet Laureate. This puts three local artists in contention for the honor."

"So, you know one, and are familiar with the work written by the other two," he said.

"No, not really, but they must be talented. After all, they've been published."

Rory wasn't so sure that publishing a poem in a magazine qualified them as talented. He'd reserve his opinion until after hearing their readings.

Once they were on the road, he asked, "Why would Winterset need a Poet Laureate? What would he or she do?"

Esther spent the full twenty-minute trip to Old Orchard Restaurant explaining the Arts Council. Who did what and who didn't make money writing poetry and the need to advance the arts within Nebraska. Rory listened with half an ear, happy that he'd made her happy. *Thank you, Bryce Mansfield.*

He knew more than he needed to know by the time they pulled into old Orchard's drive. Rory was only too familiar with the establishment, harboring a haunting and vivid memory from his visit to the wine cellar last winter. Ten miles from town and surrounded by a working orchard, the restaurant was the town's only fine dining venue. The apple orchard sparkled with white lights turning the bare trees into a fairy land in the winter's night. The gardens and pond were outlined in the landscape.

When he presented the tickets for the Guild's private party to the hostess, Rory realized that because this evening's event was special, the restaurant was closed to the general public. A sliding panel closed off a large section from the dining area, making a smaller, more intimate setting. At one end, a velvet curtain hung behind a raised platform. Small round tables faced the temporary stage where a stark podium and several empty chairs stood. A spotlight lit the area; otherwise, the room was empty.

Rory heard murmuring voices coming from another direction.

"The guests are having cocktails in the bar," the hostess explained, handing him a printed program. He passed it to Esther as the hostess continued, "There is a reception hosted by the Literary Guild before the readings and a celebration for the award recipient after the presentations. You'll want to join them in the bar." She gestured toward a doorway. "If you'll select a table, I'll reserve your seats until the readings begin."

Rory noted the reserved signs on the tables. "Pick a spot, Esther. I'd suggest somewhere near the platform so you'll be able to hear everyone clearly."

After taking a moment, she indicated a spot in the back. Relieved that she'd picked a location where he wouldn't have his back to the room, he took her elbow and gave it an affectionate squeeze. They followed the hostess to their table, waited while she placed the tented reserved placard in the center, then followed her to the bar.

The murmurs grew as they entered the bar area where the crowd had gathered. The Guild members were easy to identify—tuxedos on the men, jewels on the women. In his tweed jacket and wool slacks Rory wondered if he was underdressed and slipped the hat from his head. Esther smiled sweetly, appearing to be unaware she was the only woman not dressed to the nines.

"Which one is Phoebe Sheehan?" he asked, leading her into the throng.

Esther craned her neck to look for her client in the crowd. "I don't see her, but she'll be easy to identify. Look for a woman in her seventies with white hair. And if you're close enough, you'll notice the dog hair on her clothing."

Dog hair? Rory spotted Mayor Becker and his wife, Sophie, across the room and raised a hand in greeting. "Do I detect disapproval?"

"No. But Phoebe is devoted to an aging beagle named Rosco. And Rosco has a shedding problem. It's hard to miss."

"This from a cat lover who regularly overlooks cat dander?" he asked.

"Commander does not have dandruff."

Rory laughed. "I could use a drink."

"I'll take a white wine if you manage to snag a waiter."

"Why don't you join the Becker's and I'll order drinks at the bar?"

She agreed and they separated, Esther joining the mayor's party and he going to the bar. Waiting his turn, shoulder to shoulder, and two deep in the crowd, he concluded that not only were literary types formal, but they were also thirsty. He ended up standing behind a lady with snow white hair. He wasn't good at guessing age, but from Esther's description, and all the dog hair clinging to the lady's evening jacket, he presumed it to be Phoebe Sheehan.

He was about to introduce himself when he was elbowed off center by a woman dressed in a man's tuxedo. Bending close to Phoebe's ear, the woman growled. "This is ridiculous. You have some nerve."

Rory wasn't happy with the wait either, but it was typical that while the wine was free, and flowing, it was hard to get a drink.

The woman grabbed Phoebe's arms from behind, pulled her back from her position at the bar and barred Phoebe from turning to face her. "You can't truly believe you'll be named Poet Laureate?" she charged, her volume rising as she continued the rant. "Plagiarizer. You're no better than your father. Remove your name from consideration or I'll expose you for the fraud you are."

With a whimper, Phoebe wretched her arms free, sputtered a response under her breath, and fled, knocking Rory into the man standing behind him.

"Hey." The man gave him an angry scowl.

"Sorry." Rory looked in the direction Phoebe had taken, but she was gone. Her accuser huffed off in the opposite direction. Rory addressed the man, "I am sorry. Can I order you a drink?"

When he finally had their drinks in hand, Rory joined Esther standing with the Beckers. He handed her a Chardonnay. "Guess who I ran into at the bar?"

She raised one brow in question.

"Phoebe Sheehan," he said. "She seems nervous."

"Dignitaries at three o'clock," Mayor Becker said under his breath, and turned to greet a party-of-three tuxedo-clad, blue haired academics. The mayor, a natural politician, met each with a handshake, a smile, and offered introductions all around. Rory was glad not to share the limelight.

Discreetly, Rory asked Esther, "What time do the readings start?"

Esther took his arm to silence him, then exchanged a pleasantry with a man whom she identified as the director of the Academy of Mid-Western Poets. He'd have to wait for the answer.

Rory used the time to wonder where Phoebe Sheehan had gotten off to, who the woman in the tuxedo was, and what her argument with the poet could be. He wanted to share what he had seen and overheard with Esther yet didn't want to do so with others within earshot. He'd wait until they took their seats in the other room.

After a full hour devoted to hob-knobbing, everyone finally headed to the presentation room and the ceremony began. The Guild members sat at the front tables. A particularly distinguished looking gentleman stood at the podium. Rory held Esther's chair as she took her seat. "What is it that you are so anxious to tell me?" she asked.

"In a moment," he said, "Do you have the program?"

Esther pulled the pamphlet from her bag and handed it to him. "What are you looking for?"

"A woman in a tuxedo." He opened the program and

scanned the contents. It contained a short bio for each featured poet, including an author photograph. Phoebe Sheehan, retired librarian, Winterset Community College graduate, would read two selections from her chapbook. Her photograph was more glamor shot than portrait—and dated because her locks were more brunette than white.

Perry Benson, Winterset Library Poet-in-Residence, would present two works from his collection titled, *Midwest Muddle.* His picture revealed both arms tattooed from forearm to wrist, giving him the appearance of a shouting Prisoner-in-Residence at a state penal institution.

And last but not least, Lillie Anderson, comparative literature professor, Winterset Community College, reading from her published work, *Wildfire Lies.* Professor Anderson's author shot confirmed she was the tuxedoed assailant—but not why she'd threaten Phoebe.

He turned to Esther. "I overheard Lillie Anderson and Phoebe Sheehan in the bar. Anderson accused Sheehan of plagiarism and following in her father's footsteps, whatever that means. She said that if Phoebe didn't admit her fraud, she, Professor Anderson, was willing and able to expose her." Esther's face clouded as he continued. "It sounded more like a disagreement about Phoebe being considered for tonight's award than to the actual plagiarism. I'm guessing it wasn't Lillie's poetry in question."

"Are you sure?"

"Yes. And Professor Anderson manhandled Phoebe Sheehan."

"What does that mean?"

"Grabbed her by the arms and retained her against

her will. You know, manhandled."

"To be politically correct you should use the term strong armed."

Rory opened his mouth but decided it was better to remain silent.

The waiter appeared, lit the candle on the table centerpiece, then took their orders for wine. When he stepped away, Rory said, "I've always heard the academic world can be vicious but didn't believe it. Plus, this Lillie Anderson is dressed like a man."

"How does a man dress?" Esther asked.

Rory cleared his throat and studied the program.

"There's Phoebe now," said Esther gesturing to the white-headed woman making her way up front to join the dignitaries by the stage. She stumbled, then reached out to a nearby table to steady herself. "It looks like she's drunk."

"She wasn't an hour ago," he said, "but a couple stiff ones..."

"She's having a hard time finding her way." Esther stood, hesitating and placing a hand on his shoulder. "I think I'll see if she's okay. It might just be nerves."

Rory let her hand slip away. Patrons milled around in a confused manner, taking time to find their assigned seats, and seemingly reluctant to end conversations they'd started in the bar. He watched Esther thread her way through the tables and make her way to Phoebe. With an arm on the poet's shoulder, Esther helped she take a seat by the temporary stage and sat next to her, their heads bent in conversation. He wondered at the exchange. Soon she returned.

"Well, is she drunk?"

"No. But she isn't feeling well. She says she started

to feel ill this afternoon."

"Presentation jitters then?"

The man at the podium tapped the microphone and a loud thump exploded from the overhead speakers. "Looks like we might be starting," Rory said.

Esther fingered her pearls. "I think it's more than being nervous or simple stage fright. Phoebe looks pale and if she complained that she felt nauseous…after all, she was in the bar trying to get a soda to settle her stomach. Which she didn't manage to do. You were there along with the crowd, it was chaos. I think I'll order her a hot tea."

Esther waved at a waiter as he passed. Failing to get the waiter's attention, she stood. "They'll be a minute getting started. I'll just pop into the bar, order the tea, and be right back." Before Rory could object, she was gone.

The guests slowly took their seats. The man at the podium thumped again. "Testing. Testing. Can everyone hear me?" The guests at the tables quieted. Those roaming made for their seats.

"Good evening, ladies and gentlemen. Welcome to the Winterset Literary Guild Awards banquet. I'm George Martin, Guild President." There was some modest clapping, and more chair scraping. "We have a lovely evening planned for you. Our State Poet, Adeline Yost will open, followed by three Winterset distinguished poets: Phoebe Sheehan, Lillie Anderson, and Perry Benson. From these talented poets, one will end the evening as the first Winterset Poet Laureate." Gentle applause followed. "But first, let me introduce the literary board members." He motioned for the front row to stand, and one-by-one introduced them, followed by more clapping. Rory hoped Esther would hurry. He didn't want her to miss the presentation.

George Martin introduced Adeline Yost who, along with him, had a seat by the podium on the stage. Still no Esther. The overhead lights dimmed, and Adeline read a poem about open space and shooting stars that ended in glowing horizons. Rory was impressed with her melodic voice but thought poetry ought to rhyme. Less along the lines of "By the shores of Gitche Gumee, By the shining Big-Sea-Water", and more "high-diddle diddle, the cat in the fiddle."

Where was Esther? Should he check on her?

Yost finished and introduced Lillie Anderson. The professor mounted the stage with encouragement from the crowd, then confidently crossed the stage to join Adeline at the podium where she accepted the accolades with grace. Her tuxedo clad figure was a stark contrast to Adeline's simple long skirt and flowing tunic top. In Rory's mind the long coarse hair falling past Lillie's shoulders was ubiquitous in academia, her suit a blatant statement against the role women played in a male dominated world. He recalled the menace in her voice as she accosted Phoebe Sheehan in the bar. Professor Anderson would make a formidable enemy.

As the spotlight highlighted the poet, Adeline Yost explained the structure for the piece Lillie had selected to read. "From her chapbook, *Wildfire Lies*, Professor Anderson will read a *villanelle*."

Villanelle? It sounded as menacing as her accusations in the bar. Rory listened but continued to be more concerned by Esther's absence.

"The villanelle," Yost explained, "is a most difficult poetic form. Many artists avoid them, as it can be quite intimidating. The form has nineteen lines, adheres to a particular structure, and offers a rhyme scheme."

*Good. A rhyming poem. Right up my alley.*

Adeline continued, "Five three-line stanzas, followed by a four-line stanza. You will notice the first and third lines are repeated three more times throughout the poem at dictated locations. Composing a villanelle is no easy feat. It is so difficult to write that I, myself, have only done so, once. And, I have no intention to attempt a second." There was mild laughter. She paused for effect, then announced, "Professor Lillie Anderson, reading *The Plains Echo.*"

Adeline stepped from the spotlight, allowing Anderson to step to the microphone. She looked out over the room and waited for a silence to settle over the audience. When all was quiet, she took reading glasses from where they were tucked into her cummerbund, put them on, situated her printed page on the podium, and began.

Rory wasn't impressed, but what did he know? Anderson had a stage presence and a flair for the dramatic. And Adeline Yost had set the tone by announcing the piece's excellence. It was as Anderson raised her voice in the required repeated first stanza line that he saw Esther step into the room. Moving deftly through the tables with a large mug between her hands, she threaded her way to the front tables where Phoebe sat and drew the audience's attention as she advanced. So intent was Esther in keeping the sloshing contents within the mug that she didn't notice the disturbance she created.

Her advance, however, didn't escape Anderson's notice. The professor's reading glasses slid down her nose and she glared over the rims. Clearly flustered, she said to George Martin. "Mr. President, are you going to allow this interruption? Must I ignore this blatant attempt by Phoebe Sheehan to undermine my poetry reading?"

Red-faced, Mr. Martin stood and stammered, "I a…assure you. Th…this is not the conduct expected from our members." His focus on Phoebe, he demanded, "Miss Sheehan, are you quite finished?"

Phoebe, taking a gulp from the mug, froze. From Rory's position at the back, he watched her rise. Once on her feet, she swayed and put a hand on Esther's shoulder, and steadied herself. Esther took the mug from her hand.

"George…" Phoebe croaked, drifting to the left before righting herself. "George…" She fell forward and collapsed into a heap before the stage.

The audience gasped. A black clad waiter appeared from nowhere and rushed to the crumpled poet. He bent over her for a moment then announced, "Call an ambulance."

George Martin took over the microphone. "Is there a doctor in the house?"

Wide-eyed, Esther met Rory's gaze.

The detective nodded. Then reached for the light switch and flipped on the overhead lights.

Chapter Three

Clarence Thacker poked his head through the open doorway to the WPD dispatch office and caught Sergeant Powell checking his cuticles. "Sergeant," he asked in his deep and solemn voice, "anything new?"

"Ambulance was called out to Old Orchard." Unconcerned, Powell continued his grooming.

"I caught that on the radio. Any details?"

Powell glanced up. "Some lady collapsed at the poetry reading. She's on her way to Winterset Memorial. I understand your roomy was there."

Naysmith at a poetry reading? It was true they shared the apartment. But they weren't joined at the hip. There was no reason why he would know Rory's plans for the evening.

It wasn't unusual for the two men to go days without seeing each other. Naysmith, the department's only detective, worked a standard nine-to-five schedule unless there was a hot investigation going on, then he worked around the clock. Thacker, a patrolman, worked a rotating schedule so the two men spent little time together in the apartment. They shared the lodgings, the gym setup on the ground floor, and tolerated a kinship with a tabby named Commander, which Rory had adopted after its owner's death. Or maybe it was that Commander tolerated them?

"Poetry seems a strange entertainment, even for

Rory," Thacker said.

"Chief worked that out for him. Pawned off the tickets before Naysmith knew what was happening."

The phone on Powell's desk rang. While he took the call, Thacker checked the roster. He still had an hour left to his shift and wanted to know who was coming in to relieve him. Things had been quiet, and he had plans for when he got off at ten. If there was time, he'd study for the criminal investigator test. He waved at Powell and headed to the computer station where the patrol officers entered their reports. "I'll be doing paperwork."

Powell's voice followed him down the hall. "Seeing that Ho-Chunk girl when you get off?"

Thacker didn't reply. The sergeant had an opinion on everything, and his choice in companions was not Powell's business.

\*\*\*\*

Rory stood with Esther, the Beckers, and Guild President Martin, waiting for the EMTs' arrival. Phoebe rested on the floor, where an off-duty nurse tried to keep her comfortable. After she collapsed, the poetry reading had followed suit. The guild president could hardly ignore the woman lying there, even though it was a unique and memorable evening. Thankfully, after the first shock, the guests sat quietly, or had found their way back to the bar.

Phoebe Sheehan was conscious but disoriented when the EMTs arrived, did a quick, professional check, and said her blood pressure was elevated. She complained that she felt lightheaded and kept a grip on Esther's hand.

When they loaded Phoebe onto the stretcher, Esther said, "She shouldn't be alone at the hospital. I don't know her family, but we should notify someone."

Mayor Becker agreed. "Everyone has a family."

"She has friends," said Sophia Becker. "She spent enough years at the library to know most people in Winterset. But I never heard her speak about family."

Esther picked up Phoebe's few belongings, then shrugged into her coat. "That settles it; I'll ride with her to the hospital. Rory, do you mind?"

He wasn't thrilled, but it was his civic duty to look after the Winterset citizens. Unfortunately, Phoebe Sheehan fell into that category. "I can follow the ambulance and make sure you get home once she's admitted."

After the ambulance left with Phoebe and Esther on board, the waiter came to Rory. He held out a small clutch purse. "This was under the chair where Miss Sheehan was sitting. I looked inside. All her identification is in there. She'll need it to check-in at the hospital."

Rory wondered how the medical professionals had progressed as far as the ambulance without seeing her insurance card. Perhaps Phoebe was known well enough they didn't need to bother with things like insurance or kin. He took the wallet from the waiter, thanking him.

It contained the usual: driver's license, library card, Medicare card, and three major credit cards. No card naming an emergency contact. Sophie looking over his shoulder as he rifled through the papers, finally, said, "Phoebe never married and had no children. So, I don't know who you'd notify."

"Siblings?" Rory asked and pulled out twenty-six dollars from the change compartment.

"Her house is up the road," said the mayor. "I

believe she has a housekeeper. The Sheehan mansion is too large for a single woman to manage. The housekeeper isn't a relative, but she may know how to contact one."

Rory gazed at Sophie in amazement. "There's a mansion in Winterset?"

She laughed. "McMansion is more like it. Michael Sheehan was a professor at the community college. In his teaching days, he bought the old Webster mansion on County Line Road. It was quite the place at one time: gardens, carriage house, the works. The Websters were Winterset's land barons. Now, they're all gone. So, it sat idle for a long time. Then Professor Sheehan bought it."

"Purchasing a mansion would require deep pockets. Is the family wealthy?"

Sophie filled him in. "Michael Sheehan has a sad story. While with WCC, the community college, he wrote a novel and made quite a name for himself. I imagine it was the royalty money that allowed him to purchase and renovate the old place. There was a scandal, but way before my time. He wasn't a happy man. His wife died from some female ailment when she was young, and he never remarried. There were three children, a girl, that would be Phoebe, and two boys. They grew up and left home. Well, Phoebe returned but not until after the tragedy."

"I believe there was a tragic death," the mayor added.

Sophie frowned, "As I said, it was before my time. I don't remember the details. And the house, is way out there, not a place included in my childhood haunts."

Rory tucked the purse inside his jacket. On the stage, Lillie Anderson was heavy into a heated discussion with

President Martin. The body language made it obvious the professor was upset. He wondered what it was about, but to Sophie, he said, "I'm only concerned with the present. I think the DMV will have a listing that contains Phoebe's emergency contact."

He pulled out his phone and called his friend, Thacker. After two rings, the rookie answered in his deep melodic voice, "Hey, boss."

"There's a problem at Old Orchard Restaurant," Rory began.

"It was on the radio. An honoree fainted."

"More than that, I'm afraid. Phoebe Sheehan is on her way to Winterset Memorial. No one is quite certain what is wrong. I need a next-of-kin just in case. Are you anywhere you can access the DMV database and check for an emergency contact?"

"At the station. I can get whatever you need."

"Good. Call me when you have the information." He disconnected.

Lillie Anderson finished with Martin and glared at Rory. Under her penetrating look, he grew uncomfortable. What he had to do with the situation was beyond him. To the Beckers, he said, "I better go rescue Esther from Winterset Memorial. Thacker is ferreting out the emergency contact information."

"Good idea," said Mayor Becker. "There's nothing else happening here tonight.

Before Rory left the parking lot, Professor Anderson came through the front door and crossed to her vehicle. She left disappointed, no doubt, as the recipient of the award remained unnamed. She hadn't lavished in the limelight; Phoebe's collapse had seen to that. Anderson started her car, backed out, and then laid rubber leaving the parking lot. Rory thought disappointment didn't begin to cover her mood.

The Sheehan mansion was on his way back to town. He was surprised he'd never noticed it since the golf course area, just a little further out, had been annexed by Winterset and both fell within the city limits. But as Rory drew near, he could see thickly planted poplars shielding the mansion from the road. The name on the mailbox confirmed it as Sheehan's. He turned in. The graveled drive led to a lavish, brick home where he stopped under a canopied entry. Lights strung in the shrubbery made a dainty illuminated border leading to the front door. As he approached, he heard a crunch coming from somewhere behind him, followed by a howl.

A stocky beagle shuffled from the bushes, took one look at Rory, and lifted his head toward the moon. Another howl followed.

From the shadows, a lithe female stepped forward. Her features were distorted by the lighting below, and he couldn't read her expression. She wore jeans, a long T-shirt and was without an overcoat, although the night was crisp. "If you're looking for Miss Sheehan, she's not here."

"Do you live here?" he asked.

"Who wants to know?"

"Detective Rory Naysmith, miss." He pushed the fedora back. The beagle moved to sit at his feet and bawled again. "Is this your dog, ma'am?"

"No."

"This is the Sheehan home, is it not?" Then, when she didn't respond, he added, "Are you acquainted with Phoebe Sheehan?"

"Why do you want to know?"

The beagle looked up at Rory, large baleful eyes, and a pitiful expression as if he had the same inquiry. Rory tussled the hound's ears. "Nice looking dog."

"Miss Sheehan has gone to the restaurant down the road. I don't expect her to be back before midnight. You can leave a message with me. I can't guarantee she'll get it."

"I understand she lives here alone."

"Well, you're mistaken. Rosco and I live here." At hearing his name, the beagle moved off Rory's foot and loped over to the girl.

"There's been an accident at the restaurant. I'm looking for a responsible party to notify."

"Is Phoebe all right?"

"We hope so, but she's on her way to the hospital."

"Why didn't you say so? I'll put Rosco inside. Can you give me a ride?"

As he waited for the girl, Thacker called. The DMV record for Phoebe Sheehan named Marilyn Beauregard as her emergency contact. He'd already notified Marilyn that Phoebe was at the hospital. He'd be off duty in thirty minutes if Rory needed him.

Rory was familiar with Mrs. Marilyn Beauregard. She had been active in the first murder he'd solved in Winterset and had filed the first complaint he'd taken after arriving to take his current position as a detective. Marilyn was a life-long friend of Esther and her sister, Jesse Mullins, and therefore by association, him as well. He wondered how the two women, Phoebe and Marilyn, were connected. Indeed, they weren't relatives. But he didn't question the information. Marilyn was known for her broad appeal, and uncanny knack for being front and center in any situation.

Anxious to know what was going on, Rory called Esther's cell. No answer. Which made sense if she was in the emergency room with Phoebe. He left a message. And tried Marilyn Beauregard, got the same. Shaking his head, he thought, two voicemails, no answers, and a dog named Rosco.

Rory waited impatiently for the girl to finish securing the dog and the house. Time stretched, and he began to wonder what was taking so long when she finally appeared from the back wearing a colorful jacket and carrying a beaded sack. Opening the passenger door, she ducked her head inside. "Riding up front okay with you?"

He was taken aback by the question. "You don't want to climb in the back; it's a little messy." His city issue was the one used by the officer who was also the dog handler. The dog, a great bloodhound, had a chewing problem. The back seat cushions were tattered, the padding gone. Rory didn't expect anyone to ride in the back. The car didn't appeal to the other officers, so it was always waiting in the pool. Rory frequently picked it.

She climbed in. After she had secured the seat belt, he pulled out. "How do you come to be at the house. I mean, I thought Miss Sheehan lived alone."

"I'm the dog sitter."

"For a dog named Rosco. And you are?"

She hesitated, staring out through the window, and watching the road. Rory wondered why she hesitated, but when she answered, "Nina Mahala," she said it defiantly as if she dared him to question her.

He kept his eyes on the road ahead, letting her answer settle. He intended to find out who she was and why she lived at the Sheehan residence. "Is that a native

29

name?" He used his calm, reassuring voice, hoping she didn't take offense at his asking.

She bristled. "Am I one with the Ho-Chunk Nation? Am I Native American?" She jerked toward him. "Then the answer is yes. My family is the Thunder Clan and recognized as belonging to the Nebraska Winnebago Tribe and the Wisconsin Ho-Chunk Tribe. Like many Ho-Chunk, I don't live on the reservation."

"And not with your family."

"No."

The detective opened his mouth, then shut it again.

They finished the ride in silence.

Chapter Four

It had been a good thirty minutes since Rory
watched the ambulance pull away from Old Orchard
with Phoebe and Esther on board. Winterset Memorial's
emergency entrance was well lit, but the unit that brought
the women in was not parked at the door. Either they
hadn't arrived, or they had successfully delivered the
poet and moved out to allow space for other vehicles
needing to offload patients. He pulled to the curb where
it was clearly marked —NO PARKING— and put the
WPD placard on the dash. Turning to Nina, he said, "I'll
check with the Emergency Room. You can wait here or
come with me."

He exited the car. She followed. He badged his way
into the ER and found the EMTs at the nursing station.
Stepping up behind them, he asked, "You brought the
woman in from Old Orchard?"

They turned to him, noted Nina, saw the badge he
held up, and stepped back. The taller technician said,
"Her blood pressure spiked once we were underway. She
needed help breathing so we put her on a nasal cannula
to increase her oxygen intake."

"Good. She's here. What else can you tell me about
her condition?"

"A situation like this, we attach ECG leads once
we're underway to monitor the heart. Then we call the
hospital ER to report the situation and our ETA. It was

pretty clear we were dealing with a hypertensive emergency. They had us insert an intravenous port in her arm and told us to keep the oxygen flowing. I'm afraid she went into a coma before we arrived."

Rory looked wildly around the room. "Where's the woman that rode in with her, Miss Mullins?"

"There was a second woman waiting when we arrived. The one in the ambulance, the one that came in with us, wasn't allowed in the ER."

Rory jerked his head to face the EMT squarely. How was that possible? Incredulous, he asked, "Where did she go? Where is Miss Sheehan now?"

Marilyn Beauregard stepped out from a side room. Around her neck she wore a multi-color scarf that was held in place by a mammoth brooch. She waved an arm, sending the dozen bracelets on her arm jangling. "Detective Naysmith, over here."

He crossed to speak to her. "What's Phoebe's condition?"

"Not good."

She stepped back into the room; Rory followed. Nina mimicked his moves. Phoebe lay on a rolling hospital bed connected to multiple leads. Monitors were flashing and blood was being drawn. Technicians dashing in and out. Déjà vu. Only last summer he was delivered to Winterset Memorial by ambulance. The actual events were a blur, but the helpless feeling, the overwhelming brightness and the strange sounds were only too vivid in his memory.

"Coma?" he asked.

"So far, they are still taking vital signs and getting her prepped for whatever happens next. Blood pressure is high, and her oxygen is low."

"Do you know what happened to Esther?"

"She went to wait for you." Then seeing his displeasure, Marilyn said, "I was a little busy. They didn't want to let Esther in because she wasn't a blood relative. I have the medical POA, Power-of-Attorney, so there was no question about me.

"Has the doctor been in to see Phoebe?"

She shook her head, then noticed Nina. Raising one eyebrow, she studied the girl's face. "Hello, dear. Is everything okay at the house?"

Nina smirked. "I was with the police, there was no hesitation to letting me in."

Rory suppressed a smile. The girl had spunk. "Things look tense here but there's adequate attention for Miss Sheehan. Would you mind if I went to find Esther?"

"No." Marilyn answered crisply, eying Nina up and down.

Undaunted, Nina took a seat in the room's only chair. Scooting back against the wall, it appeared she would remain with the poet, despite Marilyn's wishes.

With Phoebe well attended, Rory grew worried about his wayward date. This hadn't been a romantic evening. He hadn't given Esther a lovely time or softened the blow for the less-than-adequate Valentine Days gift he was sure to offer her—if he found time to get one at all. Or even had an idea for an appropriate gift, whatever that might be. Some date this had turned into.

He found Esther by calling her cell phone. She in turn invited him to join her in the cafeteria.

She sat at a table by the window, the night black beyond the glass. "Sorry to make you hunt me down. I didn't have much for dinner and with all this excitement I thought it wise to prepare for a long night." She pushed a plated apple pie slice across the table and gestured for him to take a seat. "Has the situation improved?"

He sat. "Phoebe is still in triage. Marilyn is with her, and the girl that came with me." Esther tilted her head. "Long story," he said, picking up the fork and cutting into the pie. "Mayor Becker said the Sheehan home was just up the road, and since no one seemed to know who next of kin was, I thought I'd stop and see if anyone was home."

"She lives alone."

"Apparently not. I met Nina Mahala and a dog named Rosco. Both share her abode. Nina rode in with me. The dog stayed to hold down the fort. It looks pretty serious for Phoebe." He took a bite, then set down the fork. "Marilyn is health POA. Seems odd. Know about that?"

"Not really. They are the same age, probably have known each other for years."

"Usually that's a family member."

"A woman without close family plans for emergencies. If there isn't a spouse or a child, a good friend usually steps in."

Rory shrugged. He hadn't really thought about it. He always put his eldest son's name on documents requiring a family member.

"The reason I do Phoebe's taxes is because Marilyn recommended my services to her. You know Marilyn, always looking for a way to help out. I don't know this woman, except to tell you what income bracket she's in. I only started doing her taxes after I left my bookkeeping job and started freelancing."

Rory thought about it, a year, two years tops. "Well, let's hope this is nothing and you'll be filing those forms again next year."

She looked at him from over her coffee cup, "So, this Nina person?"

He pushed the pie away half eaten. "Not much to say. Pretty girl with a long, dark braid. She wears it down her back and while driving in, I noticed moccasins on her feet."

"So she's indigenous? Winnebago?"

"She says Ho-Chunk. But she doesn't have much to say other than she lives at the Sheehan mansion and is the dog sitter."

They talked for a few minutes and then decided to check on Phoebe. "She should be in a room by now," Rory said, checking his watch. "If Marilyn doesn't need you for moral support, I'll take you home."

Esther agreed there was no reason for Marilyn, Nina, and them to hang around all night. "I'd feel better if Jesse could check on Phoebe's condition in the morning, but she's not back from Toronto for two more weeks. "

Esther's sister, Jesse, an internal medicine physician at Memorial, was on Rory's special street crew. He counted on her counsel and insider information on all things health and hospital related. He had another flashback to last year's incident. He still had the limp from the smashed ankle bones and would be eternally grateful for Jesse's help.

They had no trouble getting back into the ER. The EMTs were gone but hectic bustle remained. As they crossed to the triage room that held Phoebe, the light over the door began to flash. A buzzer rang, and nursing technicians rushed in that direction. Marilyn stepped out, followed by Nina. Marilyn looked bewildered; the younger woman concerned. The room door closed behind them. A doctor reopened it and went in. A rolling cart followed. The light continued to pulse. Overhead the PA announced, *"Code blue, triage room three, code blue."*

Marilyn's eyes looked wild. Nina crossed to him and in an unnaturally calm voice said, "It doesn't look good. They called for tests, then didn't like the results. Ms. Marilyn doesn't have an answer and it appears neither do the doctors."

Esther laid a hand on Nina's arm. "Are you saying…"

"I'm afraid they're losing her."

Esther dropped her hand and rushed to Marilyn, who was leaning against the wall outside triage room three. Rory watched as she put her arms around the older woman. Their heads moved together in grief. He had witnessed it many times as a policeman. It never got easier.

The doors from the street whooshed open. A man, five-eleven, pale eyes, early thirties, stepped in. His beige overcoat was tailor made, his shoes, Italian. Rory couldn't place him but knew the swagger.

The man shook off the guard who tried to stop him. Striding to the nursing station, he bellowed, "I am James Sheehan. Where is my aunt?"

Chapter Five

The ER staff was too busy to stop and listen to James Sheehan's demands. The nurse asked him to "hold on a moment and remain calm" which had the opposite effect on the surly man. His voice rose and he flapped his arms.

Rory questioned Nina, "Have you seen that guy before?" She shook her head.

Beyond Nina, Marilyn and Esther clustered by the door to Phoebe's room. He caught Esther's eye. Her frown conveyed sadness and loss. If not for her friend, Marilyn, then for her client, Phoebe. Rory was used to death and disappointment after more than twenty-five years on the police force. He felt like he'd seen it all. Taking Esther on a date that ended in tragedy hadn't been his goal for the evening. Now, it didn't look like it would be a quick over and done with interruption, but a nightlong vigil. As a civil servant, he could at least handle the disruptive man for the emergency room staff.

Once again, he pulled out his shield. Then, stepping to the nurse's station, he flipped it open and held it for James Sheehan to inspect. "Detective Rory Naysmith, Winterset Police."

"The police. Why are you bothering me? All I want is to find out about my aunt, Phoebe Sheehan."

Rory tucked his badge in his inside pocket. "Do you have some identification, sir?"

"I don't understand this. I received an invitation to a

ceremony honoring my aunt, but after spending two hours driving, I arrived to find the ceremony canceled. I'm told she collapsed and was taken away by ambulance. I spent thirty minutes trying to find this podunk hospital, and now no one will talk to me. Where is she?" His face flushed; his eyes bore into Rory's. "Where is my aunt?"

Rory held out a hand. "Your identification?"

With a big huff, Sheehan reached inside his coat, pulled a leather wallet from his trouser pocket, and extracted a driver's license. After handing it over, he smoothed the jacket front. "Well, where is she?"

Rory examined the license, and it identified the man as James S. Sheehan, five-eleven, blue and blond, thirty-one, a Lincoln resident. "Thank you, Mr. Sheehan. Your aunt is here." He tipped his head toward the door where Esther and Marilyn stood. "The doctors are with her now. She hasn't been admitted, but it doesn't look good. They just sent a crash cart into the room."

James' jaw dropped, and his eyes widened. "Crash cart? I thought she fainted. Why won't anyone tell me the truth? No one said a word about life and death."

Rory cut him off before he started a tirade. "Don't get excited, Mr. Sheehan. Qualified physicians are with her. They'll do everything they can."

Nina, who had remained silently waiting, sighed. "Even here in Podunk, we know medicine."

James looked daggers at her but said nothing.

A nurse opened the door to triage room three. She waved Marilyn in and closed the door behind them. Esther joined Nina, taking the girl's hand, and saying something Rory couldn't hear. Level-headed, composed, common-sense Esther. Even without knowing the girl, she could lend comfort. Amazing. Maybe Sunny was right. Esther deserved more than chocolates. He abandoned his thoughts when the door opened again. The doctors stepped into the ER pod, removing their masks, and shedding their gloves.

Sheehan rushed in their direction. The doctor shook his head and picked up a clipboard from the counter. Rory joined them in time to hear the doctor say, "I'm sorry, Mr. Sheehan. Unfortunately, we weren't able to save her."

James slumped, reaching out to the counter for support, before straightening to his full height. The doctor pivoted away, checking the clipboard in his hand. "Give me a minute, and I'll answer all your questions."

The detective steered Sheehan toward the doorway. "Let's wait over here."

Surprisingly, the man allowed himself to be led away. Rory escorted him from the ER and into the waiting room beyond. After they took seats, he said, "First, let me say, I'm sorry for your loss. And second, in my experience there is a significant delay at this step. The paperwork must be filled out, and then the right people are to be notified."

"I am that person."

Rory fumbled for the right words. "What will be…Usually, there…" He ran a hand over his bald head. Sighed. "Regardless, the body will remain here at the hospital until funeral home arrangements are complete."

"What about her personal effects?"

"Those, too." He didn't mention that he had Phoebe's clutch purse and the keys. "There is a specific protocol. The hospital will hold and release the remains and personal effects once her wishes are known. That's usually a will or POA document. And in their absence, state laws concerning the body and distribution for personal effects."

James flinched. "I am the heir. There isn't anyone else."

"Calm down. It isn't as complicated as it sounds. It's just that at night"—he checked the time on his phone—"offices are closed, people are asleep. Tomorrow will be soon enough."

"Just who are those women with my aunt? I'm her only living relative. I don't understand."

It sounded like an accusation to Rory. He loosened his necktie. "The older woman, Mrs. Beauregard had a medical POA, which allowed her to make health decisions for your aunt. They were friends, that's my guess. That said, she has no decisions to make now that Ms. Sheehan has passed. So, for now, the hospital will handle your aunt and everything that came into the ER with her."

"This is ridiculous." Sheehan squirmed on the hard plastic chair, raised, and lowered his arms, adamant in his frustration. "Her only living relative."

Rory was afraid there was going to be a scene. He placed a hand on the younger man's arm. "The best thing for you to do is get a room, some rest, and return in the morning. I can recommend a motel. I'd even be willing to check—"

"What about that Indian girl?"

He had forgotten about Nina. James came out of the chair and started for the exit door.

Confused, Rory called after him. "Mr. Sheehan..." But the blond man disappeared through the loading dock door and was soon gone from sight.

Rory went back into the emergency room. Nina was nowhere to be seen. Esther and Marilyn were at the nurse's station, their backs rigid as the doctor spoke to them. Esther's hands trembled, and Marilyn watched the doctor's face.

He stepped behind them, listening to the doctor's matter-of-fact voice. "Miss Sheehan will remain in the hospital morgue while we follow protocols and then arrangements can be made. The tests have to finish up before we can file the paperwork, and they are still coming in. At this point, we don't have a precise cause of death. Yes, her heartrate was elevated, there was some hyperactivity in the rhythm strips off the EKG, but we're not sure that's what caused her death. We'll need time to evaluate. We'll know more in the morning. Your loved one isn't going anywhere."

Marilyn fluttered. Rory had seen her do it before; starting at her head, a shudder ran down her body to her toes. She was either shaken by the news—or revving up to take action. He caught Esther's eyes and jerked his head for her to step over. She squeezed her old family friend's arm before she moved away.

When they were beyond earshot, he asked, "How is Marilyn taking it?"

"She'll be fine. It was just such a surprise, and completely unexpected. Marilyn says they had lunch yesterday, and Phoebe was in great spirits. All excited about the award ceremony. And then for this to happen. It doesn't seem natural."

"It's natural for someone to have a heart attack."

Her eyes went wide. "Oh, Rory, I didn't mean that your…" In the over-bright hospital lighting, her face was colorless. Her eyes were sad. Would he ever learn not to voice his knee-jerk reactions? Silly him, Esther wasn't referring to the heart attack he'd had two years ago.

"No, I know you didn't." He took her arm, leading her to a quiet corner. "I lost Nina, the young girl who was with me. I'll need to run her back out to the Sheehan place. Do you want to stay here with Marilyn, and I'll swing back by afterward?"

"I'll get Marilyn to drop me off when she's ready to leave. I hate to run out on her. She's just lost a dear friend; I can't abandon her now."

He agreed. Leaving Marilyn in Esther's capable hands, he checked outside the ER entrance for Nina, then in the cafeteria, and finally in the visitor's parking lot. He wished he'd asked for her cell number. The night was calm as he made his way to the meditation park separating the hospital from the senior home complex; the benches were empty. The overhead lights glowed, and a mist haloed the globe. There'd be frost in the morning. It wasn't like the girl had a ride, but maybe she needed a moment alone. He didn't want to leave without knowing what had happened to her. Perhaps she was in the restroom or had gone to spend a moment in the chapel if Winterset Memorial had a chapel.

Well, one thing the hospital did have was security. He found the main entrance guard at his stand. "I'm looking for a woman, attractive, in her early twenties, one long braid running down her back. I don't suppose you've seen her?"

The guard lowered a paperback book. "As a matter of fact, yes, if she had on knee-high moccasins. Just went through the door. Not two minutes ago."

"Did you see where she went?"

"Climbed into a pickup and left. I didn't have any

reason to stop her."

Rory scratched his head, popped on his hat. "Thanks. Just in case she comes back in, ask her to give me a call?" He took out a business card and handed it to the guard, who tucked it in his book and promised to relay the message.

After taking one final look around the lobby, Rory went back out the front door, walked around the hospital to the back of the building where the emergency entrance was located, and entered through the automatic doors.

The ER guard waved him over. "Got a message for you, Detective Naysmith."

Inside he could see Marilyn and Esther seated by the nurse's station. He wondered what they could be waiting for but decided grown women, Esther especially, could take care of themselves. "Sure, what you got?"

The guard leaned over his raised desk and said, "That girl that was with you earlier? The pretty one? Well, she said to tell you she had a ride home."

Great, he'd just spent twenty minutes searching for her, and she'd already gone. Well, it was a night for inconvenience. Not that Phoebe Sheehan's death was an inconvenience, but it had been unexpected. And it had tainted the evening. He looked longingly at Esther, then tugged the fedora down snuggly and went back out into the cold February night.

Rory harbored mild guilt at leaving without his passenger. After all, they had arrived together, and should leave together. In addition, his ankle throbbed, a condition he endured after spending too much time on his feet. The award banquet followed by the hospital visit added up to too many hours standing. It was time for a good soak in the tub and a night cap.

He parked the city issue in the police lot, crossed the street to Hillard's Department Store, and used the private staircase to reach his apartment. As he drew the key, he noticed the lights on inside. Thacker must be home. Good. He hadn't seen the young officer in a few days, and they could catch up with each other, if he managed to stay awake.

The aroma of garlic mixed with pepperoni greeted him. He stepped in, expecting to find the rookie in the great room. Instead, two open beer bottles sat on the kitchen table. The two overstuffed chairs that shared space with a recliner in the living room were empty. Commander, perched along the sofa top, leaped down, and joined him as he hung his coat by the door.

"Thacker? Are you here somewhere?" No answer. The tabby circled his legs, and he bent down to greet his friend. "Where's your buddy, Buddy?"

The radiators hissed. Last year's remodeling project had converted the space so the two bachelors could share the apartment. The young officer and his friend, Axel Barrow, had expanded the living quarters by knocking down a wall that blocked off vacant offices. The area was now a second bedroom and the war room. The expansion revealed a hidden staircase to the second floor, which they professionally secured. Although not intended, the soundproof war room was great for concentration. Rory crossed to the room and tapped on the door. Then using a special key, he opened the door and poked in his head. No one.

He went back to the kitchen area and picked up a beer. Ice cold. The rookie had to be there. Rory sat, heeled off his shoes, and thought about calling Esther. As he took a sip, Commander crawled onto his lap.

He gazed at the tapestry hanging on the wall behind the sofa. The rug did more than add color to the room decor; it covered access to a private old hand-crank elevator servicing the three-floor building. A steel, roll-up door covered the elevator cage at ground level. But was a drafty, ugly shaft only protected by a retractable metal gate in the third-floor apartment. The tapestry hid the hole. In addition, a warning light above the tapestry alerted anyone in the apartment when the cabinet opened below. On Rory's second swallow, the red light above the tapestry started to flash, and shortly he heard the lift coming up.

Anticipating Thacker's return from performing the security walk-through on the lower levels, a task that kept the rent low, Rory rose and checked the pizza in the oven. Then, grabbing an oven mitt, he bent to pull the pie from the oven. When he rose, Thacker was in the room.

He wasn't alone; Nina was at his side. She ducked slightly behind the young officer.

Rory set the pan on the table. He could feel his face flush. "I guess I drank your beer."

*Why was he always the last to know?*

## Chapter Six

The overhead lights, combined with the frantic pace of the emergency room, set off steady drumming behind Esther's eyes. How did her sister Jesse manage to thrive in this too-bright, too-extreme environment? Esther's thoughts were to be as unobtrusive as possible and let those caring to life and death carry on. Marilyn had other ideas.

"We can't go yet. If we don't keep after them, Phoebe will be just one more body lying in the morgue."

Esther heard the determination in Marilyn's voice, and her heart wrenched. "Phoebe is one more loss. And you know she'll end up in the morgue."

"I mean, if we don't keep up the pressure, they'll let her lie in the triage room all night. That's not dignity, is it?"

"Oh, Marilyn. I'm sure they have rules to follow about cleaning and transporting the remains to the appropriate...." She had to stop and think for a moment. It was difficult to soften the terms for death or morgue or gone forever. A phrase too harsh would send Marilyn into another fit. They had already cornered the ER doctor twice, and both times been interrupted by something urgent requiring his attention. Marilyn hadn't had the opportunity to voice her demands. Yet.

Esther tried again. "What I'm saying is that this is the emergency room. They handle emergencies. It only makes sense that when someone passes and can no longer benefit from the staff's undivided attention, and therefore the need has diminished, and she—"

Marilyn held up a hand. "Malarkey. I'll sit here until they take care of my friend. It's only decent."

"If we get in their way again, I'm afraid they'll drive us out." So far, no one had approached and asked them to leave, but nurses and technicians had been shooting glances at them for the past half-hour. She needed to direct Marilyn's effort in another direction. "Let's spend a moment in the chapel. It's not likely that we'll hurry things along here. We could offer a prayer and take a moment to collect ourselves."

Marilyn gave her a pointed look. "If you think it's a good idea. Go ahead."

The emergency doors whooshed open, drawing their attention. EMTs wheeled in a gurney. At the same time, medical technicians reversed directions and headed for the latest arrival. Marilyn stood. "Perhaps you're right. Let's go."

The hospital chapel was on the first floor at the other end of the complex. Esther hoped her old family friend would wind down by the time they walked over. She wasn't disappointed. Marilyn set a brisk pace that slowed to a stroll by the time they reached the right hallway and closed in on the small sanctuary. Not being in the middle of the emergency room commotion seemed to give her space to reevaluate the situation. She stopped at the stained-glass door. "Do you think you could give me a moment alone?"

"Of course. Why don't I go to the cafeteria and get us coffee?" Esther gestured toward a hall bench. "I'll be out here when you're ready."

Marilyn rifled through her overcoat pockets. "I usually have a scarf. But now, I'm without an appropriate cover for my head." She fingered the brightly colored scarf that hung around her neck.

"It's a multi-denomination chapel; you don't need to cover your head. Besides, the chapel is here for you to find comfort, not to adhere to religious rules. Phoebe wouldn't care if your head is covered, and I'm sure God doesn't either."

Marilyn smiled weakly, put her hand on the nob, and hesitated. "It's been a shock."

"That's putting it mildly. Go in. I'll be waiting."

As soon as the door closed behind Marilyn, Esther headed for the cafeteria. It was close to midnight, and although open twenty-four-seven, she found only prepackaged food and coffee dispensed from machines. She got two cups, sugar packets, and paper napkins. A few employees sat at tables, but it appeared everyone was either working or in the private nurses' lounge. She tested the coffee. The best she could say was that it was hot.

Seated on the bench outside the chapel, she tried Rory's cell. When he answered, she asked, "Too late?"

"No. Glad you called. Are you still at the hospital or have you made it home?"

Esther filled him in on the delay and Marilyn's mood. When she finished, he asked, "Do you think there's any reason to check with your sister to see if being on staff gives her pull with the ER staff?"

"No, the staff is doing their job. It's pushy civilians that get in the way. There is no reason for them to alter their routine to accommodate us."

"I'm glad you see it that way. Do you think you'll

convince Marilyn to go home any time soon?"

"I do. She's exhausted. However, waiting has given us the opportunity to talk. She gave me some background on Nina." She held her breath, hoping he didn't think she'd stepped between him and his job. When Rory didn't answer right away, she began to fear she had crossed that invisible line, the one where he felt his position on the police force required him to avoid speculation and gossip. Not to mention exchanging information with civilians.

She exhaled silently when he finally came back with a reply. "What did she say?"

"That Nina lives at the mansion with Phoebe. It's an arrangement that works for them both since Nina is on parole and needs to complete a hundred community service hours. You know, as a teenager she was sponsored by the Janus Chances program? I know you feel that taking convicted criminals and placing them in trusting citizens' homes begs for trouble. But it seems to have worked out." She paused, giving him a chance to stop her if she headed into territory that he wouldn't discuss with her. When he didn't object, she went on. "According to Marilyn, Nina isn't good with people but has a natural gift for working with animals. Thus, she dog sits for Phoebe in exchange for room and board. And it gives her free time to serve out the demanded community hours."

"I see. And she is on parole?"

"I'm not sure I got the whole story, or even the true story, but breaking and entering was mentioned. Marilyn says Nina released the inmates from the city pound. I think there was alcohol and a full moon involved."

Rory chuckled. "I remember that case. And it would

explain her aversion to making friends with me. So, that was Nina. Or should I say Thacker's friend, Nina?"

"Oh, he finally told you."

"Not exactly. When I got home, she was in the apartment with him. I think I put the kibosh on their evening by drinking her beer and eating half their pizza."

"It sounds like she's a nice girl who got off on the wrong foot. Of course, she's older now and taking the straight and narrow path. Well, except for..." She paused, realizing Rory didn't need to know every tidbit Marilyn had shared. "I think getting away from her parents helped as much as the program." Then, realizing her comment was Marilyn's opinion, she winced.

Rory didn't notice the slip. They carried the conversation for another moment then disconnected.

Making herself comfortable, she sipped the coffee and fingered the pearls at her neck, the beads cool and smooth between her fingers. It had been a strange night. Rory, poetry, death, and then, despair, an odd and disquieting combination. She wished he was with her.

Marilyn's coffee was cold when the older woman finally emerged from the chapel with her face expressionless. Buttoning her coat, she said, "I'm ready."

On the ride home, Esther hoped her friend had found peace, but feared she'd only recharged her resolve to correct the hospital's priorities.

Esther didn't ask; there was no need to wind her up again.

Chapter Seven

Rory relaxed on his bed. The apartment was quiet, now that the kids were gone, and Commander curled at his feet. "It looks like our boy has a girlfriend, boy."

The cat looked at him, then scratched behind an ear. "Maybe not my first choice for the young lad," Rory said. "But who knows what someone else needs. I say, let's let it play out and see what happens. With any luck she isn't a felon."

The tabby purred, blinked twice, and crawled over the blankets to nestle against Rory's side. "I agree with you, boy"—he laid his hand on the old cat's head—"it's not our decision."

****

He was at the station bright and early the next morning, only to discover Hutchinson's Hardware Store had been hit again. Unlike the first burglary, a surveillance camera was in place this time. It pointed to the back door and if opened, the alley beyond. He didn't have much on his schedule, and a look at the crime scene while it was being processed might help solve Tom Hutchinson's problems.

Rory grabbed his fedora and made the three-block walk to the store, arriving to find Tom Hutchinson taking inventory and the WPD team collecting trace evidence. Middle-aged, a linebacker gone to flab, Tom looked defeated. "Is there a conspiracy against me? It's enough that I was robbed last week, but to have it happen again. Thank God, I didn't have the power tools back in stock yet." He followed in Rory's footsteps from the front door to the counter. "Insurance is one thing but if I don't have the inventory when someone comes in, they just go somewhere else. You might think that's no big deal. Well, I'm here to tell you, it's the beginning of the end. If they discover they can buy elsewhere, they'll buy elsewhere."

Rory removed his hat, scratched his forehead. "I understand the theft was sporting gear this time. Can you tell me anything that the boys haven't?"

"Hunting and fishing gear, clothing, ammo. They even rifled the locked cabinets. You can't imagine the paperwork involved in reporting gun theft. How am I supposed to operate?"

Rory pulled out his notebook. "It ups the ante. I understand your office wasn't touched." Tom shook his head. "The good news is you have the gun serial numbers. Why don't you get those records for me? And I'd like to know who locked up last night. But first, I'll take a look at the point where they broke in."

Tom stood beside the empty fishing rod display as if he didn't have the will to move further. The green felt background that artfully displayed the poles looked frayed and forlorn without the rods. A faded map showed the nearby fishing lakes. The man and wall were the same shade.

The break-in point was the hundred-year-old wooden door at the alley, same as last time. The metal bar Tom had added as an additional deterrent hadn't done the job. Burgled twice in as many weeks was unusual, especially with WPD running checks during the night hours when the store was closed. Brazen? Did this criminal have a personal quarrel with Tom Hutchinson?

Power tools, the original theft indicated a theft of opportunity with a quick resale and low risk of discovery. Guns were a different world altogether. Not only did the crime ratchet up in severity, but the punishment also went from a five-year maximum to the opportunity for life in prison. It didn't make sense. If firearms had been the goal, why take the power tools first and then risk a second crime? He was puzzling it through when Tom called from his office.

"Detective Naysmith, they're here." He came rushing from the office, grabbing the door frame, and using it to swing around the corner and onto the show floor. "I say, they're here. They haven't been stolen."

Rory stopped midway to the back door. "The firearms?"

Tom tried to catch his breath. "All of them. At least"—he paused to gulp in air—"I think it's all. I didn't stop to count them. The closet is full."

Rory pivoted and called to the evidence team. "Hansen. Lloyd."

Lloyd stepped forward. Hansen stopped dusting, said, "We're on it, sir."

They all clustered in the small office space. Officer Lloyd pulled the rifles from the closet, laid them, one by one on the desk. "I saw them, Naysmith," he said, stepping back and shaking his head. "I just had no idea they didn't belong in there."

Hansen recorded the serial number and wiped each for prints while Hutchinson, sweat beaded on his bow, hovered nearby. "Do you see the knives? Are the other weapons in there, too?"

Lloyd shot him an impatient look. "Give me a minute."

"Why is this happening to me? Now, I've lost two days' worth of sales and who knows how many customers."

Hansen laid a pellet gun down with a clunk. "Must have worn gloves. That's the third weapon without a print. Or he wiped them down when he moved them."

Rory pushed his fedora back on his head. "Handguns? Ammo?"

Hutchinson lurched forward. "I don't carry handguns, just air rifles and BB guns. Some Multi-Pump. If you've got—"

Rory waved him down. "Look, getting excited isn't going to help. Where's the list?"

Hutchinson pulled out a drawer and removed a ledger. "I just carry guns that you'd give your kid for Christmas or on a birthday. You know, to learn how to handle a weapon. Birds, squirrels, a paper target, that's all they're good for. I don't carry handguns. And I don't sell merchandise that could be mistaken for a handgun. No, sir. Sporting stuff; that's it."

"It appears it's all here." Hansen put an ammo box on the floor behind him, then reached in for another. "And the knives."

Tom collapsed into his chair. "Naysmith, this is the damnedest thing."

"Yeah, a thief with a conscience or a little common sense that kept him for taking the guns through the door." It was odd. Almost as if one gang member, if it was a gang, had stepped over the line by grabbing the weapons, then changed his mind and shoved them into a closet rather than putting them back where they'd been displayed. "Maybe time was an issue," Rory said. "I should be able to discover how long they were in the store from surveillance footage. They would need time to pull in, break the door, grab the loot, and then get away."

"Why move them at all?" Tom said. "I just don't get it."

"You're not alone. Hansen, still no prints?"

"No. Clean, sir."

"Let's compare them with the serial number register and verify they're all here. But I have a feeling that's what you'll find. Better yet, get someone else to do the job and you show me what you found in the alley."

The back door was splintered. The hinges were still attached but broken boards hung or lay on the concrete floor. No steel bar was going to do the trick this time. Hutchinson was in for a major redo to secure his business. The ground in the alley clearly showed tracks from a heavy trailer pulled behind a truck. Footprints crisscrossed the area. Too many to tell much, other than it was a multi-manned operation. The footprints all looked alike.

Hansen had blocked off the alley at both ends and a delivery truck honked from the east end. A hand waved out the cab window. He went to talk to the driver.

Rory examined the camera mount. It was within reach, even for him. Irritating how business owners expected the police to protect their property but they weren't willing to invest in putting the right equipment in place, so the job was doable. Hansen came back. "Man's got the replacement door. He says if we can't let him in now, he won't be back until tomorrow. He's got other jobs to complete."

Rory glanced around the alley. Pictures and casts were complete, so he didn't see any reason to hold the man up. "Let him in but put the barrier back. I don't want any more people than necessary traipsing through the area. I'll let Hutchinson know."

They sat in Hutchinson's office. Tom behind the desk still piled with BB guns, and Rory in the flimsy visitor's seat. They closed the door to keep the knocking and banging from disturbing them. "Who locked up last night?" Rory asked.

"A kid I pay to be the evening manager."

The detective took his notebook out. "Kid got a name?"

"Sure. Perry Benson."

It sounded familiar. Where had he heard that name? Then he remembered the poetry award ceremony and the competition between Lillie Anderson, Phoebe Sheehan, and Perry Benson. Had he met Benson at Old Orchard? He couldn't picture a face to go with the name. "What time do you close the store?"

"Seven. Nothing happens downtown after that. I keep a clerk and a manager on. It might take another fifteen or twenty minutes to shut the business down and stow the cash"—his eyes went wide—"I forgot about the cash." He jumped up and rushed from the room. Moments later he reappeared with a money bag. "Safe. Benson dropped it in the floor safe just like he was supposed to do." Hutchinson unzipped the bag and began counting money. When he finished, he said, "Wasn't any business last night." His voice was sad, but not disappointed.

"I think I met Mr. Benson at the literary award ceremony out at Old Orchard last night."

"If you met him, you'd remember. He's got tattoos, both arms, from knuckles to elbows, a beak nose, and a surly disposition." Rory scratched his head, but still couldn't picture Benson. Hutchinson continued, "He's only a part-time evening manager. As a matter of fact, he has several part-time jobs. I think he also works as a gardener at the Sheehan place."

"Oh?"

This was news. Yet, in Winterset everyone was interconnected in some way, babysitter, house boy, drinking buddy, partner. His experience was not to get too excited when one person linked to another—there was always an explanation. And most times it didn't make sense.

"He's been out there for a good six months. I know because I wanted weekends off myself, and he wouldn't agree to work them for me. Couldn't have the clerk work alone. He's got tattoos on his face and scares the ladies. Yeah, Benson's got a contract to keep the Sheehan grounds looking nice or some such commission."

"Do you two get along? No arguments or disagreements?"

"Sure. Why wouldn't we?"

"Just asking. What about the clerk? This theft seems personal. Just speculating."

"I don't have any enemies if that's what you're thinking. And my wife and I get along fine."

Rory wasn't sure what he was thinking. And he wasn't making progress. "Once you get that door in, you better think about moving the camera up. Maybe even put a cage around it."

Hutchinson groaned.

"Better give me the surveillance footage. I'll take it

back to the office and go over it. See if it tells us anything."

Tom made a face like getting it was the last thing he had time to fool with. "I'll give you the password, you can access it from anywhere."

Rory didn't care if Tom Hutchinson was inconvenienced. An investigation meant investigating. After taking the information from him, the detective put his notebook away, had a final word with the patrolmen, and headed back to the office.

It took considerable time to log into and figure out how to find the correct backup surveillance footage. There were two files, Counter and Backdoor. Once done, Rory diligently watched the Counter tape, starting where the store front door was locked at seven. The till was counted, the money dropped, and then Benson let himself and the clerk out. Rory fast forwarded through the "nothing happening" hours that followed. The tape ended at midnight. He switched to the second camera's tape, labeled Backdoor. He skipped the recording before midnight and began where the inside file ended. Again, using fast forward, he reviewed the agonizing footage collected at the back door. And then the picture went black.

Rory backed it up several frames and started again; this time in real-time, watching the hardware store's back door until the digital display showed 0213 hours. The picture went black. As the time ticked on, the screen remained an inky void until 0235 hours, when the hardware store was visible once again. Twenty-two minutes that might have shown the crime in progress but didn't. Rory spent time reviewing the footage: a dark room, a sudden draping by someone out of view, then complete darkness until the cover was removed by someone outside the camera's lens at exactly 02:35 in the morning.

The time was not in dispute; it was plainly stamped on the video. The criminals used the shrouded time to pull a trainer into the alley, break through the door, and grab all the hunting and fishing supplies. Plus, move the guns from their display into a closet? Trailer tracks were left in the alley and too many footprints to accurately count the intruders. Rory needed more—the missing twenty-two minutes would be perfect.

Chapter Eight

The Winterset Police Department handled law enforcement inside the town limits, but the County Sheriff's Department oversaw the entire county. The two law enforcement agencies often shared resources; therefore, it was no surprise when Petey Moss, the county coroner, dropped in at the station for a visit.

The detective answered his knock. "Come on in," Rory said and held the door wide. "To what do I owe this honor?"

Petey chuckled with bonhomie. "No honor, I had an odd request to perform an autopsy on the Sheehan woman. I wanted to run it by you."

Rory lifted one brow. "Really. Where'd the request come from? An elderly woman has a heart attack, it isn't a reason to perform a costly procedure." He took the seat behind his desk and motioned for the coroner to take the visitor chair. "Could be she died from some ailment no one was prepared for, but what good would it be to know that? She didn't have children, no grandchildren, no one is bound to inherit the disease. It's too late for her. I don't see the point."

Petey's eyes twinkled. "Same logic I ran through," he said, rubbing his double chin.

"So, who requested the autopsy? Not James Sheehan, the supposed nephew?"

"I think he might be a nephew." Petey tucked his

chin, making three-folds in the otherwise double jowl. "But he didn't make the request. From what I understand, he is more interested in getting on with the estate than he is in exploring the reason for his aunt's death. Or should I say more interested in what she left behind than why she passed away."

"You're going to make me guess. Okay. I give up. Who?"

"Marilyn Beauregard." Petey leaned back, the chair creaking out another protest. "She has the legal right to request an autopsy because she was named in the advance health directive Phoebe Sheehan signed back in November."

"I thought the health directive purpose was to appoint someone to make decisions if you were incapacitated and couldn't make them for yourself. Am I wrong?"

"You don't get more incapacitated than dead."

"Good point." Rory scratched his ear, grimaced. "So, what prompted Marilyn to request an autopsy?"

Petey grinned. "Toxic alkaloids."

Rory whistled. "Didn't see that one coming."

"My guess is she didn't either."

Rory reared back, steepling his fingers on his chest. "So, talk to me about alkaloids."

"How much time do you have?"

He grinned. "Give me the short elementary school version."

"Alkaloids are organic compounds that have been used as medications and calming agents for centuries. Some are harmless, others not so much. Most are stimulants, but their use in pharmaceuticals is well-known: antibacterial, anti-inflammatory, local anesthetic, hypnotic."

"Don't tell me she took some medicine that didn't go down well."

"Many plant species produce the compound. It can be found in flowering plant leaves, stems, roots, or even fruits. Alkaloids are in everyday foods you eat and drinks you ingest. Coffee? Caffeine is an alkaloid, as are opium and morphine."

"So, a bad cup of java."

"There's also strychnine, quinine, and nicotine. Alkaloids in pure form are colorless and odorless. Quite often with a bitter taste. And there's cocaine, the narcotic drug which has the opposite effect from morphine. It produces a euphoric, hyper-aroused state that can lead to ventricular fibrillation and death."

"You're saying Phoebe Sheehan overdosed on cocaine?"

"Not quite. I'm trying to give you some background, what it is and what it can do."

Rory took out his notebook while Petey continued, "Some alkaloids are illicit drugs, and some are poisonous. But others are just addictive stimulants we humans knowingly partake in: smoking, double mocha lattes, tomatoes." He cocked his head. "Flowering plants commonly grown in Winterset include a dozen opportunities for a would-be killer. Harvest enough poisonous alkaloid and you can mix a lethal cocktail for our Ms. Sheehan."

"Then it was poisoning?"

"Yup. The questions that remain are what and when. I'll start the autopsy this afternoon. The blood tests taken at the hospital last night indicated the toxin. I'll let you know when I isolate the culprit."

"Like you said, 'poisoned from what and when.' I'll wait to see if I can add the who."

After Petey left, Rory contemplated toxins. What and where? He'd need to discover the answers. According to Petey, there were a hundred everyday plants that could supply the alkaloid used to render Phoebe nauseous, unconscious, and ultimately dead. Rory checked his watch and found it was just after lunchtime. He felt a need to check on the Sheehan mansion and Nina, the dog sitter.

Knowing that just dropping in wouldn't be productive, he remembered Esther and Nina had hit it off. Esther would be at home doing her bookkeeping chores. He wondered if he should take her along. Who was he kidding? Anyone would have a better chance talking to the girl than a middle-aged police detective whose normal communication mode was interrogation. He decided to pick the bookkeeper up.

Together, they enjoyed a comfortable drive to the mansion. It was a sunny day, and although the temperature hovered in the lower forties, there was no wind. Just coming into February, he was glad for the break between winter snows. December and January had been mild, but too much time indoors made him antsy for a walk in the country. Most years, there was a blizzard in February or March just when he wanted to come out of hibernation. The storms always made him feel like a bear and helped the season drag on forever.

Before they reached the mansion, he told her about the break-in at Hutchinson's. When he finished, she said, "Tom is a prickly guy. Always ready to lend you a hand, but quick to remind you he did so."

"I wondered if someone is trying to make his life

miserable. The thefts are odd."

"In what way?"

"Too small. Almost designed to inconvenience Tom and not lucrative for the criminal. Take last week's crime—all or mostly power tools. Items that will bring in a price at a swap meet. Stuff you can sell from your car trunk or online. Pieces not easily traced. It feels like kids. The replacement cost for the hardware store's back door is almost more than the merchandise lost. And to hear him tell it, just one more nail in his coffin."

His stomach dropped. Coffin. Great, he had referenced death. But then, he didn't suppose she had forgotten. Esther watched the scenery pass. What was she thinking? He didn't know.

Finally, she said, "That's interesting. Do you suspect local kids? A prank not a crime?"

"Oh, they were crimes all right. Just not the kind committed by hardened criminals."

"And we're going to talk to Nina because…." She let it drift away. Then, in his peripheral vision, he saw her upper body turn to face him. "Nina is a suspect in this crime?"

"I want to get a feel for the living arrangement out there. And something Tom Hutchinson said this morning made me think about Perry Benson. He was a part-time gardener for Phoebe Sheehan, and that means Nina and Perry know each other. I'd like to understand the dynamics in their relationship."

"Marilyn knows all the parties. Why don't you talk to her?"

"She has a unique interpretation on relationships. And I'd like to reserve hearing Marilyn's opinion until I've collected some facts myself."

He wondered if Esther knew about the autopsy. And if she did what she thought about the request.

"I talked to Marilyn this morning," she said softly, offering an apology. "She feels responsible after the trust Phoebe placed in her, medical POA and all. I guess you know she asked for an autopsy?"

He slid his hands to the eleven and one positions on the steering wheel and tapped a thoughtful rhythm with his thumbs. Esther had an uncanny knack for reading his mind.

"Marilyn told me Phoebe was in stellar condition for a woman her age," she said. "It didn't seem natural for her to die so suddenly. Then she said if there were family to consult, they would surely request an autopsy, so she thought she should. Not that she suspected foul play, just that it was prudent."

He decided not to share what he'd learned from Petey about the poison. However, Marilyn would do that soon enough, and he did want the older woman's take on that development.

They drove in silence for another mile before Esther said, "It's odd to think we made this trip out County Line Road only last night. I wonder what happens to the literary guild's prize now?"

He didn't know and wasn't concerned about the award unless poison was used to narrow the poet laureate competition pool. His mind went down a rabbit hole, and they road on in silence. His mind ticking, he recalled his impression from the night before and the awards ceremony. Lillie arguing with Phoebe and later leaving in a huff. Perry Benson coming in late and leaving early. Phoebe nauseous even before the festivities got underway. He wondered, where had everyone been while he hobnobbed with the literary royalty?

## Chapter Nine

Nina and Rosco were on the lawn when Rory pulled the city car into the drive. She called the dog to her, then clipped a lead to his collar just as Rory parked.

Stepping from the vehicle, he called, "I see you made it home safely." He rounded the car to hold the door open for Esther. "We're here to offer condolences. I've brought Miss Mullins to keep me in line. You know how we older, brash policemen can be." He gave Esther a full wattage smile and then swung his gaze back to the younger woman. "Just a few questions."

Esther blushed, then said to Nina, "I am sorry for your loss."

Rory removed his fedora, fingering the brim. "Miss Sheehan's death was sudden and unexpected."

Nina didn't react. He wasn't sure whether he expected her to or not. She was dressed casually in jeans and sweatshirt under a short-cropped coat and with her hands buried deep in the coat pockets. A beaded sack hung from a long diagonal strap across her body. She showed no signs of grief. Well, people reacted differently to death; he knew that. Hollow-eyed and weepy wouldn't be in her character. He wondered what would happen to the girl now that Phoebe was gone. And what the older woman had meant to her.

Then, knowing Esther would be more tactful in dealing with Nina, he changed the subject. "This is a beautiful property. Would it be insensitive if I looked around?"

Waving the sentiment aside, Nina let the beagle off the leash. She couldn't very well refuse to let him look around. Rosco growled, which didn't make sense since his tail was going nine-to-ninety. Rory stepped over and gave the dog's ears a tussle. "Friendly guy."

Nina slapped her thigh, and the beagle heeled. "If he likes you, he makes noise. Otherwise, he's silent and watchful. So, it doesn't pay to discount him just because he isn't talking."

"Pretty well trained."

"If he wants to be. When he doesn't want to, he digs in the flower beds." She glanced at the arbor running from the front drive, along the house, and ending at the back lawn.

When he'd stopped on his way from Old Orchard the night before, she'd materialized from the arbor area. Looking now, he saw well-shaped evergreen bushes running its length. Or was it a pergola? What did he know about landscape structures? It looked nice but probably took substantial work. The flowerbeds waiting for winter's end along the house's brick front, were turned and mulched, and he imagined bedding plants filled the area in the spring. Maybe daffodils or tulips sprung when the season teased them from the frozen ground. But, for today, the beds looked hard and cold.

Esther said, "Someone has done great work with the grounds. It must be a full-time job."

Nina gave her a gloomy look. "There's a gardener."

Rory waited for more; it wasn't forthcoming. "Flower beds in the front, a trellised awning along this side"—he gestured with his head—"and what's around the back requiring a groundskeeper?"

"Groundskeeper sounds old-fashioned, Detective." Before he could respond, Nina continued. "Phoebe wasn't up to mowing and mulching. Instead, she loved to plant in the spring, walked the gardens in the evenings, and clipped a bud now and then when they were in bloom. We kept an herb garden, but the lawn, grounds if you insist, are tended to by a paid laborer."

"Perry Benson?"

She looked at him, black eyes flashing. Then, recovering quickly, she said, "Perry does the majority of heavy lifting, trimming, tilling, fertilizing. He's here a couple days a week. Not on a regular schedule, but year-round to take the burden off Phoebe's shoulders." She and the beagle moved down the pathway under the arbor. "This way leads to the back gardens. Not much there in winter, but you can get a feel for the expanse and effort required."

Esther and Rory followed. Gardens? More than one? He ran through Petey's poisonous plant list: daffodils, tulips, foxglove, oleander, delphinium, morning glory, apple seed, tomato. He didn't think he'd see any up and blooming and didn't know if he'd recognize them if they were. But it didn't hurt to look.

As they passed under the arbor, he noticed the hedge had been recently trimmed. Clippings lay under the spreading branches. Nina kicked the loose greenery off the pathway then stooped to pick up a branch. Rosco checked under the shrubs, then stopped, waiting for the detective to catch up.

Esther stepped forward and fell in line with Nina, asking, "Will you stay on here at the Sheehan place? Or is it too early to know what you'll do?"

Rory didn't hear her answer. However, he did notice the girl picked a leaf off each plant species as they passed. Nerves, he thought. Rosco kept up a constant doggy murmur-babble, deep-throated groans, and excited yips. Rory found it endearing and encouraged him by engaging in conversation. "Yes, I know what you mean, old boy." Finally, they caught up with the women at the walkway end.

Nina slowed once they moved past the building. A soft rolling lawn lay to their right. "Native flowers are dormant in this meadow. Careful stewardship has kept it flourishing." She waved to her left, where grasses lay on the dry earth, forming a layer to protect the flora below. "The taller reeds are allowed to dry in place in the fall and will naturally protect the young grasses that will come up in the spring. Other areas get covered with straw or wood chips. Pine needles if it's warranted. It all looks rather sad right now but come April; it springs to life."

Straight ahead, a pathway wound around some statuary and ended at a gazebo. Further behind stood a wooded area. It wasn't much to look at, but even to his untrained botanical eye, the landscape looked promising.

"I guess it's hard to appreciate in February." Nina's hands were back in her pockets. "But the gardens are lovely in the spring and summer. Mr. Michael Sheehan commissioned the gardens when he was in residence in the seventies. Those were the money years. Some fruit trees have peaked. Others are just coming into their full potential."

Around the gazebo, red berried bushes colored the greenery. "Some plants are flourishing," Rory said, indicating the bushes.

"Perry is amazing," Nina said. "There are berry-producing holly trees that supply the bird population with enough food to see them through winter. There are other winter-fruiting shrubs." She waved at a spruce row. "We cut the branches and covered the fireplace mantel. Phoebe liked to smell evergreen in the house."

Were spruce and holly on Petey's list? He watched as the women walked to the gazebo and back. He doubted Nina was alive in the seventies when the gardens were first created, so where did she get this information? His cell phone rang. Petey Moss.

"Hey, you should get out," Rory said. "It's a beautiful day."

Rosco threw his head back and howled.

Petey wasted no time. "No evidence to support death by natural causes. I'm ruling this one a murder."

"So, you can confirm poisoning? Nothing wrong with her heart?"

"Enough alkaloid toxin in her system to kill a horse. The time of death is definitely established from hospital protocol records."

"How long would it take to work in the body? Could Phoebe have ingested the toxin in the afternoon, say hours before. Or is this a poison that works within minutes, and thus administered at the restaurant?"

Petey exhaled before he answered. "I'll need the stomach content analysis before I can nail that down. But it's conceivable that she ate before going to the restaurant. She might even have had a nibble after she arrived. It depends on the substance. Some take hours before the poison signs manifest. I'd guess we're looking at hours, not minutes. How long were you at the restaurant before she collapsed?"

"Hours?" Rory tried to think through what he had

witnessed. Before the bar argument, Phoebe tried to get a ginger ale to settle her stomach. Was she already feeling the toxic effects? Her dizziness in the awards hall. The fact that she appeared drunk. "Would alcohol play a part in this?"

"I doubt she felt like drinking if she already had poison in her system. She would have felt lousy. Might have been hallucinating."

"When will you send the preliminary autopsy report to the station?"

"I'll do it when we get off the phone. Murder warrants quick notification. I thought I'd give you a heads up."

"Thanks."

After they disconnected, Rory wondered how long it would take before hearing from Chief Mansfield. Since he was at the Sheehan property; he better take a serious look for the toxin. Or the source if nothing else, and interview Nina.

## Chapter Ten

Nina and Esther went into the house, leaving Rory to wander the grounds with his new friend, Rosco. A six-foot high wrought iron fence circled the estate's outside perimeter, ending at the brick pillars of the opening gate. There was no gatehouse and no barrier to prohibit entry. The carriage house used as a garage held a late model minivan. He recorded the license number but felt confident he'd find it belonged to the late owner. The house, the grounds, and the gardening shed all appeared to be well maintained. He wandered to the back door to the house and knocked. Esther let him in.

Using his intimate, friendly voice, he asked, "Is Nina doing all right?"

"She seems to be. Come on in; she's put on a pot to boil water for tea." He raised one brow and shoved his hat back. "Tea, not coffee? Are you sure it's safe?"

She chuckled. "I'm sure you've had your caffeine allotment. Tea won't hurt you." Rosco scooted in, crossed the mud room's tile floor, and disappeared into the house. "Just follow the dog."

"Did you notice the girl picked up leaves and twigs, and who knows, poison berries?"

"Rory, keep your voice down. She'll hear."

He thought he was keeping his voice down. "I'm not sure I want a cup."

She socked him on the arm. "Shhh."

"Well, what do you think Nina's doing with those leaves? Do I need to remove my shoes?"

Esther reentering the kitchen, or what he supposed was the kitchen, and stopped. "That won't be necessary," she said over her shoulder. "Come on in."

He followed her, taking the single step up to enter the kitchen. He stopped in the doorway. It was a kitchen all right, refrigerator, stove, table, and cabinets and cupboards. But this kitchen's counters were buried in paper-stacks: newspapers, file folders, spiral notebooks, binders, tablets. Every wall held either a cabinet or had a cupboard affixed. Metal filing cabinets were wedged under a wooden table in the center. The tabletop was scattered with papers, folders, and binders. A cooking island looked more like a library cart, overflowing with books. There was one chair shoved under the table. One path led from the door to the sink, sink to stove, stove to the refrigerator, and food pantry to table. Rosco followed his pathway through the banker's boxes lining the floor to the doggy dishes by the sink.

He blew out a deep breath of air as he tried to make sense of the scene. "Phoebe used this room for an office?"

The teapot whistled. Nina smirked. "This room and pretty much the others." She stood by the stove and reached the pot without effort. "To your right, there are some mugs. They might be buried, but they are clean."

He found three and wound his way through the clutter to hand them to her. "Is there a comfortable spot where we can sit down and talk?"

She gave him a fixed stare, then said, "In the library." He was concerned about what that might look like but followed her into the house and down the hallway.

The library tabletops were covered with books and pamphlets, the bookcases full. The drapes were drawn. Obviously, the kitchen was where Phoebe did her writing and research. Was there a computer in the kitchen? He'd have to look again.

Nina sat the tray with mugs and condiments on the desk, pushed some papers into an open box, and gestured for them to take chairs. Two stuffed chairs sat by the desk; they emptied the contents from the seats onto the floor and sat side-by-side. As Nina opened the drapes, dust particles danced in the air.

Rory cleared his throat. "You're the housekeeper?" He met a wicked smile from Nina. "I mean, is there any domestic help?" Esther made a noise, and he looked in her direction. She had an expression that said she'd have kicked him under the table if there'd been a table. "I mean…" He looked around. "The house seems to be full. And dusty."

Esther made what he would have called, when he was younger, a raspberry. A glance showed her brows knitted into a frown; he amended his next question. "I mean, was it just you and Phoebe living in the house? No outside help, cooks, cleaners. Just you two, and the dog."

Nina took a seat behind the desk and looked sternly at him. "I'm the dog sitter."

"What does that entail?"

At first, he thought she would ignore his question. But then she opened the center desk drawer and removed a book. Flipping it open, she read, "Feed Rosco on a regular schedule. Walks in the morning, afternoon, and evening. Baths twice a week with additional baths if needed. Vet visits for shots and physicals twice a year.

Playtime when necessary." She closed the book with a thud. "It's all spelled out. And for those services, I receive a room on the second floor and every other Sunday off." She looked at him defiantly.

"Is that a contract?"

"Yes." She didn't offer to let him read it. He held out his hand. Reluctantly she handed it over. Then sat, arms crossed, while he read it through.

It was as she said. No money was exchanged. No start date or end date stipulated. However, there was a clause stating if her services were no longer needed or desired, she was free to remain on the property until she secured a position with another pet family that met her needs. "It looks like you are free to stay as long as Rosco is alive and healthy."

"That was the arrangement. We didn't think our personalities should interfere with his care. "

"How long have you lived here?"

"Five years."

That was an awful long time to be on probation. The girl must have worked out her required community service hours, then stayed on. "I heard Phoebe offered a Janus Chances opportunity for you. Is that true? Did Ms. Sheehan acquire your services through the Janus program?" He knew perfectly well that this was the case. He wanted to see what she would say.

"What if she did? It's a free world. She didn't do me a favor. I had a service; she had a need. So, they matched us up, and it worked out."

"So, you wouldn't say you were friends?"

Again, he thought she would duck his question. He could feel Esther's stare, and he avoided looking her way. Nina stood and walked to the window. Looking out, she tossed her braid over her shoulder. "I think you could say we grew on each other. At least she minded her own business."

Her meaning was clear. And he was aware that Esther was feeling the same way. So much for checking out the situation under the guise of offering condolences. Through the window, he heard a gas leaf blower startup. The phone on his hip vibrated. He glanced down, Chief Mansfield.

"I'm sorry, Ms. Mahala, I need to take this call."

She waved him off. He stepped into the hallway to answer. "Naysmith."

The chief sounded impatient. "I'm sitting here reading the preliminary autopsy on Phoebe Sheehan. The county coroner has ruled her death a murder. Poisoning. Did you know that?"

"Petey was by the office earlier."

"And you didn't think it was necessary to fill me in? Naysmith, this is a serious matter. Dead from suspicious means—in a public place—and with the mayor in attendance."

"I'm at the Sheehan place now, questioning the dog sitter."

"I sent the boys out to Old Orchard. They've talked to several witnesses. It's a popular opinion that Ms. Mullins gave Ms. Sheehan a drink moments before she collapsed. I asked Lloyd to bring Ms. Mullins in for questioning."

Rory's heart gave a fast, hard jump. "Chief, I don't think she is responsible for poisoning Ms. Sheehan. She didn't even know her, except to file her tax return. What motive would she have?"

"I don't think you can be objective in this case. I'll

see someone else does the interview."

"Chief—"

"No need to thank me, Naysmith. We'll get this done. You carry on where you are." He clicked off.

Great. Chief Mansfield was looking at Esther as a possible suspect. And who knew who would conduct the interview. Esther didn't have a mean bone in her body. He also knew her every movement and intention during the ceremony and their not-so-great date. What he didn't know was where she had been earlier in the day. Then an idea struck him—Axel Barrow. Esther's next-door neighbor and self-appointed bodyguard might know exactly how she had spent her day. He placed the call.

"Constable?"

"Axel, I wonder if you are still keeping an eye on Ms. Mullins?" Rory could hear country music playing in the background. "Are you at home?"

"Nope, thought I'd check out the local gossip down at the legion while Miss Mullins is out. And, yup, I'm overseeing her wellbeing. I need to see for myself that Miss Esther stays okay. She's with you, right?"

"Right."

"So, what can I do you for?"

It took a minute to explain the situation and Esther's awkward position. When he finished, Axel said, "Say no more. I'll stop by the station and have a word with the captain."

"You mean the chief?"

"Whatever. I'm your man."

Rory clicked off. Axel was unconventional to say the least, but his devotion to Esther was fact. He had no doubt her neighbor would move mountains to clear any suspicion from her name.

Rosco howled, then stepped from the kitchen and shuffled down the hallway in Rory's direction just as the front doorbell chimed. Nina came through the library doorway and gave him a questioning glare. On the second chime, Esther peeked around the library doorframe.

A resounding knock echoed down the hall. Nina moved to the front door. Through the beveled glass, Rory saw what appeared to be a man, and by the force of his knock, a very insistent man.

Rory held his breath. Lloyd couldn't have run Esther down this quickly.

Nina opened the door without removing the security chain. She said something he couldn't hear and closed it again. Then, turning to face him, she said, "It's James Sheehan. He insists on coming in."

## Chapter Eleven

Nina led them to the library. Rory took the seat behind the desk while Esther and James took the chairs facing him. Rosco scooted next to Sheehan's feet and stared up at the man, who was clearly uncomfortable with the overabundance of paper. His eyes raked over the books on the shelves.

Sheehan looked determined, but his voice cracked. "I went to the hospital this morning to claim her body, and it's gone. Released to the county morgue." The dog inched closer. "Who authorized that? I am the heir. My father was her brother, so I am her closest living relative."

Rory leaned forward. "So, you say."

"Look, detective, it's a fact." He pulled an envelope from the inside pocket of his blazer. "Here, look at the note I received from Aunt Phoebe, inviting me to the awards banquet last night." He removed a sheet from the envelope, holding it out.

Esther rose and took the letter from his grasp. Then, glancing at it before handing it to the detective, she said softly, "Typed."

Rory glanced over the one-page document. "It is computer printed. Hardly proof she wrote it."

He waved the envelope at Rory. "Look at the envelope. Postmarked in Winterset."

Nina snorted from the position she'd taken in the

doorway, then slipped into the hall. Rosco watched her go, as did Rory. He gestured to Esther to follow her.

After giving him a wide-eyed stare, she rose and left the room.

"So, tell me how that worked," Rory said. "Without warning, you receive an invitation from your aunt, and after being estranged for years, you drop everything and rush to Winterset to bury the hatchet?"

James squirmed, inching to the chair edge. "Take a look at my identification. Driver's license, credit cards, library card…." He patted his pockets. "We didn't have a hatchet to bury. My father and his sister had different opinions. They had a falling out. It started when my grandfather left the place only to Aunt Phoebe, not to both of his children. My father and I didn't have much to do with her, but it doesn't change the fact that she was my aunt. I am the only living relative." He opened his wallet, pulling out some plastic cards.

Rory lifted his brow. Lillie Anderson's words came back to him: *Plagiarizer. You're no better than your father.* "Do you remember your grandfather?"

"Sure, an old man, an English professor, and author."

"How old were you when he died?"

James squared his shoulders and raised his voice, "I don't see what that has to do with being in Winterset. Why can't I—"

"Do you remember coming to this house as a child?"

"Yes. But I would have been young. Too small to have many memories, just hazy impressions. I'm an only child, and as there were no cousins, visits were lonely. It was a drafty old place and not much fun for a boy. I remember this room. The books." He rose with a huff, handed the cards to Rory, and tripped over Rosco in the process.

"What about visiting after Ms. Sheehan inherited the place?"

James gave him a look that indicated that hadn't happened. Rory made a mental note to check the newspaper archives for articles about Michael Sheehan, grandfather, local English professor, and author. Taking the identification, he flipped through them, then handed them back. There was something James wasn't saying. "What did they tell you at the hospital?"

"Enough. According to the hospital and the HIPPA regulations they seem delighted to quote"—his eyes narrowed—"I don't have the authorization to know anything. The paperwork is sealed, the tests are confidential, and the body is now the county's property. That's when I decided to come out here."

"And what did you hope to find?"

"I don't know." Slumping back in the chair, James ran his hands through pale blond hair and swept it back from his forehead. "I had to go somewhere. The motel by the freeway is okay, but I couldn't face going back there so early in the day. This was the family home...." His gaze fell on the bookcase. "I guess I thought I'd find a welcome here. Maybe closure. I wanted a connection. I didn't expect to arrive too late to speak with my aunt."

Before Rory could ask who he thought he'd find to welcome him, being that Phoebe was gone, the leaf blower again sounded from outside. He twisted to look through the window behind him. A man in a camouflage hoodie chased loose clippings off the walkway. The man straightened and looked in the window. Haunting black eyes held Rory's in a defiant stare.

What was wrong with people? Was everyone surly and suspicious? Rory gave a terse nod, and then brought his attention back to the nephew. "I think we need to verify your claim before we decide on your welcome."

James looked past Rory to the lawns. "Who are those women?"

This time, Rory followed his gaze to where Nina and Esther stood talking with the gardener.

"They were at the hospital last night," James said. "And what gives them the right to be here, now?"

"The younger woman is Nina Mahala. She lives here. Furthermore, she has a contract allowing her to stay with or without your aunt. The other woman is Esther Mullins; she's…." Rory had to stop for a moment. How did he explain who Esther was? She wasn't Phoebe's friend or relative. Then again, he didn't need to explain anything to this man making an unsubstantiated claim. "Ms. Mullins is with me."

"Police?" James asked, picking up a book from a pile on the end table next to him. When he opened it, a leaf floated to the floor.

"No." Rory's phone vibrated. He unclipped it and looked at caller ID. Thacker.

"I need to take this." Putting the phone to his ear, he said, "Are you on the job or trying to place an order for pizza delivery?" And after listening for a moment, he added, "She's with me now. I'll see she isn't caught flat-footed." His brow furled. "Say, I need a favor. I'd like to send a man down to the station, Phoebe's nephew, James Sheehan. It would help if we expedited a background check and verified his identification." He turned and gave James a thumbs up. "Thanks, I'll send him down."

He disconnected and addressed the younger man.

"You'll probably need to spend another night at the motel, but we can help sort things out at the police station in town. Do you know where that is?"

Receiving a positive response, he walked James to the door and waited while he pulled out.

Once the car was gone, Rory took the outside walk around to the back of the house with Rosco at his side. There, he found Esther standing by the mudroom door while Nina talked to the gardener. Their exchange appeared amiable, and Nina was smiling. It was the first time he'd seen joy on the girl's face. Even with Thacker the night before, she had been sullen and reserved. He wondered if there was a relationship between the two, one more than work related. Or perhaps, a toxic connection?

When Esther looked in his direction, he waved her over.

She bent to greet Rosco, then said, "I've met the gardener, Perry. He seems sincere."

"An honest gardener? How unusual."

She wrinkled her nose. "I just meant he seems nice. He and Nina seem to have a friendly working relationship."

"He's not competition for Thacker then?"

"Oh, I don't think so." She stood and gazed back at the couple. They were sharing a laugh and looked very comfortable with each other. He guessed Esther also noticed because she added, "How serious do you think Thacker is about this girl?"

"I don't have any idea. He's never brought a girl around before."

"Oh." Esther watched them with a keener eye. "You don't suppose…."

"I don't want to speculate."

"And James Sheehan, how did that work out?"

He filled her in and then turned to matters closer to his heart. "After the poison was discovered in Phoebe's system, the chief sent some boys out to the restaurant to talk to the employees. Several mentioned you brought the cup to Phoebe." He watched her facial expression go from confident to bewildered.

"They don't think…I wasn't… Oh, Rory, what does it mean?"

"It means you will be questioned. Mansfield thinks it would be best to have someone else do the interview." She frowned; he continued. "It's just routine. All avenues have to be explored. No one believes you are a murderer. So, you don't need to worry, but you'll be required to answer questions sometime today. For now, I doubt they know where you are."

He knew she had nothing to hide. The late poet and Esther barely knew each other. Esther was more intimate with Phoebe's taxes than she was with the woman. And what motive would she have to want her dead?

Rosco stiffened. His nose went into the air, and with his head back, he began to bawl.

Rory bent down. "What is it, boy?"

"I think he senses your worry."

"I'm not worried. But sometimes the boys at the station can be tactless. I wonder who'll do your interview?"

Esther took his arm. "Why don't we head into the station and get it over with?"

After turning Rosco over to the dog sitter and saying their goodbyes, they headed for the car. When they reached the front of the house, two WPD units sat in the drive. Lloyd, Hansen, and this year's rookies, Black and Sorensen, waited at the door.

"Detective Naysmith," said Lloyd. "We're here to collect the food samples."

Rory let them know Nina was in the back, then sent Esther to collect her. He let them in through the front door.

"Whoa," said Lloyd, taking in the clutter, paper, and boxes. "I guess we should start in the kitchen." Rory led the way. Black and Sorenson brought up the rear.

"This might take a while," said Lloyd, rolling his eyes. "Not much room to move around." Not the smallest man, Lloyd stepped in, turned, and knocked a paper pile to the floor.

Black stooped to pick them up, bumped into the cart stacked high with books, and sent them tumbling down the other side when he straightened. While Black wrestled with the books, Sorensen started on the refrigerator's contents. Hansen took samples from the food pantry, and Lloyd tackled the canisters on the counter by the sink.

Rory tried to stay clear and not impede their progress. "I had a look at the foliage in the garden earlier," he said. "I don't know if I'm qualified, but several species looked poisonous to me. They warrant a second opinion. And there's a potting shed in the back gardens."

"Gardens?" asked Lloyd. "How many gardens?"

"Enough that Phoebe employed a gardener. And the possibility that this job is going to take a while. You might want to call in more help."

Lloyd huffed and reached for another canister. "How does anyone live with this mess?"

Rory found his way to the only chair, sat, pushed his hat back on his head. "One man's mess is another man's treasure."

Hansen sent Black to retrieve more evidence bags from the cruiser. "I hope no one is eating food from this kitchen."

Assuming it was a rhetorical question, Rory didn't answer. Then he remembered they'd had the tea. "The dog sitter fixed us a drink when we arrived."

They stopped and stared at him. Finally, Lloyd asked, "You know Sheehan was poisoned?"

Yeah, he knew about the poison. The thought never occurred to him that they were in danger. He felt fine, no dizziness, no nausea. What did Petey say—two to twenty hours. Nah, Nina had a cup with them.

Lloyd moved to a cupboard, kicking a box in the process. "Gee." He straightened the box and shoved another to make room to get where he wanted to be. "I'm not so sure it's a good idea for you to be here, Naysmith."

Rory shot his arms into the air. "I'm just watching."

"Chief wants to question everyone that attended the literary awards ceremony last night. That'd include you. And several witnesses already testify Ms. Mullins gave Ms. Sheehan a drink before she collapsed." He raised one brow at Rory.

"We were on our way to the station when you arrived." Rory lowered his arms and knocked an envelope to the floor. "Ms. Mullins doesn't have a motive; she barely knew Sheehan." How many times had he repeated that?

Lloyd made a noise. Rory wasn't sure if he was dismissing the statement or agreeing with him. Maybe Lloyd was right; he shouldn't be in the area while they collected the samples. No reason to do something that could be questioned later. They didn't need his help to do the job right. His eyes raked across the paper stacks and landed on the pile Black had knocked to the floor earlier. One envelope caught his attention. He picked it up. Printed in fancy script letters across the front were the words *Last Will and Testiment of Phoebe Orla Sheehan.*

He glanced at Lloyd and found he was preoccupied with collecting, as were the other men. Rory slid the document from the envelope. It was a will, all right, drawn by an attorney and dated two years earlier. He flipped to the last page. The record was notarized, signed, and witnessed. Except for Phoebe, he didn't know the signees. He went back to the first page and began to read.

On page one, Phoebe Sheehan named Esther Mullins as the independent executrix.

His heart sank.

He'd found a motive to commit murder.

Chapter Twelve

Rory closed his eyes and tried to clear his thoughts. Tangled in jumps and starts, he couldn't wrap his head around Esther being named as Executrix to the estate. It didn't make sense. And boy, oh boy, did it complicate the situation. Maybe he didn't know her the way he'd thought. He stood abruptly, shoved the document into the envelope and back into the pile.

After clearing his throat, he addressed the room at large, "I'm on my way to deliver Esther Mullins to the police station. If you fellows don't need my help, I think we'll be on our way."

Lloyd grunted. Hansen stuck his head out from the pantry. "Ms. Mullins is on Chief Mansfield's suspect list. It wouldn't hurt to clear her before the chief works up a full head of steam." Rory grimaced, Hansen added, "He mentioned turning the case over to the Sheriff's department, her being a friend and all." The officer blushed. "Not that I believe she could be involved."

"She's not. All the same, I need to beat Mansfield to the punch."

Lloyd said, "Don't expect to see us any time soon. We'll be here a while, and then we'll need to deliver the samples to the lab at the courthouse."

Rory went out through the mudroom and found Esther sitting on the stoop. Out by the gazebo, he saw

Nina with Rosco at her heels. The gardener was nowhere in sight.

Esther looked up at him. "It's peaceful out here. No wonder Nina likes it so well."

He held out a hand to help her up. "Did she tell you that?"

"Not in so many words. She did tell me that before the incident that led to her Janus Chances placement as live-in dog sitter, she shared a trailer with her parents."

"Out on the Winnebago lands?"

"She described it as small and cramped. Never a moment's peace with relatives moving through the place at all hours. Her parents work at the Bingo Hall."

He wasn't surprised. A good many tribal members worked at the Winnebago Casino in one capacity or another. He was more interested in how her Janus Chances placement came about. But first things, first. "We need to head back to town. There is an item that I'd like to discuss with you before we go to the station for your interview."

"Okay." She wiped her palms down her thighs, squinted at him, but didn't ask.

As they walked along the house to the front drive he said, "Did you see what Nina used to make the tea?"

"No. Does it matter?"

He shook his head and thumbed his fedora up. When they hit the city limits, he said, "Are you familiar with the Krebs and Smith law firm?"

"Not really. They've had offices on Main Street by the courthouse for years. I know they handle probate and civil law, but I've never been in their office. Grandma had a holistic will and I handled that myself. So, if you're asking do I know about probating a will, then my answer is yes."

"I think it's time we introduce ourselves to a probate lawyer."

"I thought we were going to the police station to answer questions about last night's awards ceremony."

"After."

"What aren't you telling me, Rory?" He grinned at the windshield. She leaned toward him. "Is this about James Sheehan?"

They parked by the police station. Rory waved at Sunny through the plate glass window, ignored the parking meter, and led Esther down the street to the Krebs and Smith, Family Law office. A bell tinkled over the door as they entered. A young girl in a severe navy suit greeted them from behind a mahogany counter. Rory thought she looked about twelve years old.

He took out his shield and laid it on the counter. She lifted her chin, smiled sweetly, her eyes never leaving the computer screen on the desk. "Do you have an appointment?"

"No. I'd like some information. Krebs or Smith will do."

"I'm afraid neither is in. If you'll leave your name…" She didn't finish the request, instead looked at the shield for the first time. "Oh, you are the new detective. Sweet. I'm Millie Krebs. Perhaps I can help. Are you looking to draw up a will?" She pulled out a drawer and fingered the folders. She found the form she was after and pulled it out. "Just fill this out and I will have Mr. Smith contact you."

"Are you related to Mr. Krebs, Attorney at Law?"

"My dad." Her face lit with a cheerleader smile; head tilted—no pom poms waved.

Using his warm and amiable voice, the one he reserved for children, he said, "I have some general questions."

"Awesome. That's my department." She ticked up the charm wattage. He wasn't sure she was old enough to work in a law office, even if she was related to the boss.

"This is Ms. Mullins. I believe her friend Phoebe Sheehan had a will done by this firm."

When Esther opened her mouth to object, he raised a hand to silence her.

Millie beamed at Esther. "How nice." Her head tilted in Esther's direction.

"So, my general question is"—he paused to capture her full attention—"do you keep a will copy here or is it recorded at the courthouse?"

The question seemed to confuse her. She batted her eyelashes. A dainty, pink tongue slipped out between perfectly glossed lips. "I believe the will is returned to the client. It's their responsibility to produce the will for probate." She grinned like she had answered the winning Quiz Bowl question.

Rory smiled. "And your position with this firm would give you the ability to verify that Ms. Sheehan was a client."

"Naturally."

"Would you check to see if there is a client record for Phoebe Sheehan? And at the same time verify if Michael Sheehan did business with your firm? I'd be interested to know in what year."

His shield still lay open on the counter. She ripped off a post-it and stuck it to the brass. "Would you write those names down for me?"

When Millie left them alone in the reception area, with a promise to return as soon as she had the requested records, Esther scowled at him. "What are you after? I hope you're not duping that dear child."

He explained about finding Phoebe's Last Will and Testament. "But that's crazy," she said, sinking into an antique chair in the waiting area. "I don't even know her, why would she name me as the Executor to her will?"

"Executrix."

"Whatever. I tell you, my only contact with her was filing her taxes last year and the year before. She didn't even bring the information to me. She sent it to the house by courier after Marilyn Beauregard hooked us up. I took the forms out to the estate for a signature once they were ready, but I didn't get beyond the front hall. Honestly, I talked more to her at the restaurant last night than I ever had." She paused, then added, "If it's true, wouldn't she have notified me?"

The door opened, the bell tinkled, a distinguished gentleman in his forties and wearing a stylish trench coat, entered. He seemed confused to find them sitting in the reception area. He held out a hand to Rory. "Roger Krebs. Do we have an appointment?"

"Detective Rory Naysmith, WPD." Krebs glanced around. Rory imagined he was looking for his daughter and added, "Miss Krebs stepped into the filing room."

The lawyer slipped off his coat, revealing a three-piece suit, ivy-league tie knotted at his throat. He tossed the overcoat onto the counter. "What can I do for you, detective?"

"I believe you did some work for Phoebe Sheehan. She passed away early this morning. This is Esther Mullins; she is the executrix stipulated in the will."

"Do you have the will with you?"

"No, but I've seen the will. Unfortunately, its existence may create a problem."

"Why don't we step into my office." He led the way, motioning for them to take seats, while he went to search for documents. Or more likely his daughter.

****

Clarence Thacker chewed the inside of his cheek. He had run a search on James Sheehan, but the man hadn't shown up to discuss the results. No outstanding warrants under James, Jamey, or Jim. No conceal and carry license issued. He felt there should be more to find than IRS and DMV records. So, what were Sheehan's secrets? He wished he could talk with Rory.

Sitting at the patrolmen's shared workstation, he was concerned that Rory hadn't come in or called him back. It had been hours since he'd given the detective a heads-up on Chief Mansfield's orders to pick up Esther. She needed to come in and clear the air about her involvement in Phoebe Sheehan's demise. Or, more likely, her lack of involvement.

He had a hard time accepting that the death was murder, especially if Esther was involved. And doubly concerned since the death involved the landlord and current employer for Nina Mahala, the girl he'd just started seeing. The thought made his collar feel tight. She was different from anyone he'd ever dated. Older, otherworldly, mysterious, and somewhat exotic. That, and the beautiful thoughts she shared when they were together.

Not only hadn't Rory brought Esther in, but the boys collecting the foodstuffs from the estate hadn't returned either. He checked the clock; it was almost two.

Extracting every possible piece of evidence took time. He knew that, but today it seemed time stood still. Shortly, the guys coming off patrol would want the workstation to file their reports. He crossed to the window, looked out at the street, and then glanced at the dispatcher. "Is that our city car?"

Sunny spun to face the window. "Sure is. That's the one Detective Naysmith is driving. It's been there almost an hour."

Sergeant Powell stepped behind him and laid a heavy hand on his shoulder. "He and Miss Mullins went over to the courthouse."

Courthouse? That didn't seem right. "Did you see him go into the building?"

Sunny answered, "Esther's with him. I doubt he'd be checking on a nasty autopsy with her in tow. 'Course, he has his own ideas about courtship."

Thacker smiled. Naysmith certainly did. But who was he to judge? "Maybe they went on down the street."

Sunny clicked the computer mouse; her social media feed came up on the monitor, and a kitten video danced across the screen. "Maybe he took her on down to Bailey's Jewelry, and they're pickin' out wedding rings. And tomorrow we'll see a double rainbow and find a wee laddie."

Behind them, Sergeant Powell gave a throaty laugh. "Right. Does that sound like our detective? My money is on them walking the long way around the block while getting their stories straight. That's more Naysmith's style."

Sunny gave him the evil eye. "We can't all be wild romantics like you, Dicky."

"Shucks, Sunny. You know my wife would never let

me hear the end… I didn't… Oh, you're just…" He gripped Thacker's shoulder. "Oh, mind your own business." He dropped his hand and, red-faced, went back to the day sergeant's desk.

Even Thacker knew Powell took fresh flowers home every payday. He thought it was sweet. Like something his dad would have done for his mom if he could have managed. Thacker thought relationships should complement the parties, each finding a quiet way to complete the other. Rory and Esther were two parts making a whole. And he wondered when Rory would figure out how he really felt about Miss Mullins.

He returned to the workstation and began packing his papers. He had almost decided to call Nina for an update on what was going on at the mansion when Sunny held up a ruby lacquered nail. "In-coming."

Through the plate-glass window, he watched the detective and the bookkeeper cross the street. A tall, blond man stepped into their path before they reached the curb on the station side.

"Uh-huh," sang Sunny. "Ya got trouble, my friend. And that starts with T"—both arms swayed above her head, her ample, jean-clad backside wiggled to the beat—"and that rhymes with P, and that stands for Powell—"

Mansfield's voice boomed through the intercom, "Ms. Gomez, when you are finished entertaining the troops, I suggest you locate Naysmith."

Thacker's gaze went to the six security monitors on the wall over the civilian pass-through window. Chief Mansfield's face stretched from edge to edge on the center screen. Distorted by his proximity to the camera, flared nostrils dominated his icy expression. He was not happy.

Thacker shook his head. Uh-huh. Thanks, Sunny, for planting that show tune in my brain. Slumping back in the chair, he mumbled, "Trouble in River City? They don't know what trouble is."

Chapter Thirteen

"I've been patient, Detective." James Sheehan stepped between Rory and the door leading to the station house. "If you two think you can join ranks to shut me out, you're mistaken."

"Please, step aside." Rory glanced quickly at Esther before taking her elbow. He didn't know if James had heard the rumors. News traveled fast in Winterset, and by this time, everyone might know that she was a person of interest in his aunt's murder. He wasn't going to discount James' ingenuity, either. "No ranks. Your concern is noted."

"Since my arrival in this godforsaken place, I've been given the run around. What is this place?" He looked directly at Esther. "What did you have on my aunt? How did you weasel your way into her trust?"

Esther bristled. "What do you mean?"

"You know what I mean. It's easy to mislead an elderly woman, especially one desperate for acceptance." His eyes narrowed. "I'll find out, you know. You won't be able to hide."

Rory stepped forward, deliberately moving into the younger man's personal space. "Mr. Sheehan, I suggest you move aside and let us pass."

"Oh, I'll let you pass, but don't think I don't know why you're blocking my every move."

Esther, eyes as wide as saucers, faltered. "But I… I

didn't even know her."

Rory tightened his grip on her elbow. "Step aside. Now." He shouldered his way past James, but as he and Esther made their way toward the station, Sheehan stayed close at their heels.

"Sure," he called after them. "Good story. In this one-horse town, I imagine everyone knows everyone. People will talk, you know."

The station door opened and Esther's neighbor, Axel Barrow, stepped out, greasy hair pulled back in a loose ponytail, washed-out jeans slung low on his hips, with the lingering scent of cigarettes in his wake. He raised his chin in greeting. "Hey, Constable. Miss Mullins. Is this fellow bothering you?" His bushy unibrow dipped, and steel gray eyes bore into James Sheehan.

"Thanks, Axel, but I think Mr. Sheehan has said what he had to say. Haven't you, Mr. Sheehan?"

"For now."

"Go on in, folks," said Axel. "I'll escort this hombre to his car."

Esther mumbled her thanks as they slipped past Axel and into the station. "I hope he doesn't do anything crazy," she said, looking back over her shoulder at the street.

"I hope he does."

She glared at him. "Rory."

Through the vestibule window Rory could see Sunny at the dispatch desk. "Hopefully, Mansfield is still in. Let's get this thing over with."

"We should keep an eye on Axel."

"He's a big boy." Secretly he thanked Axel for appearing at the right moment. It would be harder to talk

Chief Mansfield down with the nephew shouting accusations at Esther. Axel's timing was impeccable.

They entered the chief's office moments later. Mansfield, seated behind his desk, grunted an impatient greeting as they took chairs facing him. Esther appeared nervous, but Rory was confident they could establish her alibi and dispel the chief's concerns. "I understand you're interested in having Miss Mullins interviewed concerning Phoebe Sheehan death."

"That was earlier," Mansfield said, shifting position and relaxing into his chair. "It looked pretty dicey with Miss Mullins handing a drink to Miss Sheehan just before she was overcome by a lethal poison."

"So, you're not interested in her any longer?"

"Didn't say that." He wore a sly smile. "However, I've had a talk with Petey and he's confident the poison would have been administered before the award banquet began. He's still working on a timeline, but for now, Esther is not considered a suspect in Phoebe Sheehan's death."

"She'll be relieved."

Esther waved a hand between Rory and Mansfield. "Excuse me, gentlemen. I'm right here where I can hear you."

Mansfield blushed. "Sorry, Esther. This business makes me uncomfortable. I don't want you to think I asked to have you picked up on a whim. No way did I think you were responsible. But no stone unturned, as it were, and I have to answer to the Winterset citizens. As well as the mayor. How would it look if I hadn't taken action? People would think I played favorites."

"Chief?" Rory asked.

Looking to be on a roll, Mansfield ignored him.

"People jump to conclusions. I gave you tickets to the awards banquet, and I'd hate to have to admit that to the mayor."

"But," Esther interrupted, "Mayor Becker was at the ceremony; he knows how Rory came by the tickets."

"There's that, and your neighbor, Axel," the Chief said. "He gives you a solid alibi for earlier in the day. Actually, quite a detailed account."

She looked confused. "Is that why Axel was here? Did you interrogate him?"

The chief cleared his throat. "Let's say, he came in on his own and we had a few words."

Over Mansfield's shoulder, Rory looked out the window. Under the graying sky, Axel leaned against his pickup truck with the appearance of closely monitoring activity around the station. As Rory wondered at Esther's alibi, Axel raised two fingers to his forehead, and saluted.

*Uh-oh. The guy really did keep watch on Esther.*

"Tell me," Mansfield asked Esther, "how did Phoebe Sheehan happen to name you in the will?"

"I really don't know," she said. "I can't say we were friends, and you have to know I don't profit from her demise. Well, not much, just a small fee to handle the estate."

The chief cleared his throat. "Even so, I would appreciate it if you would stay and answer a few questions for the record."

Rory stood. "Thacker is here, I'll have him handle it."

Mansfield nodded. "That should satisfy any doubts, but truthfully, there's no need to do it today. It might be best if someone other than Officer Thacker conducted the interview."

Rory stood. "We don't know what motivated someone to murder Phoebe. I'm afraid Esther, you could be next in line."

She scoffed. "Why?"

He gave her a pointed look, "Until we understand the situation better, I'd like Axel to keep an eye on you."

"He hardly needs encouragement. I swear that boy is underfoot all the time. Really, Rory, he's next door if I need him."

"All the same, this is a murder case, and I'd rest easier knowing we could count on him."

Mansfield leaning forward to pick up a document from his in-box. "I'm glad this is all settled."

"But, Chief Mansfield," she countered, "Axel has his own life and I hardly see the need."

Without looking up, Mansfield shook his head. "Rory will sort this business out. But, until then, don't leave town."

Chapter Fourteen

After they left the station, Rory drove Esther to Marilyn Beauregard's townhome. The old family friend opened the door and waved them in, air-kissing Esther as she passed through the portal. Then she moved into the kitchenette area, waved a hand, and indicated they should join her at the table. "Honey," she said to Esther, "you look distressed."

Rory pulled out a chair for Esther. "We just came from the police station. And before that, we were at Krebs and Smith, Family Law."

Marilyn looked earnestly at the younger woman. "So, you know then?"

"Why didn't you tell me?"

Marilyn crossed to the counter, emptied the coffee pot, and started a fresh one before answering. "I thought there would be ample time for you to get to know Phoebe before needing to perform any legal duties for her."

"Chief Mansfield thinks I have a valid reason to do away with her."

"That's ridiculous. Phoebe needed someone to handle her affairs. She didn't have anyone, you know. She'd been estranged from the extended Sheehan family for years. When she had her will done, you had just completed her taxes."

Esther straightened her back. "I remember you insisted that I do her taxes."

Marilyn waved her off, bracelets jangling at her wrist. "I only wanted to help. Phoebe had such an unhappy life."

Rory interjected, "Why unhappy?"

"Oh, that business with her father." Bracelets clinked as she swept a hair strand off her forehead. "Wild allegations. The college dismissed him without proving a thing. So, there he was, alone, raising his small children. And then no job and the scandal."

Rory and Esther exchanged puzzled stares. Finally, Rory broke eye contact, turning his attention to Marilyn. "I think you better start at the beginning."

"I'm sorry if I've put you in an uncomfortable position, Esther. At the time, I couldn't think of another person who would do right by her. So, I did Phoebe a simple favor and suggested you."

Esther pressed her lips together. Rory could see she wasn't convinced it was a favor she intended to keep.

The older woman took the seat across from them, folded her hands, and placed them on the tabletop. "You can decline to serve. The court will appoint someone else."

"I may have to." Esther's voice sounded apologetic. "I can't profit from a crime."

Marilyn cocked her head. "What crime have you committed, dear?"

"Well, if you believe Chief Mansfield, I poisoned your late friend."

"Oh, poppycock."

He knew the situation wasn't funny to Esther, but he pictured her going toe-to-toe with young James Sheehan, and suppressed a smile.

"So, Marilyn," Rory said after blowing on the hot

brew. "What can you tell me about the business with the father?"

Marilyn showed reluctance to share the information, folding and unfolding her hands, then studying her knuckles. Rory knew she delighted in knowing what no one else did and waited for her to reveal the story. He wasn't disappointed.

"Michael had three children. Phoebe was maybe fourteen at the time," she said, scooting forward on her chair. "Jamison, sixteen. Another son was older and, unfortunately, drafted to serve in the Asian war when he was nineteen, maybe twenty, named Gregory. He had already gone off to boot camp. They were quiet, respectful children. There was a nanny leftover from earlier when Michael's wife died, and he was raising three small children on his own. Without tenure, times were hard. There was talk about the young live-in nanny."

Esther held up a finger, signaling a stop in the narration. "Wait, I'm already lost. So, Michael is the wifeless professor, raising three children on an assistant professor's salary, yet they live in a country mansion?"

"The mansion came later. First came the novel."

Rory looked at the clock over the stove. It was five-fifteen, cocktail time somewhere. "I don't suppose you have something to cool this coffee?"

Marilyn smiled knowingly. "For you, detective, a little whiskey."

Once she had spiked their interest and their coffee, she continued. "The academic world is unique. To be a literature professor and expect tenure, you need to publish even at the community college level." They nodded. Even Rory had heard this bit before. "The need was there, and Michael Sheehan produced a manuscript. Who knows how long he had been writing, polishing, perfecting this work? There were rumors that it existed, but no one had seen or read the manuscript. Then one day, *voila*, he had a full-fledged novel and a publishing contract for *Willow Creek Woman*."

"That was the title, *Willow Creek Woman*? I'm not familiar with it," said Esther. "So, he penned a novel. What is wrong with that?"

Ignoring her, Marilyn continued, "There was a nice six-figure advance, and Michael purchased the estate on County Line Road. The book sold well, and Winterset Community College rewarded him with tenure."

"That sounds like happy-ever-after," said Esther.

Marilyn harrumphed. "It didn't work out that way. First, Gregory died in the war, leaving the whole family broken-hearted and devastated. Then another professor came forward, claiming the work wasn't Michael's but that of a student she'd been mentoring. There was a fuss. Then an investigation that led to nothing, but the damage was done. The book went on to do quite well; however, his reputation fell into ruins. Eventually, the college let him go."

Rory said, "I thought you couldn't remove a tenured professor?"

"They made his life miserable. The son, Jamison, went off to college while Phoebe stood by her father, remaining in Winterset. She eventually took a position at the public library, but privately she was a recluse along with her father. The book royalties allowed them to live quite nicely, but I imagine it was a lonely existence."

Esther paused with her drink halfway to her lips. "The place is lovely."

"It is said that the real author was a Native American living on the Ho-Chunk lands. I believe the nanny was indigenous. But, although no lawsuit was ever filed, the rumors persisted. The stigma eventually kept Jamison from returning to Winterset after completing college."

Rory frowned. "Was the professor who came forward Lillie Anderson?"

Marilyn rose and went into another room, returning with a hard-bound book. "I believe it was Professor Anderson. You can borrow my copy." She handed the book to Rory.

He accepted it, flipped it over to read the description on the back cover, then added, "If she was so reclusive, how did you come to know her?"

She patted Esther's hand. "That's when I met your mother. We both came to know Phoebe because we had a mutual interest in horticulture. We even served on a committee or two together. Phoebe had an uncanny knack for gardening."

Rory glanced at Esther. "We saw the gardens earlier."

"They are amazing." Marilyn poured an extra shot into her coffee cup. "No matter the season, there is always native flora in bloom."

Rory remembered the berry bushes by the gazebo. "How familiar are you with the local flora? Meaning, toxic and non-toxic?"

Marilyn snorted. "Chief Mansfield can't really believe Esther is responsible for Phoebe's death?"

Esther slumped. "He might not have if there hadn't been a dozen witnesses that saw me hand her a drink just before she was taken away in an ambulance."

"What would be your motive?" Marilyn demanded.

"What could you possibly gain by killing her?"

"There didn't seem to be any reason to believe I had one." Esther swallowed hard. "…until the will showed up."

Marilyn wagged her head. "But you're not a beneficiary. I don't understand."

Esther sunk lower on the chair. Rory said, "There's a problem. The will we saw today gives Esther unsupervised authority over Phoebe's worldly goods. The house and the assets go to the college and the library because they are beneficiaries. However, everything in the house and on the grounds is controlled by the independent executor. Meaning Esther can sell, donate, or keep as she sees fit."

"Oh, dear. That is a problem."

Esther ran a finger around the coffee mug rim. "I don't see why. I can administer the estate without prejudice." She gave Rory a sly smile. "Unless I'm in the hoosegow."

"Oh, my," Marilyn said. "Then you should know that when Michael died, he left the mansion and its contents to Phoebe and a generous cash settlement went to her brother, Jamison. It's my opinion it was an equal split. However, doing so caused a huge rift between the siblings. Jamison claimed their father hid a treasure in the house, which unfairly left a sizable chunk to Phoebe. Totally, crazy, there was no fortune. I knew Phoebe. Between her salary at the library and what few royalties the novel still earned, she struggled to pay the bills."

Rory leaned back, studying her face. "And you think Jamison's son, James, is here to find this valuable item, the fortune, and claim it as his rightful inheritance?"

"The thought strikes me as a possibility."

"That is crazy," said Esther. "Not only did we see the gardens today, but we were also inside the house. If there's a priceless item in there, it will never be found."

Rory wasn't so sure. He opened the book and scanned the copyright page. He couldn't wait to get back to the apartment and crack the spine.

Chapter Fifteen

It was around midnight when Thacker unlocked the door after attending the open-mic night at Kenny's Koffee Shop. The apartment was quiet. He dumped his jacket, wallet, and keys in the bedroom then returned to the great room, taking a seat in the recliner. Commander leaped from the sofa back to the floor and padded across the wooden planks. Shortly, Thacker heard lapping at the water bowl. Usually, Rory's bedroom door was shut, and the cat closed inside with him for the night. Tonight, the feline was still wandering around.

The young officer wasn't sure what to think about the poetry read at the open mic. Nina had talent. Even if he didn't understand the Bohemian-Ho-Chunk-feminist message portrayed in her poetry, her passion was laid bare. Steamier and angrier than he would have expected from her. Certainly, nothing he would care to have his mom read. All the same, he was proud to be present and hear Nina offer her words to those assembled. That Perry Benson had also been there made him uneasy. He accepted Nina's explanation that they were only friends but felt an underlying current running between them. Thacker was good at reading people, and what he took away from Perry said the man had an agenda. He couldn't stop worrying whether Perry was interested in Nina or using her for personal gain. And if she unwittingly helped him, would she end up in serious trouble?

Unable to shut down his mind, he checked the war room—the lights were out, the computers purred, so he made his way to bed. After tossing and turning, he had a crazy dream filled with tumbling leaves and fire pits and grossly loud chanting. Then a cow bell rang. The more it rang, the faster the leaves churned. Then he realized it was his cell phone chirping. Not quite awake he reached for the nightstand, knocking the phone to the floor. Fishing it out from under the bed, he looked at caller ID.

*—unknown—*

A quick glance at the clock, 3:40 AM. "Thacker," he said. The voice at the other end was faint and he couldn't tell if it was male or female. "Who is this? Can you speak up, I can barely hear you." Again, a whispered response. "Look, it's after midnight, either speak up or call back in the morning." He should have hung up, but curiosity won. He waited.

After a moment the voice, desperate this time. "Clancy. Clancy, it's me, Nina."

"What's wrong?"

"There's someone in the house. I can hear them downstairs and I'm afraid to go down to investigate. People know that Pheobe died. Maybe they don't know I live here. I don't want to call the police. I don't want to be attacked in my bed."

"Where are you now?"

"In my room on the second floor, in the back," she hissed. "There's a lock. I can probably move the dresser and block the door." Her breathing was ragged, like she'd managed to lift a heavy object, or forgot to breathe. "What should I do?"

"Where's Rosco? Is he barking? Growling?"

"No. He's at the door pointing. You know, tail out, staring intently, and one front paw slightly up."

"Lock the door. Don't make any unnecessary noise." He shook his head, trying to think. "Do you have a gun?"

She answered with her usual spirit. "No. And I wouldn't use it if I did."

Laying the phone down, he switched to speaker mode, pulled a T-shirt over his head and looked around for his sweater. "What else is on the second floor? Can you go down to the first without attracting attention? Can you get out onto the roof?"

"I don't think I can leave without taking Rosco with me. I don't want anything to happen to him." Her voice faded in and out.

He pulled on jeans, grabbing his boots and socks. Any noise that carried up had to be substantial. "Look, I'm on the way. Stay where you are. If it sounds like the intruder is coming up, or if you start to panic before I get there…" He didn't want to think about that and swallowed hard. "It will only take me"—he looked at the clock again—"ten minutes. Can you manage ten minutes?"

She made a croaking sound. He heard a deep inhale. "Nina, just stay on the line with me. You don't have to talk. Just don't hang up. I'm leaving now."

He half-walked, half-ran to the gun safe, and retrieved his firearm. Ten seconds later he locked the landing door and flew down the stairs to the street. "Are you still there?" he asked her.

"I'm here," she said but sounded distant.

"All right. I have to pop into the station to get a unit. I want the light rack to clear the road or I'd take my truck.

You, okay? Ten minutes."

After leaving the station, Thacker switched on the cruiser's light bar but not the siren. His heart thumped in his chest while his mind spun in nightmarish directions. Nina was okay, for now. He could hear her rapid breathing as soon as he attached his cellphone to the cruiser's speakers. But why hadn't he told Rory where he was headed, even if it was late? He'd do it as soon as he reached the house.

He paused at the mansion's open gates, noting the light over the front door was out. Dark and shadowy, the brick home didn't look any different than any other mansion-sized home on a wintry night, large, foreboding, and impenetrable. Light showed through a first story window on the right and illuminated an arbor. He'd been to the residence before, but never inside, and couldn't picture where Nina was hiding.

With the unit's lights out, he eased onto the drive, stopping well away from the door. Bringing the cell to his mouth, he murmured, "Nina?" and waited for her to respond.

"Yes. I'm here." Her voice sounded hollow as if she'd moved into a closet.

"I'm just inside the gate. There's no vehicle parked out here. I can see light through the windows flanking the entry door, but the other first-floor windows are dark except one on the right, maybe halfway down."

"My room is above the library in the rear."

"On the right or the left? The side yards are filled with shadows. If I keep the headlights off, I can see enough to follow the drive around to the carriage house."

She spoke quickly, "He's still down there. I can hear him."

"Stay calm. Can I get in from the back?"

She didn't answer right away. When she did her voice was raw. "Don't drive up to the house. Walk around following the drive, I'll turn on a light in my room, so you'll know which window. But the kitchen door is locked"—her voice rose in panic—"Oh, God. I don't know if it's locked. I don't know how he got in."

"It's all right. I plan on coming through the front door. As soon as I've cleared the area, you can come down."

"What if..." After a deep breath, her voice switched back to a whisper. "All right, Rosco and I will come down the front stairs. But Clancy..."

"Yeah."

"No one can walk through the house with the lights out. You'll need our help."

The phone went dead. Nina sounded calmer, more herself. Maybe not in control, but certainly relieved. So, he took a few seconds to organize his thoughts, called the station and reported the break-in, saying he had everything under control and didn't need backup. He hoped he was right. Then he eased the cruiser door open and climbed out.

The night chill slapped him. He pulled out his service revolver and slipped the safety off. Crouching low, he wove a staggered path to the corner of the house, then down the brick front to the door. With his back to the wall, he held the gun ready, and peeked through the glass side panel. The decorative window shattered the entry and hallway into kaleidoscope images. He saw no movement and reached for the knob, turning it. Locked. Inside, he heard activity.

If the front door hadn't been the intruder's entry

point, he needed to look elsewhere. He slipped back to the corner and down the right side to a window where light pooled on the pathway. Again, a cautious peek. The far wall held bookcases from floor to ceiling including an old fashion library ladder that wheeled down the wall on a metal track. He saw no one.

The wind picked up, howling down the arborway and setting his nerves on edge. Where was Nina? Had she crept down the stairs with Rosco? Were they at that moment waiting in the hall? He tested the window. It moved. He slid it up slowly and slipped through.

The intruder was waiting on the other side.

"Officer Thacker." James Sheehan's snarky tone made Thacker flinch. "It's a little early for a social call. Or should I say, way too late?"

Nina sat in an overstuffed chair by the desk, her flannel bathrobe draped to the hardwood floor, arms folded across her chest. Rosco sat at her feet, gnawing on a bone. "He heard us coming," she said, giving James a distasteful scowl. Then glancing down at the dog, she added, "Rosco was no help."

Thacker lifted his chin and lowered the gun. "Mr. Sheehan. What are you doing here?"

Phoebe's nephew shook a book by its spine and tossed it onto the floor. "I've done everything you have asked. Waited at the motel. Presented myself at the police station. I even put up with a background check." He took another book from the table, did the shake-it-thing, tossed it, and reached for the next. "Still getting the run around. Still waiting. This is my family's home and I've come to take possession."

"At three in the morning?" Thacker holstered his firearm. "And entering through the library window?"

"It's my house and I didn't know anyone would be here."

Thacker scoffed. "I suppose you normally carry a soup bone around with you."

James shrugged. Thacker's eyes narrowed. "What exactly are you doing?"

James didn't look at the police officer as he picked up a book. "I would think it's obvious. I'm looking for Aunt Phoebe's will."

Chapter Sixteen

Rory woke to find he was in bed fully dressed. *Willow Creek Woman*, the book he'd fallen asleep reading was on the floor where he'd let it slip. A shower would put things right. The hot water was a welcome pick-me-up. He reviewed his plan for the day, which needed to include interviewing Perry Benson, the young poet connected to the hardware store, the Literary Guild, and the Sheehan gardens. He wasn't so sure Benson didn't have a stronger hold on Thacker's dog-sitter girlfriend than the younger man wanted to admit. He didn't expect Benson to come clean about the girl, but it was time to question him about the break-ins at Hutchison's Hardware. So far, Benson had managed to avoid the detective's efforts. If Rory had his way, that would end today.

Dress slacks, clean dress shirt, sporty tie, and he was ready. Opening the gun safe, he noticed Thacker's firearm was missing. He hadn't seen him the night before, so either he left early again this morning or hadn't come home. He missed the days when they worked side-by-side,

He looked out at the station. Two cars sat in the back lot, and last night's snow had disappeared. With any luck, the day would warm up. He ripped the day off the desk calendar and frowned at the new date. Valentine's Day was closing in. He didn't even want to think about

Sunny and her efforts to force him to make a declaration. Esther wouldn't appreciate showy, over-the-top, mushy schoolgirl stuff. He knew her better than Sunny, and she would hate it. He rubbed his bald head. *Or would she?*

Today's tasks included an interview with Professor Lillie Anderson. She had threatened Phoebe at the literary banquet and warranted a special look. Now that Esther was in a precarious position, he needed to check out the professor. He didn't know the community college schedule or if faculty had regular hours. He weighed his options. Benson was young and might be anywhere. Sunny was undoubtedly at the station, and he didn't feel like dodging her jabs. Lillie Anderson should be at work—so, community college it was.

Winterset Community College sprawled over one hundred acres northeast of town with two dozen one-story buildings surrounding a tall, multi-storied building with a fountain. He followed the main drive onto the campus and found the student center and the administrative offices. He parked in the visitor's lot and fell in line with students walking toward the yellow brick building. He wondered if he had arrived mid-class. The morning was gray. The cloud cover looked like snow, although the temperature hovered in the upper thirties. He remembered his college days when he preferred classes later in the day to accommodate morning sleep-ins.

He hoped that Professor Anderson had office hours, if not classes. He consulted the directory board; she was on the second floor. Passing the glass-walled student union with its comfortable seating and cafeteria tables, Rory climbed the stairs to the balcony level, followed the hallway around, and found the door marked Professor

Anderson. He tapped lightly before opening it.

She stood at the window with her back to him. Her wiry gray hair fell to her waist in a single plait. Momentarily he pictured the Willow Creek Woman, then she turned, and pale Anglo skin dispelled his thoughts.

She cocked her head and invited him in. "I expected to see you yesterday, detective."

He swiped his hat from his head, fingering the brim. "And why was that?"

"I thought for sure you expected me to make a run for it." Her eyes were large and sad. "I'm afraid I didn't make a good impression on you."

He was intrigued. "Public gatherings are never the best place to form opinions on others. Some people are naturally gregarious, while others are awkward and intimidated by the unstated expectations that surround them. I try to view things without prejudice. I prefer to meet someone in their natural habitat before forming an opinion."

Uncertainty drew a line across her forehead. "I guess this is, as you say, my habitat. It has been for more years than I care to admit."

"Mind if I sit?" He moved into the room. She indicated an uninviting wooden chair and took her own behind the desk. He sat, placing his hat in his lap. "So, did you think about making a run for it?"

She laughed. "No, detective." Her mirth softened her features. "I'm too old, and my conscience is clear."

"Can you expound on that?"

"I don't see any reason to play games. Phoebe Sheehan and I were not best friends, and I won't pretend we were." He waited, and she continued, "I've spent my life submerged in literature and debating social injustice.

Phoebe dabbled at what she hoped would bring her respectability and restore decency to her family name. But it was too late. Her father managed to destroy any credibility she might muster."

"You both were being honored at the ceremony. I understood that the Literary Guild—"

"It's hardly a literary society. Not in the true sense and purpose."

He feared she would lecture him on the topic and cut her off. "Can you tell me about the literary honor Winterset was awarding? How were you selected, and what expectations did you have? Even what happens now?"

She stared at him, and he thought he could see gears turning behind her eyes. Students moved in the hallway outside, and through the window behind her, he watched the first feathery snowflakes begin to fall.

"I've mentored many students here at Winterset Community. My disenchantment with Michael Sheehan began in the eighties when we were assistant professors in the English department. We shared dreams and aspirations. There was a movement on campus to start a student journal and publish the students' work and highlight their political concerns. Worldly concerns, what a laugh. Every college student sees reform as a sacred duty. We were idealists pretending we could establish a national poetry competition like that established in '78 in the United Kingdom. Too young to see its futility. Too full of ourselves to doubt we could." She looked into the middle distance. He didn't know what she was thinking.

"And did you establish a student journal?"

At first, she didn't seem to hear him; she shook

herself back to the present. "In the eighties, I was still considered a poetess. Gender equality came much later, as did recognition. Michael Sheehan had the good looks, the following, the student body and faculty's trust."

"A trust he misused?"

"Exactly. While I poured heart and soul into the journal, balanced the student's concerns, and typeset the publication, Michael was busy deceiving us all."

Rory saw the old wound was still raw. He didn't understand how it could fester for over forty years.

"Phoebe was a child at the time, no more than twelve, I understand. So, you couldn't have been very old." He did a quick calculation, arriving at an age between twenty-five and thirty. Then, remembering Marilyn's comment, he added the usual seven years it took to gain tenure and decided her current age had to be seventy-two. She looked older.

"I suppose you wonder why I'm still teaching. For me, you could say it's a life calling. And I have tenure. They can't force me out before I want to go."

"I understand it was tenure that caused the whole ruckus."

"Putting your name on another's work isn't a ruckus. It's dishonest. It's cheating in the worst way by stealing her heart and soul."

"It was a girl then."

"Of course, it was a girl, naive and innocent. He betrayed her. But not only did he steal her work, but he also stole her heritage." Rory thought about the passages he'd read in Sheehan's book the night before. Interesting, heady, insightful. What he'd read didn't feel like a young girl's ramblings. Or was he, as Lillie thought all men were, discounting the fairer sex?

"The minute he published it was obvious he had plagiarized. I'd read it before. But when I confronted him, he denied it. Then dared to accept tenure based on the writing's merits. So, I lost my opportunity and had to submit for tenure the following year."

Rory rubbed the back of his neck. Furthermore, the theft wasn't the whole crime. Michael's success in finding an editor and a publisher willing to take his book to print had sidetracked Lillie's career. Or worse, society's criminal dismissal because she was a woman must have devastated her.

"You saw it as your duty to expose the fraud?"

Her eyes blazed. "Yes. Wouldn't you?"

"Poetry is your chosen form." He frowned. Form? Expression, literary writing style? He wasn't sure how to ask an intelligent question.

Professor Anderson was unruffled. Perhaps there were no stupid questions in the academic world. "I've had success with poetry. But unfortunately, the longer forms challenge me with their lack of form. Poetry is concise. No wasted words yet filled with images and emotions. You should sit in on my lectures, detective."

"Perhaps I will. But back to my questions. First, can you tell me about the literary honor Winterset was awarding? What expectations did you have?" He took out his notebook. "And what happens now?"

They spent another thirty minutes discussing the benefits received from being featured in the literary magazine as the three local poets, Phoebe Sheehan, Perry Benson, and she, had. The greater honor was the chance to be appointed Winterset's Poet Laureate. With Phoebe's untimely death, Lillie didn't know what would happen to that opportunity.

By the time Rory donned his fedora and left, he felt Lillie's grudge against Phoebe wasn't strong enough to move her to murder. She genuinely disliked the other woman, but poison took planning and premeditation. His assessment told him she'd be a heat-of-battle, hot blooded killer—if she was a killer at all.

As he stepped from the student union building, snow flurries came in earnest. The ground was too warm for the snow to accumulate, and the walkway was melting slush. The campus had finally come to life. Students hurried inside to avoid the weather, joining their friends. He passed a man huddled in the corner beside the door, whose face was hidden behind a red scarf. Rory pulled his collar up against the moisture and walked briskly to the car. While waiting for the engine to warm, he called Thacker, hoping for help locating Benson.

"Hey, how's your day look?" he said when the young officer answered. "Thought I'd catch you at the apartment this morning, but you had already gone."

"It's a long story."

Rory heard a thump, then squeaky wheels. "Are you at the apartment?"

"Again, a long story." Then lowering his voice, Thacker said, "It's my day off. I'm at the Sheehan place. I can't talk freely."

"I need a small favor."

He answered in his normal full bass voice, "I'm your man."

Rory knew he could count on Thacker. There wasn't even a need to dangle a carrot, but he did anyway. "Since you're there already, I wonder if you'd like a reason to stay?" He was only too willing, and Rory continued with the request. "I haven't heard back from the lab, so I'm guessing they didn't find a contaminated or suspicious item on the estate." He paused, hoping Thacker would jump in. He didn't. "In the meantime, I've talked to Lillie Anderson, and I'd like a chance to interview Perry Benson. That's where you could—"

Thacker interrupted. "Funny you should bring up wills."

Huh? He wasn't talking about wills. What was going on? Movement in the rear-view mirror caught his attention, and he watched the man in a red scarf pass by before he answered. "I'm in the parking lot at the community college, maybe thirty minutes away. What's going on there, buddy?"

Again, it sounded like furniture scrapping the floor. "Is someone with you? Someone besides Nina?"

Without hesitation, the younger man answered, "We were talking, and it seems likely that Phoebe Sheehan had a will."

Crazy. Thacker knew there was a will, and he knew what it contained.

"Is someone there looking for the will?"

"Yes, that's what Ms. Mahala and I thought."

Ms. Mahala? Moon-struck Thacker wouldn't call Nina *Ms. Mahala* unless he were trying to send a message. The only thing that made sense was that someone was in the house looking for the will, and the rookie didn't want to admit one had been found.

"I can be there in thirty."

"Perfect. So, you agree it's likely to be here. We'll keep looking." Thacker disconnected without saying goodbye.

Rory scratched his forehead. Perry Benson? James Sheehan? Why not just come out and say who was there?

Chapter Seventeen

Esther felt awkward assuming the responsibilities for a woman she barely knew. Rory and the attorney, Roger Krebs, assured her the will had been legally executed according to state laws and recorded with the county. Someone needed to take the immediate details in hand. Being named the Estate Executrix left Esther to deal with the burial and the funeral arrangements. Since the autopsy was completed, Phoebe needed to go from the county morgue to a funeral parlor without delay. Additional advice from Mr. Krebs was in order. She'd made an appointment for ten, then called Axel to share her plans.

"I know you are taking this assignment to protect me seriously, Axel," she said when he answered.

"Yes, ma'am."

"It's nonsense. But to make the job easier on you, I thought I'd share my schedule for today."

"Yes, ma'am."

"I will leave here just before ten for a visit with the lawyer downtown, then onto Miz Sheehan's place. I expect to be out there for the day and always around other people. I think even Rory would consider my plans safe, so you can conduct your activities as you see fit, but I won't be needing your protection."

"The constable said—"

Her foot started to tap. She switched the phone to

the other ear and cut him off. "I know what Detective Naysmith said. I have this under control. If I feel uncomfortable at any point, I'll call. Okay?"

"But Rory—"

"Not today, Axel. Understood?"

\*\*\*\*

Millie greeted her with enthusiasm, showing her into the lawyer's office. "Dad… Mr. Krebs, I mean, will be with you in a moment. Can I get you some coffee?"

"No, thanks. Can I ask you when the baby is due?"

Millie paled, then smiled sweetly from behind thick lashes. "I didn't think it showed."

"I'm afraid you are blessed, a woman who glows with pregnancy."

Having foregone marriage and motherhood, the traditional roles for women worldwide, Esther felt jealous. Then she remembered how happy she was with her lot—accountable to no one, a business owner, and with enough cherished friends to feel loved. Plus, she always had Rory. The thought made her smile.

Laying a hand on her belly, Millie said, "I can hardly wait, we're so excited. But it's still four months away. Luckily, she isn't expected until my husband graduates."

"The time will go quickly. You need to enjoy your time before the baby comes. From what I hear, it's years before you'll have another moment to yourself."

"That's what Daddy says. Then he usually goes into lamenting his little girl lost." She rolled her eyes.

The door opened, and Roger Krebs entered carrying a folder. "What do I say?"

"That business is business, and I don't have a talent greater than the gift of gab," Millie said as he frowned at her over his glasses. But he didn't fool either woman.

Millie scampered out cheerfully.

"I'm sorry if she was bending your ear," attorney Krebs said.

"She's a wonderful girl. You're lucky to have her working with you."

He cleared his throat and gestured for Esther to take a seat. After settling behind the huge shipshape, executive desk, he withdrew a sheet from the folder. "I have a standard contract for handling probate." He passed the paper to her and withdrew another copy. "I know the big firms in Omaha charge for every little thing. There can be extra steps but in the long run most cases go down the same course and to make it more reasonable we here at Krebs and Smith offer a package price."

Esther read along with him as he detailed what would happen, when, and the final dollar amount. "If this looks in order to you, we can sign a contract and our firm will handle probate for you."

"I have no questions about the fees. But I don't know what I need to do as Executrix."

The formalities finished he covered the duties Esther would need to address if she chose to accept the responsibility to execute the estate. To her surprise the list included pet care, managing the house, notifying the family, and arranging for funeral and burial. Krebs made a special point of telling her the first thing she'd need to do was locate the important documents outlining Phoebe's wishes for any and all things.

"Those documents include the Will, the latest bank account statements, investment statements, deeds, birth certificate, marriage certificate, divorce decree, if any, life insurance policies, and keys to the safe deposit box or home safe. Is there a home safe?"

"I wouldn't know."

"Do you know if you are named on the bank accounts?"

"No." Her stomach did a flip-flop. "I can't imagine why I would be."

He frowned and again looked over his glasses at her in earnest. "If you're not named on the accounts, the estate will eventually reimburse you for expenses, but in the meantime, you'll need to cover expenses with your own funds—or find a family member willing to foot the bill. But that's only until the accounts are transferred to the estate and you have full access to the money. And naturally, you'll receive a court decree appointing you executrix. It's all included in the package here at Krebs and Smith." He pushed the contract toward her again.

"What happens to Phoebe if I don't agree to execute the will?"

"The county will see that she is buried."

That made her uneasy and she tried to recall the amount in her personal checking account. Handling her grandmother's affairs had been easy, she knew what the plans were. They had shared a checking account for years. Her sister and her mother were both alive and willing to help her work through the tough decisions. She had an inkling about Phoebe's affairs because she had access to her income taxes. Locating banking institutions and the named beneficiaries wouldn't be a problem. But managing and securing the estate? It felt like a daunting task.

"Because Phoebe named you in the will, you have first rights to execute her wishes. If you decline, and you can, the county will try to locate a blood relative willing to act as executor. Sometimes that happens quickly, sometimes not at all."

Esther had a sinking feeling. What if the county dumped Phoebe in a pauper's unmarked grave? Or James Sheehan muscled his way into the mansion and stole everything valuable? She pictured Rosco wandering the countryside howling at the moon.

"If I take the job on, can I change my mind later?"

He nudged the paper again. "Yes."

Esther took the pen he held out. After she signed, he said, "Make a check out to Krebs and Smith for five-hundred dollars. We will bill the estate for the balance once probate is complete, and funds are available. In the meantime, this will get the petition started."

"Is there anything else I need to know?"

He shook his head and stood, extending his hand. "I will have Millie copy this document for you, as well as the will. Do you wish to wait, or should I have them couriered to your home?"

"If it's no bother, I'll take the copies with me."

Esther sat in the reception area, looking out the window, watching the light snow flurries. She wondered if she should have consulted Rory, but decided he would encourage her to do what she felt was right. This felt right.

Millie came out with a sealed envelope. "Dad says to tell you that he will file the petition for probate this afternoon. And he encourages you to secure the house as soon as possible."

"Even before the funeral arrangements?"

Millie shrugged her shoulders.

Okay. Secure the house. She didn't suppose the body was going anywhere. She, if nothing else, needed to verify that Nina would stay on at the house now that Phoebe was gone. And she needed to pick up the keys and let the dog sitter know about the will. She had a lot to do.

****

Rory drove through town and out County Line Road enroute to the Sheehan property. He didn't think Thacker was in trouble per se, but he'd been interested in summoning him to the estate. He ruminated on the situation but couldn't come up with a feasible explanation. The young policeman and Nina were there along with someone else. He hoped it was Benson because that would save him from searching for the young poet.

The flurries cleared, and the day, although cool, had the brilliant midday sun that he'd missed in January. It was too early to have spring fever—yet he wished spring would come. The short days and long nights left him depressed, longing for a fresh breeze and an early sprouting meadow. He even envisioned crocus blooming. He shook his head; too much time spent with poets.

He glanced in the mirror in preparation to turn into the Sheehan drive. A jeep crowded up behind. Rory goosed the gas pedal, sped past the turn, fishtailing on the gravel shoulder. The vehicle zipped past. He could have sworn the man in the red scarf sat behind the wheel.

He paused to steady his heartbeat. Finally, he put the city issue in reverse and backed up, turning onto the drive just as Esther came from the other direction and pulled in behind. He led her around to the carriage house, passing Thacker's cruiser and a rental sedan parked on the drive at the front door. Once they parked, he asked,

"Did someone from the estate call you?"

She wore a puzzled frown. "No. What's wrong?"

"I don't know. Thacker's in there with Nina, and I had a strange phone call." He brought her up to date as they approached the mudroom door. "I don't know if I've driven to the shoot-out at the O.K. Corral or if I've been summoned as a referee."

"Before we go in"—she wrinkled her nose—"I need to tell you, this morning, I engaged Roger Krebs to handle Phoebe's probate."

"I figured you would. Anything else I need to know before we blow the doors open?"

His comment brought out her smile. "I sent Axel to scour the countryside for packing boxes."

"Remind me to tell you about Professor Anderson later." He squeezed her elbow. "Ready?"

The door gave way as he twisted the knob. They entered, stepped through the paper stacks leading through the kitchen to the hallway, then followed the noise down the hallway to the library. Rory unbuttoned his overcoat and freed access to his shoulder holster. Before they reached the door, he heard the commotion.

Placing his body to shield Esther, he scanned the room. Rosco slept on the hearth rug, snoring. Thacker sat behind the desk reading a magazine, and to his left, Nina sprawled in the overstuffed chair still wearing a night robe.

Perched on the library ladder, James Sheehan reached for a book. He froze in mid-stretch and said, "Good afternoon, detective."

"Mr. Sheehan." The detective thumbed the fedora's brim up. Rosco grunted, rolled onto his back, and looked up at him with one eye open. "Are we late to the party?"

James pulled a book from the shelf, shook it by one corner, and then tossed it to the floor. A good six feet from release to hardwood, the book landed with a thud. He reached for the next. This time, his shake dislodged a leaf. He watched it flutter to the floor, then threw the volume down after it. The book hit a small wooden table edge, dislodged a paper pile, and ricocheted under the desk.

"Mr. Sheehan, I suggest you come down from there."

"My house. My library."

"I can have you arrested for destruction of personal property."

"You don't get it. This is my property." He almost lost his balance, grabbing the rungs at the last moment and avoiding a topple. "You've had me certified. Don't you remember? And now, I'm looking for Aunt Phoebe's will to make it all legit."

Rory caught Thacker's eye and lifted one shoulder. The young officer remained silent but raised his brows as if to say *beats me*.

"I can't talk to you while you're up there. Come down. Let's discuss this like civilized gentlemen."

He was afraid James would refuse, but instead, he made his way down, kicking the books at the bottom farther into the room, and sat on the third rung.

"Phoebe had a will prepared by a firm in town. Yesterday, Ms. Mullins and I visited them, and they verified it exists. This morning, she retained them to petition the county to probate the will."

James' mouth fell open in a fair imitation of a fish before he jumped up and shouted, "Ridiculous." Slamming an open palm on the ladder rung, he spat,

"You can't do this."

"What is it you think I've done? Your aunt had a plan in place, including a will, asset distribution, and named beneficiaries."

"Let me see the will."

Rory spread his hands, palms up. "I don't have a copy. Although, there might be a copy here in the house somewhere. However, I can tell you it is registered with the county clerk, so there's no denying its existence."

James didn't falter. "You may have the will, but I have a codicil."

Thacker, Nina, and Esther looked confused.

But Rory understood. James had made a move and was about to declare checkmate. He gave him the evil eye. "Do you have it with you?"

"No. But I can produce it. Which law firm drafted the will?"

"I'm afraid you'll have to contest the will. It's already moving forward in probate."

James eyed him suspiciously, then straightened his back, plastered a confident expression on his face, and raised his chin. "We'll see. You haven't heard the last from me." Tripping over the books scattered around his feet, he made a hasty exit, but not before glaring at each in turn.

When the front door slammed, Rory asked, "Okay, who wants to tell me what was going on in here?"

Nina spoke for the first time. "James broke in through the library window around three o'clock this morning. I called Clancy, and he came to save me."

"Clancy?" said Rory, amused. Esther shot him a look. Thacker pinked. Rory cleared his throat, "Clancy can be helpful. But I don't understand why you two let

Sheehan dismantle the library."

"He was agitated," Thacker answered, "but otherwise, harmless. I thought rather than argue with him, we should stand back and let him wear himself out. Mr. Sheehan seemed genuinely surprised to find Nina in the house. I think he's used to bullying. When we didn't back down, he only knew to go on blustering. What makes me wonder is that he came prepared to deal with Rosco." On hearing his name, the beagle threw back his head and howled.

Nina slapped her thigh. He looked at her with baleful eyes and scampered over to her chair. She rubbed his head. "Good boy."

Thacker added, "I was worried he'd move beyond this room."

Rory's gaze ran over the library's contents—scattered books, boxes, papers.

Nina said, "What do you think he was after?" She stood, adjusting the tie at her waist. "Surely, more than the will?"

"What did he mean when he said he had a codicil?" asked Esther.

After hesitating for a moment, Rory moved to the bookshelves, selected a large dictionary, and took it to the desk. Checking the index, he opened it and ran a finger down the page. "Codicil—noun. An addition or supplement used to explain, modify, or revoke a will."

"That means—"

Thacker stopped her by holding up a hand. Then, he held down a button on his cell phone and asked, "What is a codicil used for?"

A popular artificial intelligence voice filled the room. "*A codicil is a testamentary document similar to but not necessarily identical to a will. A codicil is used to revoke the person currently named as the executor and appoint a new executor. In some cases, it can revoke the person currently named as the beneficiary and name a new beneficiary."*

"Oh. My. God." Esther's eyes were the size of Rosco's water bowl. "What nerve. Can he do that?"

Rory shrugged. "I think it's safe to say he will try."

"I think it's safe to get on with the day." Nina tapped her thigh. Rosco snorted, and nails clicked on hardwood as he followed her out and down the hall.

After they left, Esther crossed to the ladder and picked up the leaf that had fluttered to the floor during James' search. Rubbing it between her fingers, she studied it.

"What have you got there?" Rory asked.

She raised her gaze to the top bookshelf. "I don't know, but it was in a book."

"Interesting." He took it from her, shoving it into his pocket. "Since I'm here, do you want some help this morning?"

She didn't need to accept his offer; her eyes said it all.

Chapter Eighteen

"I want to sort Phoebe's papers," Esther said. "The lawyer says I need to find her important documents. I brought boxes if you'll bring them in from the car."

After retrieving plastic bins from her trunk, Rory stopped in the kitchen. "Can I make a suggestion?" She nodded. "Thacker and Nina can finish going through the books on the library shelves. They will be more respectful than James, and you can ask them to organize those on the floor. Meanwhile, you and I will check the other rooms on this floor."

She agreed. "I warn you, there are countless rooms, including a formal dining room, pantry, sunroom, casual day room, and a formal living room."

He sighed. "I suppose every room is stuffed with paper." He gazed around. "Where do you want to begin?"

"Here in the kitchen," she said. "If Thacker and Nina finish the library, I think I can tackle the kitchen. But I'll be the first to admit I can't work under these conditions. It's no wonder Phoebe sent her tax papers to me. If I'd seen this mess before I took her on as a client, I wouldn't have."

"Are you thinking twice about handling the estate?"

"Nephew James has my dander up. I would tackle this job just to keep him from gloating."

"Important papers, huh? So how do we sort it out?"

"Separate the wheat from the chaff. Trash, receipts, papers." After glancing at a few, she picked up a handful and said, "Better make that trash, legal documents, requests, unopened mail, and correspondence. Just toss like items in the same bin. I'll sort them out later."

"I think I can manage unopened, legal, and advertising."

"It's a place to start."

Rory found a dolly in the mud room and moved the boxes from the kitchen into the hallway. It helped but not much. Luckily, Esther had coffee ready.

After an hour, they had cleared the table and moved to the serving cart.

Handing the original will to Esther, he said, "This needs to go to Krebs before he can file for probate. If there's a safe in this house, don't you think she would have kept this there?"

"Grandma kept her will in the kitchen. She always said that if it were in a safe box, no one would have the key to open it. She got so many questions about the envelope she'd marked "when I'm gone" that she threatened to keep it in the freezer. Naturally, she pooh-poohed the idea that there was anything worth leaving."

"Freezer, huh?" He stood and crossed to the freezer, opened the door, and rummaged through the contents. It was surprisingly empty, with a few frosted-over ice-cube trays and a package containing Dixie-cup-sized vanilla ice cream. "Is there a deep freeze?"

"Look in the mud room."

The deep freeze was buried under blankets and old coats. He had to wrestle the lid up. Then leaning in, he worked his way through the freezer-wrapped parcels to the bottom. Knocking the ice off a six-by-nine-inch plastic container that looked odd, he pulled it free. With a thud, the freezer's lid dropped back to seal the contents in its icy cocoon. He pried the container open.

Inside were pages wrapped in a beaded cloth. He removed the one on top but couldn't decipher it. Stepping back into the kitchen, he held it out to Esther. "It's handwritten, but I don't know in what language."

After examining it, she handed it back. "This was in the freezer?"

"I guess for safe keeping. There are several more packages."

"Strange place to use as a filing cabinet." She looked around, pushed a brunette lock that had fallen onto her forehead back into place, and added, "Well, maybe she needed a place where she'd be sure to find them."

It sounded reasonable to him. "Do you think it's Sioux? I think the Ho-Chunk are a Siouan-speaking people." Esther gave him an astonished look. He smiled. Well, he knew odd things. They came in handy, handier than one could imagine. He cocked one brow. "The Ho-Chunk tribe seems to have come up a lot lately. Do you suppose…?" He glanced toward the hallway and then motioned for her to follow.

The books were back on the shelves. A small leaf pile sat on the desk blotter. The young couple lounged in the stuffed chairs. Rosco ran to meet him as he held the page out to Nina. "I came across this in the mud room."

She took it, glanced over the paper, and handed it back.

Thacker craned his neck to get a peek. "What is it?"

"I think it's written in a native American language. I hope Nina can identify it."

"The Ho-Chunk," she said, "have about a hundred

native speakers among their elders. Keeping the old language alive is important to the Nation. But if you're asking if I recognize it, I can tell you I don't speak or read *Hocąk*."

Thacker opened his mouth to add a comment, but a gas snow-blower erupted and drowned out his words. Rory looked out the garden window—Perry Benson had arrived.

Rory wanted a word with the young poet. Although Benson was around the back, he decided to check out his vehicle first and went out through the front door. A pickup with attached flatbed trailer was parked on the drive. The detective walked around the rig, kicked the tires. It fit the bill for the hardware heist, yet nothing appeared suspicious. It might be a gardener's trailer and nothing more.

He heard the blower in the back and headed around under the low hanging arbor formulating questions as he went, until he was nearly through the overhang and into the gardens. He stepped onto something loose, and combined with his body weight, the object suddenly rolled forward. Momentarily losing his balance, he slipped backward. The fir trees dipped wildly and blocked his vision, then sprang up in an arch overhead. In a flash, he was lying on his back. The gas engine abruptly stopped.

Rory laid there for a moment catching his breath.

"Hey, man, you okay?"

Rory couldn't see Benson. Lying under the arbor and suffering from wounded pride, he hoped Benson hadn't seen him either. No luck.

"What happened, man? Let me give you a hand."

Tattoos ran up the arm that reached down to help

him up. The winter vest zipped to his Adam's apple didn't cover the ink that wound around his neck. The dark eyes held humor.

"I've been practicing that maneuver for a while now," Rory said. "I guess the sleet threw my timing off."

"Seriously, man. Nothing broken?"

He dusted his knees off. Checked his ankle. He wished he could leap up but knew that wasn't going to happen. "I guess I stepped on loose gravel, and it threw me. Careless. Yet, all parts are still functioning." He grabbed the hand and let the younger man pull him to his feet. "Rory Naysmith, WPD."

"Perry Benson, gardener."

"Are you also, Perry Benson, poet?"

"Guilty." The younger man moved back, giving him room to recover or to distance himself from Rory's inquiry. He wasn't sure.

"I was at the award ceremony Thursday night. Quite an honor for you. Congratulations."

Perry's expression changed. Rory wondered if he would deny being at the awards banquet. But then he said, "Being recognized by the local guild is a start."

"From what I understand," said Rory, "it's quite an honor to be among the finalists. But what would I know, I'm just a policeman." He tried to make it sound friendly. Perry didn't buy it, so he changed tactics. "Who knows, you may have become the first Winterset Poet Laureate, but then disaster struck when Phoebe Sheehan went down."

His eyes flashed. "If you're okay, I'll get back to my chores." He turned to go.

Rory followed close on his heels. "I'm also the detective looking into the break-ins at Hutchinson's

Hardware."

Perry stopped.

"Gardener, writer, night supervisor," Rory said. "Might as well add butcher, baker, and candlestick maker."

"I like to stay busy." Perry made his way from the arbor. "Look, I need to finish here and get on my way."

"Sure. Don't let me hold you up. I'll stop by the store tomorrow and take your statement."

The young gardener picked up the blower and yanked the cord. The engine roared to life.

Rory glanced at the library window. Nina, face expressionless, stared out. Esther stood behind her, frowning.

## Chapter Nineteen

The Golden Leaf Diner had been the community hub for as long as Esther could remember. On Main Street, the casual restaurant with its padded booths, bottomless cups of coffee and all-day breakfasts still drew a crowd. Dishing up heaping plates and encouraging friendly chatter, the diner was the place for people to linger in conversations with neighbors as well as conduct town business.

Today, the diner had one empty booth in the back corner. Esther took it, tossed her coat onto the bench, and slid in so that she faced the door and could see who came in and who left. She'd called a pow-wow with Marilyn, intending to solicit help with the Sheehan house. And although there might be a hundred lovely objects there, it'd be impossible to find them among the disarray. Perhaps there had been a method to Phoebe's madness, but Esther didn't see it. Not only were the rooms filled with papers and souvenirs, but they also contained every correspondence her father, Michael Sheehan, had handled throughout his long life.

Yesterday she'd uncovered a box containing English papers he'd graded in 1982. And then, a box containing the Valentine's Day cards Phoebe had received from her second-grade classmates. Reading through them and matching the names to those she knew in town had been fun. She even wondered if Rory would buy her one this year. But fun had no place in her plans—she needed to find funds to sustain the household.

Before the coffee arrived, Marilyn entered. She moved briskly, as if impatient. "I've about thirty minutes before heading out to the hospital." She slipped from her coat, unwound a colorful scarf from her head, and took the seat opposite Esther. "What's happening on the murder investigation? Progress? Arrests?"

"If there is, I'm not privy to it."

Her eyes danced with mischief. "Just thought I'd ask. Dating Rory has to have some benefits."

"I'm meeting a locksmith at Sheehan's in an hour. He's changing the locks."

"Oh, is that necessary?"

"Yesterday, James Sheehan broke in through the library window, claiming he didn't know anyone was in the house. Well... it's a long story. But suffice it to say, trouble seems to be his middle name. And after what I witnessed yesterday, I don't trust him. So, rather than waste time looking for keys and worrying there might be copies floating around the county, I'm having them replaced. I might even install a security system."

"What do you need me for?"

Esther brought her up to speed. "According to the attorney, there is no question the will is valid. I need to liquidate Phoebe's possessions, stuff that doesn't require a title change, including all the furniture, jewelry, and the houschold items. My problem is the ongoing expense needed to pay the utilities."

"Why is that a problem? Phoebe wasn't destitute. There should be money."

"Oh, I believe there is, but I don't have access to it until the will goes through probate."

"How long will that take?"

Esther shrugged. "Attorney Krebs' advice is to keep the estate running as normal. I can use my funds, which the estate will eventually reimburse, or find a beneficiary willing to advance the money."

Not warming to the problem, Marilyn asked, "Who are the beneficiaries?"

"The community college and the Winterset Library."

"Oh, goodie," Marilyn scoffed. "Government institutions, operating on budgets. Good luck with that."

"I talked to the administrator at the college this morning. Although she was pleased to hear about Phoebe's gift, her hands are tied, and there are no funds available until after the annual budget review in July. I can't wait six months. However, she said she'd be glad to send around a memo and check their charter. So, that thought produced zilch to zero. And the library's help might be even harder to acquire."

Marilyn waved for refills and picked up the menu. "Should we have pie?" Then after a moment, she dropped her palms on the tabletop and made the bangles at her wrists chink. "I'm sure you'll figure out a solution."

Esther leaned forward. "That's exactly why I asked you here."

When the waitress brought the coffee pot, announcing an apple pie had just come from the oven Esther ordered two slices, then said, "I have in mind a garage sale. Not to sell the items that would be valuable to the library or the school, although I can't see they'd have an objection to turning pots and pans into cash. Besides, it would help to see what else is there. And keep the estate going without borrowing money from the bank."

"Esther, don't you have money?"

"I do. But I don't want to spend it. The biggest problem right now is all the stuff in the house. Yesterday I took half a dozen plastic bins out there. It took less than an hour to fill them. Burning old utility bills is one thing, but Michael Sheehan's writings would probably interest the college. The estate library is filled with beautiful books. The Winterset Library—"

Marilyn interrupted, "I get the picture. What are you asking me to do?"

"I need administrative help in organizing and selling off the household goods."

Marilyn rubbed her hands together, and rings clinked, and bangles jangled. "It might be fun."

After the meeting at the diner, Esther swung by the grocery and collected a few packing size boxes. She arrived at the Sheehan place at twelve-thirty and after finding Nina and the beagle gone, let herself in.

She hadn't known what to tell Tom Hutchinson when she'd called about the security system's needs, offering the door count, and mentioning the outbuildings. He suggested replacing the main door locks and hanging cameras at the front and back. When pushed, he suggested his man work up a quote when he got there. As she waited for the locksmith, she counted the outbuildings. Carriage house. Gazebo. Gardening shed. Had she told him about the gardening shed? Would it be advisable to install a camera in the gazebo—it was an open structure? The money issue remained a problem, she wished she'd talked to Hutchinson about financing or delayed billing.

Transferring the empty boxes from the car to the mudroom, she was dismayed at how few she'd brought. Who knew the grocery store staff routinely broke them down and bundled them for recycling? However, the manager said he'd have a fresh supply after restocking the shelves in the morning. In response, she'd promised to swing by early, adding another chore to her growing task list. This job severely cut into her accounting business hours. She'd have to manage.

At precisely one o'clock, she heard a pickup pull into the drive. The vehicle downshifted, coming to the back and she stepped out to greet him. "Why, Perry, I didn't expect you today."

The gardener gave her a disarming smile, his black eyes twinkling. "Didn't you order the locks changed?"

She was dumbfounded. Then finding her voice, she said, "Tom Hutchinson is sending...don't tell me...Are you here to install the new hardware?"

He made a deep bow, bending at the waist and removing a watch cap from his head. "At your service."

"Forgive me, I was expecting...well, I'm not sure who I was expecting." After regaining her composure, she added, "New locks will set my mind at ease. Are you prepared to estimate the needs for the security system, or will someone else be coming?" She looked toward the front drive, but unfortunately, the evergreens and the arbor hid it from view.

"That would be me, ma'am." He reached back into the truck and pulled out a bag. "I'd like to change the locks first if that's okay with you. Front, back, and the carriage house doors. Does that sound right?"

"Sounds perfect."

He walked around the truck's bed and lifted a

toolbox over the side. "Lead the way."

Perry started at the front door, adding a deadbolt and a new tumbler lock. She watched as he performed the job. But when he finished and started for the kitchen, she felt he could do without her supervision. "Why don't I get started on another project?"

"Suit yourself, ma'am. You're not bothering me."

"It's not that I don't enjoy your company, but there is a lot to do inside." His expression said he understood.

The library almost looked livable. The books were back on the shelves and the papers, previously scattered over tabletops, had been placed inside bins. Granted, the hoard was all still there, but containing them worked wonders. Esther sat down at the desk and booted up the computer. When the prompt for a password appeared, her heart dropped. She typed "password," nothing doing. "Rosco" and "beagle" didn't work either. She opened the middle drawer, and in the pencil compartment, a post-it had "Big-Voice" written on it. She typed it in; *Voilà!*

It didn't take long to discover the operating system was old and the processor slow. She'd need to sell enough "fluff" at the garage sale to cover the cost to replace the computer. And then sell that computer before she dispensed the estate assets.

She scanned the directories looking for a folder that might contain an inventory or Phoebe's records. Not finding an obvious choice, she settled for checking Phoebe's email. Interestingly enough, her nephew James Sheehan wasn't in her contacts. That made her wonder. She found an address book in the drawer, but flipping to the S section found no Sheehan, James, or otherwise. Curious.

There were numerous files containing poetry. But

unfortunately, there didn't seem to be a rhyme or reason for the titles or directories. Then again, what did she know about poetry? She was better with numbers. Discouraged, she moved to the second order of business, finding the safe.

A home that size, built for the gentry, undoubtedly had one. Since her only experience with personal safes was the kind found in hotel rooms, she immediately wanted to check the closets. The library didn't have one, but it had several cupboards. None contained a safe. Then there were the safes you saw in movies, hidden behind the artwork, buried in the wall, and under the flooring. So many walls, rugs, and closets in a sizable home. She set off to investigate.

When Marilyn's Cadillac crunched up the drive, Esther toiled in the formal dining room, opening and closing cabinets and inspecting beneath the floor coverings. Before she got the Persian rug back in place, the older woman burst through the front door, calling, "I'm here. And I've brought reinforcements."

Marilyn's boot heels echoed in the hallway. "My goodness, the boxes. Esther, where are you?"

"In here."

"You'll never guess who I ran into downtown. I didn't know how I would get all the containers into the car and... Gee, there is stuff everywhere. Where is here?"

"Dining room. Second door on the left."

"Well, I was trying to wrestle them into the trunk. I'd already filled the back seat, you see, and he just walked up and said, are you Mrs. Beauregard? And I said how did you know, and... Oh." She stopped in the doorway with a plastic bin in each hand. Her mouth gapped open.

"It's all like this, Marilyn. Can you see why I need help?"

"Yes, dear. But I'm trying to tell you I brought help."

Behind Marilyn, with a superior glint in his eye, stood James Sheehan.

Chapter Twenty

"There is so much to do," said Esther, eying James suspiciously. "And you've brought Phoebe's nephew?" Her voice strained, she added, "How nice."

She recalled James' threats from the previous afternoon. Well, he could bluster all he wanted, she was going forward with the estate liquidation. And if Marilyn and Rory were right, he was determined to find a hidden treasure somewhere on the grounds. It didn't make sense that Marilyn had befriended him. Although, she was known to keep friends close and enemies closer.

"So, dear, where do we start?" Marilyn asked.

"I could use help deciding what items will bring a better price in an estate sale than at a consignment shop."

Esther looked over her shoulder toward the formal dining room where mahogany wainscoting rose three feet from the hardwood floors. It was her favorite room with cream-colored walls above the paneling, tasteful landscapes on the interior walls, and large windows facing the grounds behind the house. "I've been going through porcelain in the dining room, but the amount is overwhelming." Only a tiny white lie, she meant to do that, but later.

The older woman shifted the bins to rest against her hip. "Why don't you wait until after the sale? Any unsold items can always be sold on consignment."

"True," Easter agreed, leading the duo back into the

larger room where they could sift through glassware, silver, and porcelain. James moved past her and over to the huge china cabinet. "James," she said as he reached for the cupboard door. "I'm planning to unload the cabinet. Furniture will do best at auction, and we'll need to empty all the pieces. Marilyn, why don't you start by clearing the table so we can see what we have?"

James grunted but didn't respond. "Marilyn," she said, her gaze not leaving James' face. "You can supervise your helper while I work elsewhere."

She wasn't about to admit they'd interrupted her search for a hidden safe. Exasperated with their interruption, she backed against the decorative paneling, and accidentally pushed the baseboard with her heel. The panel gave way, and a minuscule gasp escaped her lips. What the heck? Neither Marilyn nor James appeared to notice her surprise.

"Is Nina around?" asked Marilyn, placing the bins on the table. "We could use more help."

Not wanting to move, and afraid the panel would drop, or pop while they were in the room, Esther froze. "I don't think..." she looked around unsure how to distract them. "Today is adoption day. I guess she and Rosco are at the animal rescue facility." Seeing Marilyn's frown, she added, "Janus Chances helped her become a regular volunteer there. I think she's happiest spending time with the animals."

"No doubt that is true. She'd probably adopt them all given the chance," Marilyn said. "But how'd she get there? She doesn't drive."

"Then someone must have picked her up," said Esther. "She wasn't here when I arrived."

"A friend, a relative, Thacker perhaps?" suggested

Marilyn playfully raising one brow. "Or that gardener poet?"

"It wasn't Perry Benson. He's out back changing the locks." Behind her back, Esther slowly ran her fingers along the panel's edge, trying to examine the board behind her without drawing attention. It had budged, she was certain. But it was now back in place. She definitely wanted to investigate, but not until they left the room.

Marilyn leaned forward. "Esther is something wrong? You're wearing the strangest expression."

"No, why do you…" There was a tap at the window and Esther turned toward the noise. "Oh, good grief," she muttered under her breath. "Nothing is wrong, Marilyn. It's just that everyone keeps popping up and I'm not accomplishing what I need to."

The family friend glanced at the window and smiled. "I'll see what Axel wants while you tend to important matters."

Marilyn swept past her, opened the French doors leading to the brick patio, and stepped out. Esther locked eyes with James. "Why are you here?"

"To help, of course."

"You don't fool me, James. Lending a hand is the furthest thing from your mind."

"All right," he admitted, "I'm here in case my inheritance turns up. You can get a restraining order against me, if you want, but it won't keep me away."

Esther took a deep breath. Except for being a nuisance, he hadn't hurt a soul. He'd made a mess in the library, yes. But he hadn't punched holes in the walls or dug up the flower beds—yet. "I don't want you wandering around the property. You came with Marilyn. You stay with her."

He opened his mouth, but before he could respond, Marilyn returned with Axel.

Still against the windows and shielding the loose panel, Esther shook a finger at him. "I told you I don't need your protection today, Axel."

He hung his head. "Yes, Miss Esther, but you didn't tell the constable."

It was true, she hadn't talked to Rory today. "All right as long as you're here, find Perry Benson. He's someplace out back, probably at the carriage house, installing new locks. Find him and see if he needs help changing them or hanging security cameras."

Axel flexed his hands, exposing the fingerless gloves he always wore in the winter months. "It would be my pleasure to accept your assignment now that Ms. Beauregard is here to run interference."

He pulled black aviator glasses from atop his head and situated them to hide his beady gray eyes from view. Esther could see her reflection in the lens. But it wasn't until he started to walk away that she noticed the black suit, white shirt, and thin black tie beneath his sleeveless ski vest.

James carefully set a gilt-edged soup tureen on the table. "I would be more help in the carriage house. Any objections if I help the men?"

"I guess not," said Esther.

Once the men were gone, Marilyn said, "What does Axel mean by interference?"

"There have been some odd happenings. And now that Phoebe's death is definitely established as a homicide, Rory is afraid I might be in danger." Marilyn sunk onto a dining chair, listening as Esther continued. "James Sheehan may or may not be who he says, and until Rory can clear that up, he thinks we should assume there is a valuable item among Phoebe's things. Rory suspects, whatever *it* is, plays a part in Phoebe's death and places me in the line-of-fire now that I'm handling the estate."

"Ridiculous."

"Worse, he asked Axel to protect me. A bodyguard. As if Axel doesn't already watch my every move." Wrinkling her nose, she added, "I couldn't ask for a more considerate neighbor, but I don't need a babysitter."

"So, you don't think James would harm you?"

Unwilling to move away from the wainscot panel, Esther leaned against the windowsill and analyzed her feelings toward Phoebe's nephew. They didn't include fear. "He's all bluster. Rory thinks there's something fishy about him. Yet, I don't think he will hurt me."

"He can be charming," Marilyn agreed, "but other than being insistent, he hasn't done much beyond complaining."

"He did break in and rifle through the library books. I don't trust him."

"Why would you send him to change locks if his honesty is in question?"

Esther scoffed. "Frankly, he's more sneaky than dangerous. Since it's hard to be villainous when you're in plain sight, directing James to secure the grounds might sidetrack his bigger plan to dislodge me. Or harm me if you believe Rory."

"He hasn't found the item, or he'd be gone. Wouldn't it get his goat if we found it first? What does he say it is? And more important, how valuable?"

"He doesn't say, so I doubt he knows. More worrisome is a codicil he claims to have and says he plans to use in blocking me from selling off the assets."

"Well, let him try. No silly paper can stop you." She waved a hand, dismissing the notion and sending the silver bracelets on her wrist jangling. "Besides, if we get started, we'll have the sale underway before he gets a foothold." She added a wink. "You should have seen your face when you opened the door and there we were."

Her glee unnerved Esther. "Why don't you see if he really went to the carriage house while I get started?"

Esther waited a beat after the door closed behind her friend, then turned toward the paneling, running her hand down until she discovered a push-latch slightly above the baseboard. One press, and a three-foot section swung open to reveal a hidden space, its depth equal to the window ledge above. Inside were two chambers, the upper with a biometric safe, and the lower a slim wire rack holding three colored folders. She tried the safe first. No luck. The last person to close it had spun the dial.

After closing the panel, she took the folders to the table and spread them out before opening them. The first contained documents for repairs, a receipt for a roof patching in January, an estimate for chimney repair. She flipped the next folder open. Poetry. Glancing though the pages, she didn't know whose work it was as none were signed. However, the handwriting indicated they had been penned by a single person. It might be Phoebe's work, Nina's, or someone else's altogether. The third folder was empty. She wondered at the need to keep them in a hidden compartment.

A noise indicated someone had entered the kitchen. She quickly gathered the folders before Marilyn saw them. However, it wasn't her friend. The dog sitter swept into the room, dropped her beaded sack on the table, crossed to the wainscoting, and accessed the hidden panel. Squatting, she spun the dial and opened the safe.

"You knew about the safe?" Esther asked, amazed.

"You're still here?" Nina said over her shoulder.

"If it's any consolation, I'll be gone as soon as possible."

The girl took a small box from the safe, stood, and held it out to Esther. "Phoebe kept more jewelry in the safe."

She craned to look around the girl. "What else?"

Nina tossed her braid and stepped forward blocking any hope Esther had of discovering the contents. "Nothing much. A few pieces Phoebe thought valuable. Old papers. Birth certificates and marriage licenses. Death certificates."

"Whose death certificates?"

"Father, mother, brother. I don't know, I'm just the dog sitter."

For someone who didn't care, the girl seemed to know a lot. "Nina, I'm the executor. I should know about the safe."

She shrugged and handed the box over. "There's also a war medal and a few rings."

Esther fanned the folders. "What about these. Why hide your poetry?"

"They're not hidden. I keep them here, so they don't get misplaced. Phoebe did as well."

"That I can understand. Safe guarded so they don't fall into the wrong hands. The father's shame influencing his daughter's actions, and in turn her obsession influencing you."

"The accusations were unfounded."

"Unfortunately, speculation that he used another's writings overruled the facts." She raised a brow challenging the girl to dispute her observation. "His family was treated like outcasts. Deceit and fraud leave a nasty taste."

Nina crossed her arms over her chest and vigorously shook her head.

Esther held out a hand. "I'll take the combination for the safe."

## Chapter Twenty-One

The war room was dark and windowless, but Rory loved the solitude. Here he could concentrate undisturbed by the bustle at the police station. A private sanctuary made from a discarded office, two makeshift desks, enough filing cabinets to contain his old notebooks and the case files. After settling onto an office chair, he booted up the computer. He'd finally come to respect technology but still didn't understand it. If the beast would continue to do its magic, he'd continue to use its talents.

A tentative knock sounded at the door, then the lock mechanism clicked, and Thacker stuck his head in. "Commander is lying at the door. A dead giveaway you're in here." A golden streak slipped between his legs, leaped onto the desk, and the old tabby settled on Rory's keyboard.

"Where else would I be? Did you bring the background information?"

The younger man stepped in. "For the record, I don't feel right investigating Nina."

Rory held out a hand to accept the folder from him. "You'll get over it."

"Is it because she's…?" Thacker's voice trailed off as if too embarrassed to finish the accusation.

"She lives in the household with access to food supplies and connected to the Janus Chances organization. That should be enough reason."

The rookie knew better than to think he'd singled out Nina because she was Native American. If she'd been Armenian or Irish, she'd still be on his person-of-interest list. "I understand why you need to dig into the others' backgrounds, but—"

"Enough. Objection noted." Rory glanced down at the page containing information on Nina Mahala. "Not much here. Relax. You know me, suspicious by nature." He looked up and found Thacker's face flushed. "No need to blush like a schoolgirl; I won't railroad her yet."

He thought he'd said it mischievously, but Thacker collapsed into the other chair, defeated. "What? What did I say?"

"It's not anything you said, it's what I haven't told you."

Rory frowned. "You better come out with it. Nina didn't poison the old lady, did she?"

"No."

"Well, what have you learned that could be so damaging?"

"It's not so bad as it might look bad. I mean suspicious because withholding information could make her appear guilty."

Rory studied his face. "Bad enough to reveal a motive for killing the landlord."

Thacker swallowed hard.

He lowered the paper to his lap. "Come now. Just tell me."

"Nina lives on the estate."

"Yes, this, I know."

"She honors her ancestors' traditions, like preserving the earth and caring for animals. "

He rolled his hand, indicating Thacker should get to the point.

"Nina's clan… Well, in her family, the women were taught to grow, gather, and process food. The knowledge passed from one generation to the next. You know, roots and leaves that are used for medicinal purposes. You've probably noticed her collecting them?" When the detective agreed, Thacker continued. "Nina thinks it's important to follow the tribal beliefs."

"Okay. That doesn't seem unreasonable."

"No, I didn't think so either." The young officer ran a hand through his unruly hair. Short auburn tufts stood on end. "It's about her family."

"They live on reservation land and work at the tribal casino. Again, no surprise there."

"Nina doesn't think so. Her parents barely make ends meet. Worse, they abandoned their traditional values, bowing, as Nina says, 'to serving the white man.' "

The detective cocked his head. "That's for them to sort out. Working for the tribe must have its privileges, although living on the reservation might be challenging with job opportunities limited, and alcohol abuse rampant. Nina would know that, growing up out there."

"That's the rub."

"Huh?" What had Thacker discovered?

"She didn't grow up on the reservation. Her mother was born on the Sheehan estate, and so was Nina." Their eyes met. "Nina's grandmother raised the Sheehan children. It seems the professor brought her with him when he moved into the mansion as a housekeeper-nanny, although she wasn't much older than Phoebe."

After a moment, he added, "There's more."

Rory stood, running a hand over his bald head. The page fluttered to the floor. "Let's have it."

"She's buried in a small graveyard behind the gazebo."

"So, the grandmother was considered family. Behind the gazebo, you say. Isn't there a grove or a wooded area…" He frowned, starting to pace as he thought through the news. "Have you been to this grave?"

"Marked with a single name, Nani. Which, if my research is correct, means mother. It's the most recent grave. There are a few others, all unkempt and dating back to before Sheehan purchased the property."

"Okay. I see where this is headed." He took four steps, pivoted, and took six steps back, and stopped facing his friend. "Are you sure? Have you asked Nina about it?"

Thacker shook his head sadly. "Not yet. She doesn't like to talk about family. I know her mother is called Aponi. I've never met her."

"It could mean Nina knew a family secret and used extortion to gain permanent residence in exchange for her silence. Blackmail is a nasty business. Maybe Phoebe had had enough, and Nina saw fit to do away with her."

The young officer winced but didn't add credence to the idea. "I also learned that Aponi took up the household duties after her mother's death. By that time, there was no need to live in, and she came on weekdays to oversee the household. When Michael passed, Phoebe inherited and immediately let the housekeeper go."

"But Phoebe couldn't sever ties with Nani's granddaughter."

"Maybe Phoebe felt obligated since the mansion

was Nina's childhood home."

"Hmm," Rory said, starting to pace again. "Anything more?"

Thacker checked his notebook once more. "Aponi eventually married Pierce Crouching Bear, a Winnebago. He doesn't seem interested in tribal beliefs or being one with nature though he moved them to the reservation. Before that, Nina and her mother weren't allowed to live there. That part is a bit murky."

"We should interview the parents. What about the Janus Changes connection?"

"The program is well respected. The only odd thing I uncovered is the graduates display an uncanny loyalty to each other."

"Like the dog sitter and the tattooed gardener?"

"Nina and Perry Benson, yes. But also, others. It's like a fraternity or a brotherhood—one for all and all for one."

"Musketeers? Robin Hood and his merry band? The Masons and their secret handshakes?"

Thacker shrugged. Rory stopped, took a deep breath, and slowly expelled it. Had he missed an essential element in the hardware store break-ins? What if the robberies were committed by such a brotherhood, not for financial gain, but to foster *Esprit De Corps* among its members? It would explain leaving the guns at the store and why the stolen merchandise had yet to turn up in pawn shops. But if so, who was Robin Hood? Who pulled the strings?

He swung toward Thacker. "I'd like a list containing those placed by Janus Chances, and to interview Nina's family. Which do you want to tackle?"

The rookie hung his head.

"Okay, dealer's choice it is. You collect information on the Chances youth. I'll visit Aponi and Crouching Bear at the Bingo Hall."

When the door closed behind Thacker, Rory stooped to pick up the printout on Nina. Commander lay curled atop the page, purring.

"You're right, boy; this doesn't look good for Nina."

Chapter Twenty-Two

In was mid-afternoon before Rory headed to the Winnebago Reservation, thirty miles to the west of Winterset. Although he hadn't visited the native-run casino, he found the signs easy to follow. Once there, he located the bingo game in the convention center without trouble. He stopped in the doorway and gazed over the set-up. Cafeteria tables sat end-to-end in rows and were sparsely populated. The few players present in the room concentrated on the game sheets in front of them. On one wall, a podium stood on a stage. In a glass enclosure, ping-pong-sized balls performed somersaults and handsprings as if auditioning for the show. Large monitors hung to the stage right and left, displaying the bingo numbers already in play.

Seated at the podium, the caller reached for the next ball, positioned it in his hand, and called, "B-ten." His voice erupted through speakers mounted from the ceiling and on the flashboard monitors B-10 lit. A muted sigh rose from the tables.

The detective thumbed back his fedora as a large man approached. "Let's see your receipt." He wore a uniform, dark slacks, and a dress shirt, hair trimmed close, and jaw shaved. If he was Winnebago, Rory didn't see it. However, the badge on his chest plainly said Security.

He removed his hat. "Detective Rory Naysmith,

Winterset police."

"This is reservation land. You have no authority here."

He cleared his throat. "I'm looking for Pierce Crouching Bear. Or his wife. I have a few questions concerning a private matter."

The guard squinted. "You should seek him through the Tribal Police."

"I'm not here on a police matter. A friendly chat is all I'm after today. Do you know if he's working?"

The guard grunted yet looked around the hall. "Not that I've seen."

"What about an employment office?"

"Wait. There he is over there." The guard pointed toward a massive man in the far corner by the refreshment window. "No one is allowed in the Bingo Hall unless they purchase a game package. I'll let you in, but only to talk to Crouching Bear. You have your chat, then leave. Understood?"

"Got it." Rory flopped the fedora onto his head and headed toward the concession window weaving through the tables and floor workers selling pull tabs and game sheets. Four feet from the burly man, he stopped. "Are you Mister Crouching Bear?"

Reluctantly, the man stepped away from the window, and his conversation with a plump kitchen worker. "Who wants to know?" Pierce Crouching Bear was about his age, with a strong jaw, a short haircut, and coal-black smoldering eyes. "Don't tell me you left a jacket on the bus."

Surprised, Rory said, "No. Did you find one?"

Crouching Bear's eyes narrowed. "Did you read the rules? Once the doors close, I lock them until time for the return trip."

"I came by private car."

"What, then? I got things to do."

"It's about your daughter. That is if you are Crouching Bear."

The big man's eye color changed from smoldering to glowing. "I'm Crouching Bear, yet I have no daughter."

"Nina Mahala? I understand your wife, Aponi, had a child. You, in turn, brought them to live here on the reservation."

He drew his lips in a stern line and clenched toaster-sized fists. "If it's my wife's child, you must ask her. Nina Mahala is not my blood."

Rory stepped back, widening his stance. "So, Nina wasn't welcome in your home?"

"That one," he spat, "was nothing but misery. Constant whining, finding fault where there was none. I claim a wife, not her daughter, a self-appointed Earth maker. That girl might be young in years, yet she is old in the ancestral ways. She thought herself a shaman, spouted the correct living ways, collected berries for medicines, and associated with spirit animals."

"I'm told she's a passionate poet."

"What's passionate about harping on and on? Wrong drink, wrong hours, wrong job, wrong man."

Rory thought she disagreed with her mother's husband to boot. "So, she didn't last long on the reservation?"

"Always spouting off about," Crouching Bear drew air quotes, "People of the Big Voice." He crossed timber-sized arms over his chest, then puffed it out. "She weaseled under my skin."

"And you asked her to leave?"

"Didn't have to. After releasing the animals from the Winterset pound, the shaman princess ran head-first into the law. Can't say I was sorry to see her go."

A cry rose from behind, "Bingo!"

Rory checked for the source. Participants tore a page from their packs. Chairs scooted. Players moaned. Hushed conversations started as a lone player waved a paper sheet overhead. While a floor worker scurried to validate the winning card, Rory turned back to Crouching Bear. "So, no love lost?"

The bus driver jerked his head, lifting his upper lip in a sneer.

The uniformed guard crossed the floor to where they stood. "Everything all right here, Crouching Bear? Should I remove this man?"

A terse head shake.

Rory reached inside his jacket for the one document he'd brought from the freezer bundle. "I don't suppose you read Hocąk?"

Crouching Bear chuckled. "I wouldn't drive a casino bus if I did."

"Yeah," said Rory. "I understand it's an endangered language." Addressing the guard, he asked, "And you? Do you read Hocąk?"

"Some Ho-Chunk people are working to keep the language alive," he said. "A few elders still speak the old words, but the young are only interested in video games. Times have changed. Stories are forgotten. It's almost time for the spring Buffalo Dance, and there are not enough braves to perform the ceremonial dance for calling the bison herds."

"Yeah," agreed the detective. "Although not much

point now that the buffalo are all over in Yellowstone."

The large Winnebago laughed.

"I'd like to talk to your wife."

Suddenly sober, the big man bristled. "She doesn't speak the native tongue."

"Perhaps she will answer some questions about her daughter."

Crouching Bear glanced at the concession window, throwing a warning glare at the plump woman behind the counter. "Aponi will tell you the same, Nina is trouble." His eye color returned to its earlier intense smolder.

Rory tried to make eye contact with the woman working the concession. She lowered her head and stepped back from the window. Okay. Nothing else to uncover, then. "I appreciate your time, Mister Crouching Bear."

The guard escorted the detective from the convention hall. At the door, he said, "Pierce Crouching Bear is proud. You should know Aponi fairs better now that the girl has left the reservation."

Rory figured as much. Where the big man might bully and bend Aponi to his will, Nina would not easily bow or break.

Chapter Twenty-Three

The sun wasn't up when Rory turned onto the Sheehan property at seven. After spending more than a week cleaning, pricing, and displaying, Esther had advertised a four-day estate sale and opened the house to the curious. While cataloging the contents, she'd uncovered some fine jewelry and a few interesting art pieces that might make her efforts a success.

Each morning, he'd come to ensure her safety, although he didn't tell her as much. Seeing that Esther's day started well, he could dismiss his worries which said the grounds were too secluded and offered an attractive opportunity for a gatecrasher with less than honorable intentions. Once buyers started to trickle in, he'd retreat to the home office or the station to carry out his duties. Although he'd rather have stayed with her, the break-ins at the hardware store needed his attention, along with the other crimes he'd been assigned.

The cars driven by Esther and Marilyn sat by the carriage house. He pulled in alongside them, thankful it was the sale's final day. According to Esther, proceeds had been less than anticipated, leaving her both disappointed and frustrated by the picky lookers. He understood she felt more annoyed with the disposal task than the shoppers' lack of spending.

He let himself in through the mudroom, grabbed a

coffee in the kitchen, and entered the dining room. "Good morning, ladies." Marilyn smiled. Esther looked exhausted. Both acknowledged his greeting. "Ready for the finale?" he said.

Esther shrugged. "I'm marking some items down fifty percent in hopes they sell. I can't face boxing everything up again."

He handed her the coffee. "This will fortify you."

"What, no donuts? I thought you police-types had a passion for sweets."

He took a chair under the window facing the doorway. "I need to keep an eye on my figure."

"If I know you, Thacker served a hardy breakfast this morning, and you ate an extra tall stack smothered in maple syrup and a half-dozen bacon strips."

As their banter continued, he watched Marilyn leave and Nina and Rosco wander in. The beagle immediately came to him for an ear tussle.

"So, people in and out all day again?" Nina asked, stopping to finger a woven basket displayed on the sideboard.

"Can I count on your help?" Esther asked, marking down a crystal vase. "I expect a crowd."

"I'll be in the gazebo, writing." She patted the journal she carried in her beaded, cross-body sack. "Rosco will stop them from wandering the grounds."

"Good. You may take the basket if you like."

"I have others," she said, signaling the dog to join her.

Rory gave Rosco a final pat before they passed through the doorway. "Now we wait for the treasure hunters."

Unfortunately, the first person through the door was

the boy with a tattoo over his left eye. He'd come each day, looked at various baubles but not buying. His carriage and demeanor screamed "thug." So, he was probably a nice guy with a checkered past.

A pretty girl dressed in scrubs accompanied him. She called him Doug, and they appeared to be friends, although from very different worlds. Then again, in these times, there was plenty of body piercings and tattooings all around. The workers at the hospital had body art peeking from beneath the edges of their scrubs. The girl was probably among the rebel generation who wore their allegiances on their arms, bellies, or other hidden body parts. She was dainty, almost prim, and the boy was lanky and tall. The tattooed lad made her giggle.

"They're over here," this Doug said, narrowing his eyes, making the dagger inked above his brow angle down threateningly. His forehead above the blade displayed additional objects. He led the way into the dining room, where Esther had the jewelry displayed on the table. Thankfully, she locked them in the safe overnight, but they were the first things she set out in the morning. Rory thought the finer pieces were too available to thieving hands, but she deferred, declaring, "If they can't touch, they're not going to buy."

Doug went directly to the pearls. "They are over here. You don't want anyone else to get them."

"Okay," she said. "I'll look, but I only have about five minutes, then I've got to leave for the hospital." She stopped to inspect the silk scarves hanging from a coat tree, then hastily crossed to the table.

Rory stood and edged closer to where the boy stood.

Doug picked up the box and impatiently waited for his friend to join him. "Mel?" he said.

It made Rory nervous. "You're interested in the pearls?" he asked, moving to the table.

The boy didn't respond.

"She had them looked at by a jeweler," Rory said. "They are real. The string in the store showcase was a pretty close match and priced at over a thousand dollars." He paused. The boy didn't seem impressed. "Naturally, we don't expect to get that much for this strand. But you can tell they're the real deal even though they've been in a box for a long time. I think Esther wants six hundred. The jeweler said—"

"You better tell, Mel." Tattoo Boy frowned. "She's the one that knows pearls. I don't know baubles from buttons."

Mel and Esther crossed to the display together. "Good morning, Doug," Esther said.

He barely glanced at her. "I brought Melissa. She's interested in the pearls."

Mel stepped close and peered into the box. "They are beautiful," she said, "and today, fifty percent off? So, four hundred dollars?"

"Well, no," said Esther. "Some merchandise isn't marked down. The pearls are among them."

Around Melissa's neck hung a string of black pearls, the matching bracelet adorned her wrist. She took Phoebe's pearls from the box and held them to the light. "These are beautiful."

"Do you work at Winterset Memorial?" Esther asked. "My sister is on the staff."

"Yes, I know, Dr. Wallace. She's such a treasure."

Oh, boy, thought Rory, schmoozing to get a better price. Esther will never fall for that.

"I'll tell her you said so. Thanks." Esther

straightened the silver bracelets beside the empty pearl necklace box. "I'm afraid I need seven hundred for the strand. They are worth more. Did you notice the diamond chips in the clasp?"

Doug stiffened. "Isn't it a half-price day? I told Mel and she's been waiting all week."

"I'm sorry. I can get at least seven hundred from the jeweler. I think someone else will be willing to pay as much."

Mel opened her purse, pulled out some bills, and then searching the side pockets, found a few more. "How much have you got, Doug?" She dug in her purse.

"I've got a little," said Doug, slapping his pants pockets.

"Let me have it." He obliged, hunting through his shirt pockets and checking his jacket for more.

"I have to get to work. They won't be here later, but I've got"—she counted the bills, straightening them as she went—"four-hundred and eighty-eight now. Cash. I thought it would be four hundred. Would you take four-hundred and eighty-eight?"

"I've got another fifty." He handed the cash to Melissa, who added it to a fist full she held out to Esther.

Rory watched Esther hesitate. The pearls would make a great gift. He could give them to Esther for Valentine's Day, it would save her from letting them go for less than they were worth. Did she already have a strand? Would it say too much? As he mulled it over, a shadow fell on the table. He looked toward the doorway and found a frowning James Sheehan blocking the sun.

Ridged shoulders and stern expression, Sheehan growled, "Don't try to sell the house out from under me."

Esther didn't look at him, but said, "This isn't the

house, James. These are Phoebe's personal possessions. You know perfectly well I have the court's permission to liquidate your aunt's household goods."

"These are jewels," he sneered. "An estate agent should be called in. Then, after a professional appraisal, you'd have the opportunity to set a realistic price." His gaze threw daggers at her. "What else are you selling?"

Melissa handed the necklace to Esther. "I did want these. This strand would be the perfect gift for my mother who is going for her first chemo treatment tomorrow."

James snatched the necklace from Esther. "Not today."

Esther snatched it back. "Yes, today. How much do you have?"

Rory stepped between James and Esther. "Let's step into the hallway, Mr. Sheehan."

"I'm allowed in the house. What are you afraid I'll find?"

"What are you looking for, Mr. Sheehan?"

"My lawyer is filing a petition to stop any further sale until authority is established."

"Authority. Meaning until the court rules on the codicil?"

"Yes."

Rory noticed Esther, Doug, and Melissa slip from the room. "Esther has the right to sell the possessions in the house. She was named Executor in your aunt's will." He almost choked when he said, "aunt." Even if James was Phoebe's late brother's son, he hadn't been mentioned in the will by name and definitely hadn't been named executor.

Wound up in his tirade, James bellowed, "Yes, but

the codicil—"

"I'm afraid that doesn't change a thing."

"You can't throw your weight around just because you're on the police force. I have rights. I am a Sheehan."

"Sorry, James. It doesn't seem that your aunt saw fit to leave you a dime. And don't bring up the addendum; its validity is still to be established."

Esther returned. Behind James' back, she waved the cash at Rory, tucked it into the money bag, and left the room, again.

"Mr. Sheehan, I can't ask you to leave, but I ask you not to interfere."

The nephew harrumphed and took the chair vacated by the detective.

When Rory stepped outside for a breather, he found Esther by the front door straightening the estate sale sign. "So, you took less for the necklace than you intended."

She looked at him sheepishly. "I wasn't about to let James dictate the price. And after they waited all week, she told me the story."

"Story? What story?"

She cleared her throat. "Melissa's father died when she was a teenager. On his deathbed, he wrote his wife a letter declaring his love for her and their daughter." She looked down as she continued, "He said she had given him the only thing he had ever wanted, their beloved Melissa. His only wish was that he could give her the one thing she deserved, pearls to match the purity of her love." Then, glancing up, she added, "She wanted the pearls as a gift for her mother, the gift she never received from her husband. And at a time when she needs them most now that she is facing cancer without him."

"It's a nice story, Esther."

"I thought so, even if it's not true." She looked out over the driveway. "The weather is cooperating; I don't understand where everyone is?"

He laid a hand on her arm. "You like the story, and you don't like James Sheehan."

"Am I that obvious? I don't trust him and can't figure out what he's after. She left everything to the college and the library. What can he hope to gain by holding up probate and trying to replace me as executor?"

Rory had no idea. But James was after something. If only he knew what.

Chapter Twenty-Four

Rory slipped away at midmorning, leaving Esther and Marilyn to manage while he went to the apartment to study his lists. Dead—Phoebe Sheehan, alkaloid poisoning. Under her name in no particular order, he'd listed the suspects, James Sheehan, Nina Mahala, Lillie Anderson, and Perry Benson.

James seemed the most likely and therefore his first choice. Arriving unannounced after his aunt's collapse at the ceremony, in Rory's mind he had the most to gain from her death—the Sheehan inheritance. He scratched his forehead. What was the inheritance, not the rambling old mansion. The place might tempt some, but the upkeep alone would put it beyond most means. James seemed comfortable enough, but a salesman always had to hustle, making his own opportunities. Could it be that the nephew saw this as an opportunity to supplement his wealth. Or did he know there was an item more valuable than the house and the grounds. Then there was the poison—typically a woman's choice in weapons. Did James have the cunning to administer the lethal dose? Rory hadn't seen him at the ceremony, but that didn't mean he wasn't there.

He pictured the pretty dog sitter. Nina Mahala lived at the mansion. Evidence tying her to the Sheehan family through her grandmother's employment as nanny was problematic. Records didn't substantiate birth or death for the Native American woman called Nani. If she bore a child from Michael Sheehan, Rory was hard pressed to prove it. Yet the dog sitter had a contract that granted her permission to live on the estate with or without Phoebe. An odd arrangement. He wondered why the librarian would agree to the stipulation. Unfortunately, since Nina wasn't willing to explain there wasn't anyone to ask, and rumor didn't solve his dilemma. Crouching Bear confirmed Nina's obsession with natural remedies. The poison could have easily been given to the unsuspecting poet before she went to the Old Orchard ceremony.

What had Petey said about the toxin? Likely to kill any time in a window spanning thirty minutes to thirty hours. Leaving the possibility Esther administered the poison at the scene, but equally supported the theory Nina had done it earlier in the day. If so, what motive did the girl have? Revenge? The rightful heir seemed the only other explanation, and he wasn't convinced. A sulky and contrary girl, she didn't display animosity toward Phoebe.

On the other hand, Lillie Anderson held a huge grudge against the entire Sheehan household, though her actions were based on an old grievance. He was sure she had harbored a love for Michael Sheehan—a feeling he hadn't reciprocated. Lover spurned, blinded by her emotions, and heartbroken when they were exposed. It was all speculation on his part. Mixed up with it all was the jealousy she must have felt when his novel published, and she was passed over for tenure. And the Ho-chunk Nation? Where did they fit into the local librarian's death?

The third candidate for Winterset Poet Laureate was also a contender. Perry Benson seemed to touch everyone. First, he was the gardener at the estate. Second, he was a poet like Phoebe and Lillie. Third, he and Nina shared a secret. And last, and most disturbing, was the fact he was tied to the hardware store. But without means, opportunity, and motive, Rory couldn't pin that crime on him either. At this point the murderer could be anyone except Esther.

Getting nowhere, Rory decided to take the document packet found in the deep freeze to the college. Someone out there was bound to recognize the language it was written in. Lillie Anderson was his best hope for labeling the writings as rambling prose or poetry.

When he arrived, Professor Anderson was delivering a lecture. He stepped into the hall, took a seat in the back row, and listened. "A writer who is as much at home on the stage as the page." Paper rustled, and muted laughter toward the front. A single overhead light highlighted the speaker. All other lighting had been dimmed to focus the students' attention on the slide presentation behind her. Lillie ignored both, laughter, and restlessness.

"She takes poetry to audiences that poetry doesn't usually reach. Starting out as a guerrilla poet, pasting poems onto lamp posts, and handing them out on free postcards. We can learn from her determination." Lillie had warmed to her subject and Rory felt his eyelids droop. The heat in the crowded hall made it almost impossible to stay awake.

Sudden overhead lights woke him. He'd slouched low enough in the padded lecture hall seat to rest his head on the seat back and apparently gone to sleep. Straightening up, he realized he was the only one left in the gigantic room. He rubbed his hand over his jaw and gave himself permission for a good yawn. Focusing his eyes, they found Professor Anderson behind the podium watching him. "I wondered how long it would take."

"I didn't disrupt your lecture?"

"Not at all, detective. Not that much would, I can deliver this particular lecture series with my eyes closed. Are you here to see me?"

"I am." He made his way down to the front and fished the paper from an inside pocket. "You mentioned that you worked with the reservation school." She shot him a quick glance, then continued to collect her papers. "I have a document here"—he unfolded it—"it's written by hand. I can't identify the script. I wonder if you can tell me if it's Sioux."

"Sioux?" She took it from him. Her face clouded, and the wrinkles between her brows grew more defined. "What makes you think this is native?"

It was clear the paper, or what was written on the paper bothered her. The hand holding it trembled.

"I hoped you'd recognize it. I need a translator."

She thought it over, chewing on her lower lip. "Where'd it come from? Is it Ho-Chunk, is that what you're asking."

"I hope you don't think I'm trying to entrap you." She looked up suddenly; he went on, taking the sheet from her hands. "There were a dozen documents tied together in a packet and hidden at the Sheehan mansion." He paused to let her think. She still stared at the spot where the paper had been. "Should we go to your office? I'd like to understand what you know."

Raising her head, she spoke too quickly. "I know nothing."

Rory swallowed a quick retort. He'd watched too

many late-night reruns. Instead, he said, "I've found people know more than they think."

Well aware that in allowing the conversation to move from the lecture hall to Professor Anderson's office, he had given her ample time to concoct a story. He wanted her to be comfortable before he asked the next question. He intended to gauge her reaction carefully. And as he expected, she had regained her composure once they'd stepped onto her protective turf. She settled in the chair behind the desk.

He took a moment to look at the plaques, pictures, and awards displayed on the walls. "You've had a distinguished career at WCC. Is this you with the Dean?"

She placed her finger-laced hands on the desktop. "Do you think we could wrap this up, detective? I could use some time to prep for my next class."

"Sure." He moved to the opposite wall, and a picture he'd noticed on his first visit. "When was this taken?" Using the document, he tapped a framed photograph where a much younger Lillie Anderson, in native dress, posed with tribal elders. Among those pictured a young woman in a ribbon adorned skirt, a native shawl draped over her shoulders echoed a passage from Sheehan's novel—*She wore a ribbon embroidery skirt and one as a shawl. A heavily beaded binding decorated the braid that hung down her back.* The woman's face radiated strength and tribal pride. He noted an uncanny resemblance to Nina Mahala. Could this be the woman they called Nani? "It must have been during your undergraduate days. Can you name those present?"

"I don't remember."

"Surely, righting social injustice, being honored by the tribal council, and being a dedicated scholar would warrant a remembered occasion." She didn't answer. "And this man"—he pointed at an unmistakable Michael Sheehan—"this Irish scholar, with his arm around the native girl? Would this be the novelist, Michael Sheehan?" He paused, prepared to observe her slightest twitch. "Would the princess be his Native American nanny and housekeeper?"

The professor paled. Satisfied, he crossed to her desk and laid the document in the center by her folded hands. "Look closely, Professor Anderson. Is this Michael Sheehan's handwriting?"

After a lengthy pause, she said, "If you want them translated, you should leave the documents. I have friends on the native council who might oblige me. I doubt they would extend the favor to you."

Chapter Twenty-Five

Rory headed home, convinced more than ever Professor Anderson had been in love with novelist Michael Sheehan. Furthermore, she had known Sheehan and the native girl were involved, feeding the detective's suspicion a child resulted from their union. By his reckoning, jealousy led Lillie to cast doubt on his novel's origin and fueled the plagiarism rumors—which she continued to stoke. If Michael and the Winnebago girl had a child, it could be Aponi—making Nina Mahala, the Sheehan live-in dog sitter, his granddaughter.

Furthermore, facts could prove Nina is among the heirs to the Sheehan property and any treasure hidden there. This, unfortunately, was purely an assumption, or a series of assumptions, for which he had no real evidence. And if there were proof, he'd need to keep his discovery from James Sheehan until the details were substantiated. It in no way removed him or the girl from his suspect list.

Rory reversed directions, driving straight for the reservation. He passed new family dwellings, neat one-story homes, the lawns gray from the recent snows visible. The Ho-Chunk Nation had made strides to improve reservation housing in recent years. However, the Crouching Bears still lived in an older apartment building, freshly painted but with decaying litter laying ignored by the entryway. If unemployment ran high on the reservation, a working bus driver married to a Bingo Hall cook found it hard to raise their living standard. He knocked politely on the door.

Locks tumbled, and the door opened three inches, allowing a heavy security chain to stretch between them. "Aponi Crouching Bear?" he asked. She lowered her head. Behind her, the room sat quiet, the odors of boiled cabbage and rancid grease souring the air. "Detective Rory Naysmith, WPD. I have some questions."

She looked up, startled.

He cleared his throat. "No one is in trouble," he said, taking off his fedora. "Mrs. Crouching Bear, is your husband home?"

She abruptly closed the door. Rory heard the chain rattle, then the door reopened. "No," she said as she moved back to allow him entry. "He will not be happy to hear you were here."

He stepped into the apartment and glanced around. The small living room contained a sagging recliner, a lopsided TV tray, and a worn sofa. Aponi looked fit in dark slacks and a rose-colored sweater which did more for her appearance than the casino uniform had the last time he'd seen her. Her face was round and blemish free, her smile welcoming.

"What do you want to ask me?" she said, taking a woven blanket from the sofa and gesturing for him to sit. "I can speak freely while Crouching Bear is away."

He wondered if speaking to him put her in jeopardy, yet she looked unruffled. "Your husband would forbid you to answer?"

"No," she said. "But shamed at your need to speak directly with me. He insists on being a protector and provider but has lost his direction and refuses to recognize mine. He doesn't understand why the ruling council declares the Winnebago tribe the Ho-Chunk Nation." She fingered a glass bead and shell necklace at her neck. "Here, there is much idle time. My husband fills the hours with unsavory thoughts and suspicions."

He could see where Crouching Bear liked to push his weight around, yet Aponi had let him into the home they shared. "I'd like to hear about your mother."

She tentatively sat on the recliner's edge, glancing around as if she usually sat elsewhere and might get caught trespassing. "An odd request, Detective Naysmith. Surely, my family holds no importance for you."

He smoothed the fedora's brim. "Your mother served as housekeeper to the Sheehan household in the seventies. I'd like to hear how a Winnebago maiden influenced Professor Sheehan. How she ended up in his household."

"Influenced how?"

"I've read Michael's novel, *Willow Creek Woman*. A feminine mind doesn't cover the territory like a man. If we agree he wrote the novel, his thoughts were influenced by someone else. Let's say his muse was a woman."

She bristled. "It does not chronicle my mother's journey."

"But perhaps was it a story passed down to her by her mother?"

She went wide-eyed, then slowly lowered her gaze to study the hands folded in her lap. He waited while she gathered her thoughts.

Aponi began in a whisper. "Ho-Chunk men were hunters. The women were farmers, cooks, and caregivers to their children. Traditional chiefs were men, but there were a few female peace chiefs in the Ho-Chunk tribe." She raised her head, and locked him with a stare, her voice gaining strength. "*Ho-poe-kaw*, Glory in the Morning, was such a chief. Professor Sheehan traced TiKa's lineage back to her."

"TiKa was your mother, and Glory in the Morning was your grandmother?"

She covered a smile behind a delicate hand. "Yes. TiKa was my mother. I turn fifty-four this year. Glory in the Morning's soul went to the wind village in 1832. One-hundred-eighty years have passed." Her face lit with humor. "I carry her blood and call her *Gaga*, grandmother, but there are many generations between us."

"Oh," he said, confused.

"Being chief is a great responsibility. Leading the People is hard, and then she married a Frenchman, who eventually took their daughter to raise in the East, away from the Ho-Chunk."

He ran a hand over his balding head. "Yet, you are here, her descendant, and she became part of the Sheehan household."

"One longs to be among their people." She rose. "I will make herbal tea, and we will discuss these matters."

As she went into the kitchen, a shiver ran up his spine. He heard the water run, then the whoosh from the gas burner lighting. He pictured Nina offering tea made from…who knew what? He wondered if he'd forever be wary when accepting a drink without knowing its origin. From the other room, Aponi took up her story.

"The Ho-Chunk people come from here. They have always lived in this place along the river. TiKa reunited with the People of the Big Voice, renounced her French family and embraced her native name. Sadly, her blood claim was no longer strong enough to live on the Ho-Chunk lands. When Professor Sheehan discovered this, he took her in, and in exchange, she cared for his children."

"So, it was charity?"

She appeared in the doorway holding two mugs and a face filled with displeasure. "The seventies were difficult for the Ho-Chunk, Detective. Harder for those with mixed blood. Professor Sheehan wanted to help. I would not say charity, pity, or even compassion. TiKa learned the tribal traditions, became familiar with the fauna and flora in the area, and listened to the stories the older tribal members told. She hungered to understand her cultural heritage. All that she learned, she taught to the professor. In return, he saw she had a place to live." She handed him a mug.

He eyed it dubiously.

"Elderberry," she said.

He'd seen Michael Sheehan and the Native princess together in the photograph hanging in Lillie Anderson's office. There was more than an employer-employee relationship going on between them. "And along the way, their closeness led to romance," he said.

"She was a beautiful woman, Detective. But no, my mother wanted only to know her people."

He searched for a place to set the mug. Not finding a convenient spot, he pointed it at her instead. "But then you were born."

Unaffected by his argument, she said, "Is Michael Sheehan my father? Is that what you have come to ask?"

He shrugged. "If you were in line to inherit the

Sheehan estate, it would make my job easier."

"And give me a motive for murder?" She looked him square in the eye. "I do not want the estate land. My family is the Thunder Clan and is recognized as belonging to the Nebraska Winnebago and the Wisconsin Ho-Chunk Tribes. Like many tribal members, my mother and I did not live on the reservation. We still consider it our sacred home." She said it with pride like Nina had defiantly claimed her family the night they'd met.

"Do you deny being born on the estate?"

"No. I lived there for many years, and my mother has a place among the trees."

"All right, you admit a history with the place," he said. "Tell me about your mother's position in the household."

"Let's see, what can I tell you?" She looked into the middle distance, then said, "TiKa was much younger than Michael Sheehan. I did not question why we lived on the estate, although sometimes I resented the closeness between her and the children. The professor, Jamison, and Phoebe always treated me with kindness."

He allowed himself a terse nod. "Not Gregory?"

"No, he died before I arrived, a war casualty."

"So, before you were born."

She gave him a weak smile, then sipped from her mug while he mulled it over. Nina strongly resembled the princess in Anderson's photograph—did he see Sheehan in Aponi's features?

When he lifted his cup, the tea had gone tepid. "I have to ask," he said. "If not the professor, then who was your father?"

She seemed not to hear, rising from the chair to take

his mug. "My husband will return soon, detective. I must prepare for work."

Her avoidance felt abrupt. Had she lied about Professor Sheehan's relationship with her mother? While her demeanor remained pleasant, he wondered how much she hadn't said.

He tugged his hat into place and decided to try out the only Ho-Chunk phase he remembered. "*Pinagigi*, Aponi." Thank you, what else could he say? Besides, it would thrill Esther to know her efforts to educate him had paid off.

Aponi smiled broadly. "You are welcome, detective."

He saw himself out. The day was gray, but the sun had begun to set, leaving a golden glow on the horizon. He wondered how the professor had traced the lineage. Glory in the Morning was born before the Bureau of Census was established as a permanent agency to register births. TiKa and Aponi's deliveries weren't necessarily recorded with the county or noted in a family Bible. Or were they? He made a mental note to ask Esther if she'd run across one while cleaning up at the mansion.

Hmmm, perhaps his assumptions weren't just conjecture. There was every possibility Nina Mahala held a closer relationship with Phoebe than a house guest or dog sitter. That wouldn't make Thacker happy. His cell rang before he could wonder about his roommate's progress with the Janus members. He punched the icon on the dash and took the call hands-free. "This telepathy thing is working out nicely."

The young officer's voice boomed through the cab speakers. "Huh, what telepathy thing?"

"I was thinking about you, and voila, here you are."

"Oh. I thought you'd want to know about James Sheehan."

"What about him? Weren't you looking into the youthful offenders?"

"Boring stuff, boss. The program is on the up and up. No one with a bad thing to say about them. The homes offering community service projects were pleased with the program. Many sponsors encouraged others to sign-up."

"No silver stolen? No small children missing? All pets and checkbooks accounted for?"

"I interviewed enough to see a pattern. There wasn't a single negative review."

"Well, the mayor will be pleased to hear. Yet, it's hard to believe every delinquent became a solid citizen overnight."

"Maybe not overnight. Interestingly, many Janus participants bonded."

"Bonded how?"

"By remaining friends after being in the program, then mentoring those that followed. You know what I mean? Like the Boy Scouts."

"Like a gang?"

"More like Big Brother-Big Sister buddies."

Rory wondered if it could be true or if it was more like recruiting. "When we get together tonight, you can lay it out for me. For now, what's this about Sheehan?"

"James said he arrived in Winterset too late to see Phoebe at the ceremony."

"Yeah, drove in from Lincoln Thursday night with an invitation from his aunt but missed the shebang."

"It turns out he checked into the motel on Wednesday night, a full day before the awards banquet."

"So, where was he all day?"

"I'm running that down now," Thacker said. "In the meantime, I learned James lunched with Perry Benson and Doug Ryan yesterday." Rory heard a page rustle and imagined the young man searching through his notepad. After a pause, Thacker continued, "Beryl down at the Golden Leaf said, 'Those three acted as thick as thieves.' "

"Thieves, huh? So, Benson and Ryan are a bonded pair?"

Doug Ryan might be the kid with the dagger forehead. Fishy that he'd be a buddy with the estate gardener. Rory searched his memory for any interaction between the two men. If this Doug was the guy who'd been at the estate sale every day, he might have been there at the same time as Perry. Unfortunately, Rory hadn't noticed if they were together. He'd ask Esther; she'd spent significant time with the tattooed boy.

"Could be friends," Thacker said.

"Okay. Do you know what Doug drives?"

"No. But if statistics are right, it's a pickup."

"Let's take another look at the hardware store. It's a remarkable coincidence if Perry and James have a common interest. And now this Doug Ryan can be lumped in with them."

"Coincidence? Don't you always say there is no such thing as coincidence in police work?"

"I'm glad you've been listening."

Thacker heaved a sigh. Rory knew the young officer wanted to ask what he'd learned about Nina. However, that could wait. James Sheehan moved back to the top of his murder list, with Perry running a close second. Why had James lied about his arrival in Winterset? Rory could imagine Perry and his Janus comrades pulling off the hardware robberies. Was James involved? He'd had a full twenty-four hours, more than enough time to see his aunt, administer the poison, and orchestrate the robbery.

"We'll compare notes when I get home. In the meantime, see if you can find the information on Ryan's vehicle."

As he punched off, Rory wondered if James had purposely misdirected them by pretending to search for a valuable item at the estate. Perhaps he was following a more sinister agenda—one that included murder.

## Chapter Twenty-Six

Esther placed the last jewelry piece in the carrying case, disappointed it hadn't sold, yet relieved the estate sale was over. She'd made enough money to cover the immediate bills and reduced the household items to a manageable number. The unsold furniture could go to auction next week, along with the special crystal pieces and oil paintings. For now, she'd made a dent—a sizable dent.

The jewelry case went into the china cupboard. Tomorrow, she'd take it to the jeweler to sell on consignment. At least she'd found a home for the pearls. Her dream to quickly liquidate the estate had been a lark. It would be months before she dug the house out from under the items accumulated, first made by Michael, later by Phoebe. While Esther felt she'd made headway, so much remained. If only...

No, she wasn't going to shirk her duties. There was no sense wishing she'd stepped away from the job when she'd first had the chance—or that James Sheehan would take his nasty attitude and disappear.

"All the doors are locked," Marilyn said as she joined Esther in the dining room. "The only cars out back are ours. I suppose Nina is somewhere on the grounds, although I haven't seen her lately. Shall we call it quits?"

"Go home, it's been a long day." Esther offered a weak smile. "As well as a successful week, thanks to you."

"Oh, poppycock. You've worked your tail off. I shouldn't have suggested—"

"Marilyn. I understood the obligation when I accepted it. You don't need to apologize, again."

The old family friend started to object, then instead pulled out a chair, "I'll rest while you count the money. These old bones are screaming from being on my feet all day. Once everything is tucked into the safe, we can leave together."

Esther felt weary, too, but glad to accept her offer. "Now that we've pared it down, I want to go upstairs again and plan for tomorrow. The boxes in the master bedroom are filled with family photos albums and correspondence. I don't see any reason you need to stay while I go through them. The house is safe. Nina is around somewhere, and I don't plan to stay long." Unclasping the fanny pack from her waist, she plopped it onto the table. "I think we did rather well."

Twilight lengthened the shadows as Esther saw Marilyn to her car. In less than an hour, the sun would be gone entirely. She set her mental timer and headed back inside. The smallest room in the house was the mudroom. She'd start there now and work through the house in the morning ensuring every item needing disposal had been, and pieces heading for consignment were collected into a single room.

Stale air escaped from the freezer when Esther lifted the lid, letting loose the scents of molding paper, any number of chemicals, and the forest. A yew branch emitted a sharp, piercing wood scent with a heavy evergreen overtone. Nina's work. Esther raised it to her nose and inhaled deeply, curious that the girl, so reluctant to help sort items, felt compelled to bless them with nature's gifts.

After discovering the Ho-Chunk documents, Rory insisted on unplugging the freezer to allow it to defrost before exploring further. Any papers her detective still needed to take waited for him. Her search discovered letters bound with a rubber band in a brown paper bag, so old the elastic was disintegrating. She removed the letter from the top envelope. Composed in pencil and smudged until the words appeared ghostlike. The paper so thin it split at the folds as if it had been read and reread countless times. Esther studied the message that had to be fifty years old and sent from Vietnam by Phoebe's brother Gregory. According to Marilyn, Greg was drafted at nineteen, and perished before coming home to rejoin his family.

The message contained very little about the brutal campaign which the young man had survived. Instead, Greg begged Phoebe to continue sending news from home. "It's the only thing that keeps us going, sis. You can't imagine the excitement when the mail bag arrives."

Intrigued, Esther read more. "The days seem to run together, so one of the guys started a contest to break up the monotony. Every letter you get from home costs you a dollar, and you earn a tick under your name in his tiny notebook. The guy lucky enough to receive the most mail before our next four-day pass wins the whole pot. So far, I'm a shoo-in, thanks to you and Tina. Keep those cards and letters coming."

Esther closed her eyes, trying to imagine the boy far from home, living amid fear, death, and unrelenting humidity. Surely, he missed home. But who was Tina? A cousin? Or a girlfriend left behind? She couldn't recall a local girl with the name. Perhaps a nickname for Christine, Christina, Martina, Valentina, Faustina—there were plenty to choose from. And Tina could be from somewhere other than Winterset.

Esther put the letter away and rifled through the remaining pack. One, thicker than the others, contained a Polaroid snapshot with three grinning GIs. Each posed with one foot atop a sandbag, an M16 rifle resting casually on his knee, and a metal helmet pushed back as if to say, "Ain't so bad."

Beneath the photo, Greg had scribbled, "Shotgun, me, and Roach - A day in the life '62." She could see the Sheehan family resemblance in Greg's facial features. Much more than any physical traits James Sheehan displayed. Greg looked like someone, and it wasn't James. She wrinkled her nose, then suddenly the urge to check out the photographs upstairs seemed important, particularly those featuring all three Sheehan children.

The beagle poked his head into the mudroom, startling Esther. "Hello, Rosco." He looped over for a head rub. "Nina? Are you in the kitchen?" she called, slipping the snapshot into her pocket. When she heard the kettle placed on the stove, she added, "If it's not too much trouble, I'd love your special tea."

Rosco stayed with her while she replaced all but the picture in the freezer. Then led the way as Esther joined the dog sitter in the kitchen.

After setting the tea to steep, Nina said, "Still organizing things?"

"I'm afraid I'll never finish. Did you know there were more documents in the freezer?" The younger woman's head swiveled for a better look at the kitchen refrigerator. "Not that freezer, I mean the one in the mudroom."

"Do you mean beyond the Ho-Chunk documents?"

"Yes. I discovered letters to Phoebe from her brother."

Nina shrugged. "Didn't he die long ago?"

"There were two brothers, Jamison, who lived here in Winterset, and Gregory, who died in Vietnam."

"So, do you mean James' father or the other one?"

"The other one. These letters are at least fifty years old and written while he served his country. I don't suppose Phoebe mentioned him to you."

"No. Why would she, we weren't friends."

Esther studied the girl. "Of course, you were. Why else would you be here. She wouldn't have given you an open-ended contract to stay on at the estate if you hadn't been friends."

As if in agreement, Rosco woofed.

"So, it occurs to me," Esther said, "that if Jamison fathered a son, perhaps his elder sibling did as well."

Chapter Twenty-Seven

Esther glanced at her watch, it was already eight. Where had the morning gone? She'd worried over the letter from Greg and therefore slept poorly. If only she hadn't found the second photograph in the box upstairs. She picked up her phone. Perhaps Rory had already seen it, or one much like it, yet she imagined his reaction if she didn't pass along the discovery right away.

He answered with a smile in his voice. "I'm doing the sudoku puzzle. This better be good."

She pictured him seated at the kitchen table with an empty cup, and the newspaper opened before him. "I finished today's puzzle an hour ago," she said. "What's taking you so long?"

She knew his latest self-challenge was to visualize the solution. Then, once solved, he'd fill it in as quickly as possible, put down the indelible-ink pen, and stop the timer on his stopwatch. She knew he wanted to perfect the trick to show off, but it didn't matter. He enjoyed a mental challenge, and she enjoyed his desire to best her. Good luck with that.

"First things, first," he said. "I've had my morning workout, coffee, and read the news."

"And your roommate?"

"Thacker is in the shower, and as much as I'd like to hurry the young officer along, it doesn't seem prudent to interrupt a good bass rendition of *Oklahoma* and the winds sweeping down the plain. However, I'd accept an invitation to breakfast."

"I wish I had time, but I have a meeting at the library to review the Sheehan book donation. Then I need to swing by the church and put together the bulletins."

"Are you still doing that? I thought you'd cut back on giving away your free time."

"Rory don't start," she said with a sigh. "You know I enjoy helping Pastor Mark."

"I do. I just worried about your mental state."

"There's nothing wrong with my mental faculties. You think I'm going nuts from too many hours stirring the dust and trash?"

"No, there is no doubt about it; you are loony tunes. So, what's up?"

She took a deep breath. "As much as I hate to admit it, I need help, namely a strong back."

"Thacker's here."

"Very funny. You agreed to move some boxes from the master suite upstairs down to the sunroom for me. It's so depressing to work in the room where she slept."

"I'd be glad to help if you arrange your schedule to go to the Sheehan mansion before the others."

"That will work. I'll make a call or two, so no one wonders where I am."

He chuckled. "We all know how much time you devote to the estate. Give me fifteen minutes, and I'll head out."

"I'll be ready and waiting," she said. "I found something I'd like to show you."

"Can you give me a hint?"

"You need to see it for yourself."

"In that case, make it ten minutes."

Esther had every intention to leave immediately after they disconnected; instead, she took out the photograph again. Four teens, two boys and two girls. They could be friends, two teenager couples. However, the boys, both blond, looked very much alike. Possibly brothers, Greg and Jamison. One girl, also fair-headed, had facial features to match. Their sister, Phoebe. Esther felt confident they were Michael's children. However, the fourth, a dark complected girl with raven hair wasn't a Sheehan. Behind the teens stood a sign for Parris Island. Perhaps it was taken the day Greg reported for boot camp. Moreover, the girl might be Tina, a fifty-year younger Tina.

It only took Esther a moment longer to leave a message for Pastor Mark and then one for the library administrator to say she'd be by later in the day. She fingered the pearls around her neck. She'd dressed for the library meeting, too dressy to work through the piles at Phoebe's. Yet, she feared she'd never get away from the estate in time to change again. So, it was a sweater set and wool slacks, with Rory doing all the heavy lifting.

She tucked the photograph into her coat pocket, grabbed her cell phone and purse, then headed out.

The roads were clear, the sun shining as Esther turned onto the back road cut off to County Line Road. Preoccupied with thoughts for the day, it surprised her when the car jerked toward the shoulder. She quickly corrected the situation. Unfortunately, handling the strange tug that continued to pull the vehicle toward the road's edge took both hands. Even with the heater and the radio on, rubber slapping on the blacktop could be heard as she eased the car onto the narrow shoulder. After turning off the engine, the world went too silent amid a murder of crows. The radio was now quiet, and tight-fitted doors muffled all the other outside noise.

She guessed an inspection was in order. After climbing out and making her way over the loose gravel, she surveyed the situation. The tires on the driver's side looked intact. But on the passenger's side, the front wheel squatted on the ground, and the back tire sat dangerously low. She recalled Marilyn's words before the YMCA's Powder Puff Auto Repair class last fall: "You need to know this stuff, Esther."

At the time, she'd known enough about car maintenance. Regular fuel is cheaper than Premium. The tires should be inflated to forty-four pounds per square inch, and someone needed to periodically check the oil. That someone being Axel, who attended to all her vehicle's needs. Besides, being a car mechanic didn't fit her profile, so she pulled out her phone and hit the speed-dial number for Al's Auto Repair, reported her location, and secured assistance before settling in to await their arrival.

A moment later, she realized Rory would beat her to the estate. She picked up the phone to call him, but it rang instead. Ten minutes later, new rearrangements had been made with the library administrator. So, once again, she tried to contact the detective, but the phone slid from her grasp, dropping through the narrow space between the center console and the bucket seat. Her hand just fit through the opening. While fishing for it, she pushed the cell further beneath the seat. Then, exasperated and leaning over the gear shift, she thrust her arm into the hole. Unfortunately, when she strained sideways and twisted her upper body to lengthen her reach, the pearls hanging around her neck snagged on the gear shift, and the silk string snapped. Pearls spilled everywhere. She frantically grabbed at the glimmering gemstones, sending the precious beads spinning in all directions.

Esther had collected a handful of pearls but not the cell phone by the time the calvary made its way up the road, pulled in, and backed close to her front bumper. Shoving the pearls into her coat pocket, she went to greet the man behind the wheel.

He rolled down the window. "Looks like you've got a problem."

"Thanks for coming so soon," she said. "I expected the shop to send a tow truck or someone to change the tire."

She stepped back as he opened the door and climbed out. Tall and slim, he met her eye to eye. A mixture of grease, body odor, and stale tobacco assailed her. "A flatbed is the only thing when a car has multiple problems," he said as he skirted her and advanced to the sedan.

Esther followed him. "I didn't realize I had more than one."

The driver harrumphed, mumbled "women" under his breath, then added, "It'll only take a minute to load. The winch will get it onto the transport, and you'll ride back to the shop in the cab with me."

The driver looked familiar. Not so much someone she knew as someone she had seen in passing. Then again, she'd seen so many new faces in recent days. The estate sale, the law office, plus all the time and places spent on poetry awards night. "I'm late for an appointment."

"Depending on what the shop finds, an hour and a half tops, and you'll be on your way."

Esther looked past the truck, eying a beech tree grove a quarter mile down. Past the towering gray trunks lay the intersection with County Line Road. Another mile beyond that, the Sheehan property skirted the road. "Perhaps you'd drop me somewhere instead?"

"That's not allowed. Insurance and all." He didn't look at her as he rounded the flatbed and started to unfurl a heavy chain. "You can ride with me, or I can leave you here."

Her destination lay less than a mile away if she cut through the trees. Rory would worry if he arrived and she wasn't there. A simple phone call would solve that problem. As the truck's motor engaged and the chain began to rattle as it drew the car onto the transport, she said, "Wait. Please. I need to get my things."

He looked up from his task, thumbing a cap back to get a full look at her. "They're safe in the car," he barked, narrowing his eyes. A tattoo in the shape of a dagger angled down over his brow and looked even more threatening beneath the furrowed forehead. "They'll still be there when we get to our destination."

As stormy blue eyes drilled into hers, she fingered the loose pearls in her pocket and recognition stuck. She stepped back. "Doug?" she asked, not confident he was the same boy who'd frequented the estate sale. Rory had pegged him as a boy with a misspent youth and harmless and he hadn't made her feel queasy. Not like she felt now, looking into a face that projected malice. "I didn't know you worked for Al's."

"I'm not on the payroll if that's what you're saying. Yet sometimes he hires my flatbed when there's a need."

"Like today?" she said, swallowing hard, then moving another step toward the shoulder to put a greater distance between them.

"Or I overhear a call when it goes out," he said and leered at her, "and beat Al's driver to the pick-up site."

She kept her voice calm. "Perhaps I could use your phone to make a call?"

His mouth lifted in a sneer. His eyes went flat. "Not a good idea."

Esther's stomach dropped. Doug worked the winch on the opposite side, while he kept a watch on her movements. The chain groaned to pull the car onto the truck bed. She wanted to ask what he was after or why she was the target. Yet, there was a menace in his actions, and she fought to keep her growing fear in check and weighed her options. Six or eight strides away from her, the equipment would block him from reaching her position quickly. Two feet, and she'd make the ditch that ran along the roadway and separated it from the fallow field beyond.

By Esther's estimation, the embankment was too steep for the truck to enter, and the gutter too narrow to maneuver in. She couldn't be sure he wouldn't pursue her on foot if she fled but didn't have time to evaluate the pros and cons before he bellowed, "Get in the cab!"

The motor went silent when he threw the switch, then moved to tie the straps down. He shot a damning glare in her direction.

Esther perceived it as a dare and raised a brow, offering a weak smile.

She took a deep breath when he leaped from the flatbed and bent to secure the strap. Her intuition screamed, "*run!*"

So, when he ducked under the truck, she sprang for the ditch and tumbled down the embankment, thankful for her six-foot frame. Not only did her height dictate the necessity for flat sensible heels, but common sense led her to seek out those with substantial tread.

Without glancing back, she dug in, heading for the beech trees.

## Chapter Twenty-Eight

After arriving at the Sheehan place, Rory pulled around to the carriage house. Esther's car wasn't parked where he expected. It was a mild day, but he wasn't fooled by the Midwest winters—it might snow in an hour. From his seat in the parked car, he saw Nina in the gazebo and Rosco playing in the yard beyond. She concentrated on a notebook in her lap. An evergreen crown graced her head, and a native blanket wrapped her legs. She appeared lost in thought. Or composition. He didn't know how one composed poetry. He checked his watch. Esther was late, it wasn't like her.

The wind blew the branches on the apple trees in the orchard. Crows gathered on the bare limbs. Rosco set off to chase them away, and Nina lifted her head and called after him. Noticing the detective, she waved.

He waved back, then rechecked his watch. Maybe he'd misunderstood and Esther waited in the front. He decided to walk around to check and had just stepped under the arbor when Nina's screams raked the air. The crows flew down the walkway carrying horror on their wings. Rory pivoted and dashed back to the garden.

The dog sitter was no longer in the gazebo. Rosco barked wildly at the door to the garden shed. Rory dashed in that direction. Stumbled. He righted himself and drew his gun. Another scream and the beagle's hackles went up and he went on point.

Rory was at the shed in less than ten seconds. He gulped in air as his sides heaved. Adrenalin shot sky-high, kicking the door open while leveling the weapon. Nina stood against the far wall, hands to her face, eyes wild. At her feet lay James Sheehan.

"He's dead," she said, her voice barely above a whisper.

Rory bent to check the pulse. He holstered his gun and checked the body. James' body was cool to his touch with no noticeable trauma. By the amount of stiffness in the limbs, rigor had already set in. He pushed the eyelids closed before addressing the girl. "He's been dead for hours. Maybe as many as twelve. What made you come in here?"

"I... Rosco..." She couldn't seem to find her voice.

Afraid she was going into shock, he placed a hand on her arm for comfort. "It'll be all right. You can wait outside with the dog."

She nodded. Her eyes unfocused as she passed the body and through the open doorway. Rory pulled out his phone and pushed the number for WPD dispatch. When Sunny answered, he said, "James Sheehan is lying in the gardening shed behind the Sheehan mansion on County Line Road. It appears he's been dead for ten to twelve hours. I need Doctor Moss and a crime scene crew as soon as possible. No hurry for the EMTs. I'll secure the area." He clicked off and stepped in his own footsteps as he backed out.

Rory closed the door to the shed and noticed Nina sitting in the gazebo with the dog on her lap. He crossed the lawn to wait beside his vehicle. His spirits plummeted. James Sheehan's death meant he'd lost the number-one suspect for Phoebe's murder. Nina's horror seemed genuine; it would take a cold-blooded killer to fake the reaction she'd displayed. Then again, a second kill would be easier than the first. With no visible wounds on the body, this, too, might be poisoning. A second strike—Nina eliminates the competition.

In the distance, two police cruisers and an emergency vehicle made their way up County Line Road. Still no Esther. An unsettling voice started to bounce around inside his head. Where could she be? Had her need to move boxes prompted the call earlier, or had it been the item she wanted him to see? Was the object dangerous enough to warrant James Sheehan's death?

He kept one eye on the girl and tried Esther's cell again. No luck. A knot tightened in his stomach.

Petey Moss arrived filled with his usual bonhomie. "Yo, Rory. Found another one, did you?"

"Winterset, the small town where tragedy overlaps misfortune."

"You forget I'm an advocate for the Chamber of Commerce." Petey pumped the detective's hand. "There, we refer to Winterset as the hometown to happiness and prosperity."

"Not for James Sheehan. His body is in the shed."

Petey followed the detective across the lawn to the outbuilding. Still watching the gazebo, Rory said, "The dog raised the alarm. The girl and I made the discovery. We were in the shed long enough to check for a pulse. Otherwise, nothing has been touched."

Petey pulled on surgical gloves and paper booties. "All right, wait here." It wasn't long before he returned. "Rigor and body temperature indicate he met his demise during the night. On a very brief inspection, there are no apparent puncture wounds or signs of blunt force trauma." The ME rocked back on both heels, shoved his hands into the parka's pockets. "If I were a speculating man, I'd say we have another death by poison."

"Yeah, but you won't confirm without a full autopsy."

"True, my friend. However, I can concur he met with tragic misfortune."

Petey stayed while the crime scene was documented and until the body was loaded into the van. "Say, Doc," Rory said, "before you take off, how about pointing out any toxic plants?"

"Not much in bloom. Although, a few poisonous species about." He pointed at the arbor. "Take those yews, for instance."

"Really? Evergreens are dangerous?"

"Not only that, but the leaves also contain their highest alkaloid concentration in winter. As little as a cup can kill. Last year, a local farmer lost a prize bull after turning him out in a snow-covered field. The bull wandered along the fence line and nibbled on a few yew needles."

Glancing at the gazebo, he found Nina no longer writing. Instead, she watched the police activity, and the beagle roamed freely between her and the trees beyond. He wondered, "I've seen sprigs, even whole branches inside the house. Bad idea?"

Petey slowly shook his head. "Best to employ caution. Evergreens look festive draped on the mantel during the holidays, yet they, too, are deadly. Even the dried leaves can be toxic. I'd suggest the local Everything For a Dollar store and go for silk decorations."

The detective walked under the arbor to the front

drive and back after the coroner pulled out. This time he eyed the draped boughs with suspicion. With Officer Lloyd in charge and collecting trace evidence, Rory waited impatiently, and the knot in his stomach grew larger with each passing minute. When he checked again, the gazebo was unoccupied, and the dog was nowhere in sight. Surely, Nina hadn't made a run for it. She might have entered the house, but he thought the trees were more likely. Unbuttoning his jacket for easy access to his weapon, he waved at Lloyd to indicate his intention, then headed into the orchard.

At first, the trees were well tended, planted in rows, and cropped uniformly on top. Then slowly, the foliage thickened. He found the graveyard just before the woods took over. Nina knelt by a gravestone with Rosco at her heels. The dog watched his approach.

"Nina?" he said. Rosco's ears shot up. "Are you okay?"

She placed a hand on the ground beside her. "My grandmother rests here. I've come to draw peace from her."

Cold air crept down his neck, and he pulled the jacket collar up. The cemetery sat in a shaded meadow that left the ground moist, even though no snow remained. A breeze rustled the branches, and he heard small creatures scamper in the underbrush. "It is peaceful here," he agreed.

"Back at the house, the sky began to close in," she said. "Here, the air is abundant."

He nodded in understanding, but she didn't turn to face him. They continued in silence with the woods around them, then suddenly branches snapped, and birds took flight. Rosco growled and took off into the trees.

Two more whoops followed, then nothing.

Nina laid a hand on his arm. He hadn't heard her rise or move to stand beside him. Sensing movement in the trees, Rory quickly reached inside his jacket, slipped the pistol from the shoulder holster, and stepped in front. Unlocking the safety, he motioned for silence.

Another twig snap, then heavy breathing. Rory raised the weapon.

Rosco burst into the clearing with a woman at his heels. Leaves, bark, and small twigs stuck to her thick hair as she stumbled to her knees. All Rory could see was a face covered in scratches and cuts.

"Thank God, I made it," Esther said. "I'm out of breadcrumbs."

Chapter Twenty-Nine

While Rosco did a happy dance around Esther, then finally settled down to rain kisses on her face, Rory lowered his weapon. "Esther? What are—"

"Give me a minute," she said, pushing the beagle away and straightening to take in her surroundings. "I've been traveling in circles for the last hour." She brushed the mud from her knees. "Sorry, I'm late. There was a small problem with the car. Then with the tow service. We won't even talk about briars and roots."

He thumbed back his fedora. "Take your time. But tell me, did you see anyone in the woods?"

"I thought he might follow, but I didn't see anyone, didn't hear anyone. I admit my heart was pounding so loud in my ears, I could have missed him."

"Good. He?" Rory holstered the gun.

Rosco howled, and Nina raised her hand, palm down, to calm him.

As if she had just realized the girl was present, Esther smiled. "Hello, Nina. I found the estate, didn't I?"

"Yes." Nina tapped her thigh, and Rosco went to sit at her feet. "This is my grandmother's place behind the orchard."

Esther approached. "It's lovely."

"Her final wish is to rest one with nature."

The trees, the graveyard, the cold, his energy waning after the adrenaline spike, Rory raised his voice. "Ladies!

We'll make nice later. We have a dead body and too many unanswered questions right now."

"What body?" said Esther.

"Sometime during the night, Sheehan met his maker in the shed."

Esther's dirt-stained face paled. "James is dead?"

"Poison," he said. "The boys are processing the scene now. You better explain why you're tramping through the woods."

She looked unnerved, glancing between Nina and Rory before answering. "I took the backroad cut-off to County Line, expecting to get here before you and with time to spare. Unfortunately, the car had other ideas. So, I called Al's Auto Repair for a tow. Only they didn't respond."

He shifted his weight to ease the ache in his ankle; the cold, damp ground would do that. "A heads-up would have been nice."

"You don't think I had anything—"

"No. I don't think you're responsible for James' death, but others…"

Her face crumpled. He looked back toward the gazebo, but trees hid it from sight. He'd muted his radio earlier, distracted by the constant chatter, and realized he didn't know what the police were doing. He flicked it on and lowered the volume. Even though Esther was eliminated as a suspect in Phoebe's murder, she might end up as a person-of-interest in this one. High in a birch tree, a woodpecker's high-pitched whine broke the silence.

"I'm just saying you spent time here yesterday, and you'll need to account for your movements."

Esther exhaled a long, slow sigh. "After assigning

Axel to dog me? Honestly, Rory, he'll tell you when I got home and didn't leave again until this morning."

"Yup, I'll check with him. And before you left the estate yesterday?"

She balked but answered. "Marilyn stayed while I counted the money. It was dark when I…" She paused, patting her coat pockets. "Nina can confirm I left after dark, but it wasn't late. I want to show you what I found." After turning her pocket inside-out, a bead fell to the ground.

Rory tracked it until it settled in a leaf pile. "Is it the treasure?" He stooped to retrieve the bead, then rolled the pearl between his pointer finger and thumb, confused.

Esther blushed and turned to the girl. "Do you know Doug Ryan, Nina?"

"He was at the estate sale."

Rory's detecting gene kicked in. His heart quickened when he heard Ryan's name for the second time in as many days. Thacker put him at lunch with James and Perry only yesterday. "For the record," he said with a frown. He sounded more like a reporter than an investigator, yet he stood and pulled his notebook out. "Who is Doug Ryan?"

Nina took the evergreen crown from her head and laid it on the grave. Until that moment, he hadn't recognized the yew branches for what they were, instead dismissed them as pretty headdress, native girl garb, and harmless. Hmmm. Not so much. He waited.

Esther wasn't as patient. "I ask you," she said, "because Doug hijacked the call I placed with Al for help and showed up to steal their tow. I didn't know he had an agenda until he'd loaded my car onto the flatbed and advanced on me."

More startled to hear about Ryan's aggressive action than his flatbed truck, Rory lowered the notebook to his side. "What does that mean?"

Esther frowned. "I'm sorry, Rory, I lost my phone and couldn't call."

"Forget the call, how did he advance?"

"More like threatened. From my perspective, Doug acted villainous, even menacing. It wasn't a friendly exchange. Furthermore, he scared me, and I wouldn't put up with it." She continued to brush debris from her soiled slacks. "I kept my wits about me and found the opportunity to run for the trees."

"And this?" Rory held the pearl out for her to identify.

"I dropped the phone and broke my necklace at the same time. I couldn't reach the phone, but I grabbed some pearls. And thank goodness because I lost my bearings in the woods. They are a lot thicker than they appear. Once I'd been in there for an hour and passed the same fallen tree, I started to drop the beads to mark my path Hansel and Gretel style. I thought I'd follow them to retrace my way out if necessary, or you'd use them to locate my body." She held out her hand. "Thanks. I didn't know I had any left."

She went to stand by the girl. "Nina? Are you friends with Doug?"

Nina took the blanket tied around her waist and draped it over her head and shoulders like a shawl. "I've seen him at the Janus meetings. There I call him brother, not a friend."

Rory held his pen ready. "Where do you hold these meetings?"

"The location changes. I don't always attend."

"If brother, why not friend?"

She clutched the blanket edges together at her chest. "He is not a friend. Doug Ryan uses kind words to hide his angry face. Friends are truthful and do not falsely wear the Ho-Chunk dream-catcher tattoo over their heart."

"A tattoo?" asked Esther. "But Perry is covered with them, and you are friends."

"Perry wears art to celebrate his life. Doug Ryan uses it to display his desires."

Rory interrupted, "Maybe he just likes tattoos."

"No," said Nina. "He wears the dagger to intimidate. A university basketball player wears the dream-catcher tattoo to express pride for his Ho-Chunk heritage. Doug Ryan learned this and marked himself with the same, not to honor but to declare himself a fierce warrior ready for battle. He is not Native; he has no respect for The People."

The police radio crackled—Lloyd's voice instructing the officers to widen the search area came through loud and clear. "We should get back," Rory said, gesturing for the ladies to lead the way.

Nina was willing, but Esther pulled him aside. "Last night, I found a letter from Greg Sheehan to his sister. It talks about a girl called Tina, and I sorted through photographs until I came up with this one." She shoved the snapshot into his hands. "I think it is the three Sheehan siblings with a girl named Tina."

"Esther," he said, placing the photo into his notebook without a glance. "I have two murders to investigate. I need to deal with today first. How did you get away from Axel?"

She blushed, adding slyly, "It wasn't hard."

"Foolhardy, even reckless. That's why I—"

Her expression changed from playful to irritated. "What's asinine about meeting to give you new evidence?" She didn't need a dagger tattoo to telegraph her anger.

*When would he learn to use discretion along with his Officer Friendly voice?*

"Furthermore," she snarled, "I'm not helpless." With that, she stomped off after Nina.

He followed with his head down. She could huff and puff all she wanted; Esther knew he didn't consider her a fool. He should have used another word. Then again, every alternative that came to mind implied she was vulnerable. None would have made her happy.

He'd apologize once he'd sorted out the latest Sheehan death.

Chapter Thirty

Rory stopped at the gazebo. Across the yard, Lloyd had Esther and Nina corralled near the mudroom door. Esther's hands flew to her hips, and from her expression, Lloyd wasn't having an easy time getting whatever he was after.

The boys had finished at the shed and had begun to walk the property line in pairs. He wandered to the carriage house to inspect the security camera mounted under the eaves and pointed at the gardening shed. A second camera aimed at the gazebo. Recalling that Esther had purchased the units from Hutchinson and that Axel and Perry had installed them, he called Axel.

"Whoa, constable. It wasn't my fault. Miss Esther promised she'd be okay on her own."

"Axel, we'll review your surveillance techniques later. She's safe and with me. Right now, I need to know what you can tell me about the cameras on the Sheehan property."

Golden Leaf Diner activity sounded in the background; muffled voices mixed with dish clatter. "Tilt and zoom," Axel said. "If set up right, they're motion detectors. We did it right."

"Then you can tell me where the tapes are?"

"Aren't tapes, nowadays."

"Meaning what? The cameras are dummies?"

"No. Everything is stored in the cloud. Don't ask me which one. That way, anyone with a password can log in and view them."

Rory furrowed his brow. "Doesn't sound secure to me. Who has the password?"

"Miss Esther, Perry, me, and I think that pushy nephew, James, 'cause he helped put 'em up."

It was the detective's turn to bristle. "Axel, Pushy-Pants was killed last night."

"Geez, I don't mean any disrespect, sir, but he's been giving Miss Esther fits."

"I know." Rory cleared his throat. "By the way, she misplaced her car this morning on that back road cut-off from your place to County Line Road. She watched it hoisted onto a flatbed but didn't stay around to see which direction it was headed. I want you to locate it."

"I'm on it."

Rory felt certain that Axel paused to salute the phone. "Eat your breakfast, then call me when you have eyes on the car." He clicked off without getting the password. *Dang.*

The dog and the girl disappeared into the house while Esther sat on the mudroom stoop, looking sad and forlorn. He went to make amends.

She raised her head at his approach. "Today is surreal," she said quietly. "James Sheehan is dead, and I'm a suspect. I thought him a pest and a nuisance, but I never wished him ill. Never once did I contemplate doing him in."

He sat, taking her hand in his. "Who says you're a suspect?"

She jutted her chin at Lloyd, who stood by the carriage house, a cell phone at his ear. "Officer Lloyd."

As if he heard her, the policeman turned his back to them and strode into the building.

Rory cocked his head. "I can see where it might feel that way, but Lloyd's job is to secure the area and detain any witnesses."

"What could I have seen? I was too busy running from Doug and arguing with you."

Not wanting to disagree, he remained silent, giving her hand a light squeeze.

"My clothes are ruined, my car is gone, and I destroyed the only decent jewelry I own." She leaned into him, resting her head on his shoulder. "Truly," she said. "I'm no good to anyone."

He dropped her hand and took her in his arms, savoring the moment. They sat in silence while he listened to her erratic breathing settle. When their heartbeats synchronized, he lifted her chin and softly kissed her lips.

She sighed, and he said, "You still have me, one pearl, and all your friends."

Abruptly, she struggled free. "Honestly, Rory. Can't you let me feel sorry for myself?"

"Not today," He pulled her up with him. "I need your help in the library."

"But..."

"No excuses; this is a job only you can perform."

Once he had Esther sitting at the library desk, he turned on the computer. "I want the security footage taken last night from the carriage house camera watching the garden shed."

He pulled a chair around to sit beside her. While she pushed the magic keys to log into the program, he adjusted the chair so he could view the entire display.

"I'm not an expert, Rory. I can run the program, but you'll need to get the finer details from Perry Benson. Or maybe Tom Hutchinson."

"Talk to me about tilt and zoom."

She looked at him, confused. "Tilt and zoom are functions performed with the camera."

He scratched his head. "So not like in pinball, when you nudge the machine to get the desired results."

"No. Not like a pinball." She laughed. "I can see you doing the hip-nudge maneuver."

He shrugged. "Misspent youth."

"Zoom," she said, "focuses in on the image. You can use either function in live view."

"Can anyone view?"

"You'd need a password and the program."

"How often do you review the tapes?"

"They're not tapes, Rory. They are files."

"Okay, files?"

"Never. Cameras are a deterrent. If there is a problem, like…," she cringed, "like this body, there is footage to look at. Which is what we're doing, right?"

"Right."

He tucked the information away. "Let's see what you've got on the garden shed."

Esther typed, called up files, and displayed the results. Deer, badgers, and geese wandered across the lawn. Rory grew impatient with viewing endless menage of fauna. "This doesn't start at one point and end at daybreak?"

"Not really. The motion detector starts and stops the recording. It just naturally jumps forward, opening a new file each time."

"How do you know we're not missing one? Maybe

the assailant crawled on his belly and didn't trip the camera."

She made a face. "I don't think so. The camera covers a wide area and picks up almost everything. Leaves blown by the wind, maybe not, but not much else goes undetected."

"With time gaps, how can I know everything? Look at this." Pointing to the display, he tapped a file. "Twelve-nineteen, then the next one isn't until a little after three in the morning. I'd like to know what happened in the two and a half hours in between."

"I guess you can't, but no one can fool with the recordings except the administrator."

"Isn't that you?"

Esther wrinkled her nose. "I'm one. Tech support is another."

Rory shook his head. "Let me guess, Perry Benson."

"It's not as bad as it sounds. An exception log captures all sign-in activity."

"Okay. Call up the log."

"Sure."

When Esther clicked on the appropriate icon, a message flashed on the screen: *Access Denied.*

She squinted at the message, tried again, and got the same result. "I don't get it. I'm logged in and should be able to pull up the log."

Rory sat back, pausing to think through the problem. After a moment, he asked, "You've looked at it before?"

"When they installed it, Perry went through all the options with me."

"On this computer?"

"No, with his phone."

"There is an app for that?"

She agreed there was.

Rory gazed out the library window. The Sheehan security system was available to everyone with the program. But it wasn't just that; it could be controlled from any cell phone, anywhere there was service, and if you had a password. Worse, an administrator had complete control. Camera on. Camera off. An image altered. A recorded file removed.

"Maybe if I had my phone, I could show you," she said.

"No need. I have a full understanding. First, we'll watch the remaining files. Then I'll find out who is controlling this security system."

The phone at his hip vibrated. He unclipped it and checked the caller ID.

—*Esther Mullins*—

He grinned at her. "It's Axel. Things are looking up."

Putting the phone to his ear, he said, "My grandmother was slow, but she was old."

He paused and listened. Esther leaned toward him expectantly, but he held up a hand to stop her from interrupting.

"Okay," he said, looking deep into her eyes as the caller continued. His stomach somersaulted. "Yes, I understand," he added.

After disconnecting, he lowered his gaze and shook his head. Then regaining his bearings, he stood and moved to the windows. The boys were still collecting evidence. He didn't spot Lloyd but knew he was around. Esther came to stand behind him, placing a hand on his shoulder.

Rory took a deep breath. "We have a problem."

## Chapter Thirty-One

Silence wrapped around them. A tremble passed from Esther's hand to his shoulder. He laid a hand over hers. "I should take you home."

Esther looked at him, her eyes filled with dread. "It wasn't Axel, was it?"

"No." Not by a long shot.

"But it was my phone?"

"Yes."

"What is it, Rory? What does Ryan want?"

He shook his head. "Your car is in the faculty parking lot at WCC."

"What...at the college? Why?"

"It's abandoned, tires flat, doors open."

"Rory?" Her voice wavered. "What does he want from me? What else did he say?"

"This isn't about you, Esther, you or your car. It's a warning for me to step down and move away, so he can get what he wants."

Her eyes glistened. "It was Doug Ryan."

He had no doubt it was Ryan. What bothered him was being directed to leave the scene, and the women, unprotected. "I think so."

"Did he kill James?"

"I don't know that. Yet."

Overhead, he heard Nina moving around in her room. "I want to check out the car, but it's not a good idea for Nina to be alone. I will call Thacker; he can finish looking at the security files and keep an eye on her."

She tucked her head so he couldn't read her thoughts. "I'm sorry I gave Axel the slip this morning," she said. "I'll help Thacker with the files."

Figuring it was safer for her there than home alone, he agreed. "Okay. But stay close to Nina and don't let her leave. I haven't begun to interview anyone about James' murder. Call me if anyone shows up?"

The tremble moved to her lips. He followed Esther's gaze to the business phone on the desk. He picked up the receiver and got a dial tone. She managed a weak smile.

Pulling his wallet, he extracted a business card. "Yeah, I don't know anyone's number either. My cell number is on the back. Or Sunny can find me."

"I was gullible," she said. "Furthermore, I'm old and annoyed."

He rubbed her arms. "You're tired," he said, pulling her into a hug. She felt frail in his arms. Oh, Esther, kindhearted, sensible Esther. He couldn't let anything happen to her. "Besides," he said, "you're not old. I'd say vintage, and except for the dirt on your clothes, you look stunning—practically woman-of-the-manorly."

"There's no such word."

"But if there were…"

"Go on," she gave him a shove, "you're acting way too possessive. Go fetch my car and do some detecting."

He watched as she gracefully crossed the room and started up the stairs. Halfway to the top, she paused and called down to him. "I'm still annoyed that Doug took my car. I'll be doubly upset if he is involved in this estate fiasco."

Triple if he murdered James, Rory thought but didn't say it out loud.

Officer Lloyd was waiting by the detective's car. "Thacker is on his way out to stay with the women until I get back." Rory said.

"Chief wants a word with Esther," Lloyd said. "What do you want me to do?"

"I'll give him a call." He snicked the doors open. "If Benson shows up before I return, detain him. It'd be best to keep him separated from Nina and away from the shed and the house. Especially the shed."

"Sure. Benson is a suspect, then?"

"Person-of-interest. And whacking my cage."

Lloyd stepped away, grinning. Rory plugged in the phone. A call came in before he cleared the drive. "Naysmith," he said, taking it in hands-free mode.

"Whoa, constable."

"Esther's car is at WCC, Axel. I'm on my way there now. Where are you?"

"Geez, I'm still over on the cut-off. It appears Miss Esther put up a fight."

"Why do you say that?"

"Gravel's messed about. A big squiggly patch says a vehicle pulled over, and it ends at a bigger greasy spot. Multiple ruts gouged in the ditch. Looks like heel marks. Also, it looks like fight and flight, mostly flight."

"Any evidence a wrecker was there? She called for a tow."

"Al's Auto says Miss Esther called but canceled in short order 'cause she had it under control. Want me to ferret out the fellow who took the call?"

"Nope. You're sure you're at the right place?"

"Did I mention the footprints? And there's these

funny beads…" Rory heard Axel's lighter flick, followed by a deep inhale, "Kinda looks like they're from that dress-up necklace she wears sometimes."

"Pearls."

"Yup. That's them."

"Esther said she ran for the woods. Do you think you can find where she went in?"

"Ten-four, Kemosabe."

Rory then called Chief Mansfield. Even though he argued it wasn't necessary, the boss insisted Esther come in to give a formal statement. Rory agreed but said it'd have to be later that afternoon. He neglected to tell Mansfield about the car theft or Doug Ryan's actions but said Lloyd was doing a thorough job at the crime scene.

With that out of the way, he hung up to concentrate on locating Esther's abandoned car.

Offloaded, it sat in the WCC faculty parking lot, blocking two parked cars.

Professor Lillie Anderson leaned against the blocked burgundy sedan with arms folded over her chest. Her face matched the car's paint. "I'm having it towed," she said. "I understand flat tires, but keeping mine and Professor Miller's vehicles from leaving? It simply is not acceptable."

"Good morning, professor," he said, tipping his hat. "This is a stolen car. Did you find it like this?"

"I saw him unload it," Anderson snapped. "Douglas Ryan. I happened to be looking out the office window and saw he had it half off the trailer."

"What time was this?"

"I didn't look at the clock. I yelled and knocked on the window. Nonetheless, being two flights up and behind glass, he didn't hear."

"So, you rushed down?"

"Yes, and he was gone by the time I got to the parking lot."

"You can definitely identify the driver as Doug Ryan?"

"Hard not to. He's been hanging around the campus for years. He participates in the Native Medicine Wheel, which I monitor, although he isn't Native American, and he isn't a student."

"A club, then?" Rory scratched his forehead. Winnebago, Ho-Chunk, Janus Chances, how many societies were there?

She scowled at the disabled vehicle. "I've said too much. My feelings about Doug are just that, feelings, not facts. He and Benson can be unnerving. This is one more irritating act done by them."

"Would that be Perry Benson?"

She rolled her eyes. "The same."

Hmmm. Another connection between Benson and Ryan. "Did you see Benson here as well?"

"I can't say I did, yet they are usually together."

"This car could be linked to a murder. Yet, you think it was left intentionally to inconvenience you."

"I would guarantee it."

"A car stolen from someone else and brought to you? For what purpose?"

She pinched her lips together, and glowered. "How would I know why he did it? A secret vendetta, revenge, hatred. He's not rational. Take one look at him and it's evident."

Rory reseated his fedora. "That seems farfetched."

"I tell you, those two are no better than criminals."

"Okay. I'll look into it. In the meantime, your car

can't be moved."

She glanced around, her jaw set. "I have a lecture in an hour. Mind you, I don't like being intimidated."

"I'll have a team process the car. When they're finished, I'll have it removed."

She didn't answer.

"I don't suppose you have had time to have the Ho-Chung letters translated."

"No, they are still with the Native Council."

As she turned and headed back to the building, he wondered at her anger toward Doug Ryan. It was equal to the virulence she'd spat at Phoebe Sheehan before the poet awards banquet. It made him wonder who was the irrational one.

"Say, Professor," he shouted at her retreating figure. "Why didn't you tell me you knew TiKa Mahala?"

She waved a hand in the air but didn't turn.

More worrisome at the moment was why Ryan had dumped Esther's car at Professor Anderson's door. And why did Ryan insist he pick it up?

## Chapter Thirty-Two

While waiting for the boys to arrive, Rory donned gloves and went over the inside of Esther's sedan. Unfortunately, there wasn't much to find: a paper on the passenger seat contained a list of book titles and a dozen pearls beneath the floor mat on the driver's side. Her phone wasn't there—but then Doug Ryan had it. After the department's wrecker arrived, they explained the vehicle would go to the garage for forensic analysis.

Rory took the book titles and the beads, then returned to County Line Road. Thacker was in the library seated at the computer. The rest of the police were gone.

"Everything under control here?" Rory asked. "Esther and Nina still behaving?"

Thacker gave him a deer-in-the-headlights stare. "Boss?"

"The car is intact," Rory said. "However, it needs tires."

"Did you apprehend Doug Ryan?"

"Not this time. Professor Lillie Anderson confirms he unloaded it. Moreover, she thinks Benson and Ryan are out to get her."

"That's kooky."

"Agreed. Her words, not mine. What have you found on the surveillance tapes?"

"I called Tom Hutchinson for the administrator

password and started back at the beginning. James Sheehan entered the shed at about nine last night carrying a package. I couldn't see it plainly, but it was not too big, shoe box size. Shortly after he's inside, Esther exits the mudroom and drives off in her sedan."

"She didn't know he was on the estate?"

"She says not. There is a twenty-minute time gap before the next file shows Nina crossing the same area and entering the woods. I think it's to visit her grandmother's grave."

"Did you ask?"

"I thought I would see what else was on the film."

"Okay."

Thacker continued, "Nina hasn't returned when a dark figure steps from the carriage house and enters the shed. He's wearing dark clothing and never looks at the camera."

"Go on."

"That's it. There isn't much else unless you count the animals grazing. Esther said you saw them earlier."

"So, James was on the grounds before Esther left. He went into the shed with a box and never came out. Nina visited her grandmother in the woods and didn't return. A dark figure entered the shed and is still in there. Where are we, the Bermuda Triangle?"

Thacker didn't react to his sarcasm. "You arrived, and Nina and the dog were there before the body was found this morning. I've started on the gazebo files," he said. "They have a different angle on the same area."

Rory began to pace. "Changing gears, son. When Sheehan, Benson, and Ryan were at the Golden Leaf Diner, did anyone join them?"

Thacker looked up. "I didn't ask. No one said."

"Benson, Ryan, and Sheehan were together at the diner," Rory murmured out loud. "I wonder how many other times and places they met?"

"Could be anywhere," said Thacker, "anytime."

"True, and before the hardware store thefts. Possibly before Phoebe's death by poison. Definitely before James' death today."

Rory took out his notebook and flipped through the pages. "Here's the password for Hutchinson's security files. Log off and try the hardware store." He handed the notebook to Thacker. "Start with the inside camera at a time just before the store closes." Rory rounded the desk to view the monitor himself. "The file is labeled *Counter*. Last time, I only looked for the theft after closing and concentrated on the back door. I want to know who visited the store before Perry Benson locked up for the night."

Unlike the motion detector files from the Sheehan security system, the hardware store cameras recorded all. Minutes showed nothing more than an empty counter with an unattended cash register. As Tom Hutchinson had said, there was not much business that night. Then, at 1840 hours, a man moved to the checkout and placed a pair of pruning shears on the counter. The cashier appeared and stood with his back to the camera. The camera focused on the customer's chest; nothing above chin level was in the frame. He wore a winter coat opened at the collar.

"Freeze that shot," Rory said. "Dang. I can't see his face. Do you recognize those whiskers?"

Thacker scooted the chair closer and leaned in. "Negative. Do you think it is the perpetrator?"

"How about the coat? Wait. What did Sheehan have

on when he showed up at the hospital Thursday night?"

It was a rhetorical question; Thacker hadn't been at the hospital. Rory snatched his notebook from the desk and started reading through the pages. It contained no description of James Sheehan the man or the clothing he had on.

Rory scratched his head. "Why would a businessman want a garden tool?"

The rookie answered without hesitation. "Fifty-six percent of all gardeners are Caucasian men, and most are in their forties. My dad loved to putter in the ground. He said he found it relaxing."

"It's February, hardly time to set out the begonias. Go on, let's see the rest."

Thacker clicked the icon. The film advanced, showing the cashier reaching under the counter and laying a crowbar and a sledgehammer beside the shears.

"Guy's getting ready to do some damage. Who is behind the cash register? Is it the clerk or Benson?" said Rory. He tried to recall the clerk's name and failed.

"Must be the clerk. I don't see Benson's tattooed knuckles."

The customer scooped up the tools and left without paying. "Whoa," said Rory, watching as the man left through the front door. The camera focused on the countertop and captured a blurry doorway image, yet he recognized the man's swagger.

"Inside job?" said Thacker, raising his brows.

Rory's thoughts exactly, but he jutted his chin toward the monitor to indicate they should continue to watch.

The cashier moved away, otherwise, nothing. The next activity occurred at seven when Benson locked the door, counted the money, and dropped the bag in the safe. The time stamp indicated 1924 hours. Rory tried not to smile. He loved the heady tingle when things started to fall into place.

"Notice Benson's wearing a sweatshirt?" he asked. "Either he changed before closing, or he wasn't the cashier."

"Do you suppose the crowbar and hammer damaged the back door?"

"Why not just leave the door unlocked?" asked the detective. He felt a buzz growing.

Thacker squinted, pinched his lips together, then lifted his shoulders. "They knew about the cameras?"

"Bingo! So, here's what we do. You contact the security software manufacturer, ask for a hotshot top-tier engineer, and find out what shenanigans an administrator can do with surveillance footage. Erase, alter, splice. You get the picture?"

"Sure, boss. But—"

"In particular, question him about the ability to black out twenty-two minutes. And if remote manipulation is possible. Meanwhile, I'll look for the box James Sheehan carried into the shed.

They each took up their phones.

Hot on the trail, Rory didn't notice Esther until she stood beside him. "Did you find my car?"

He held up a hand and continued to speak into his phone. "So, the evidence is all logged in and no box?" He smiled at Esther, "Yes, detective's intuition, Lloyd. And no, that's all I'm interested in right now."

After disconnecting, he filled Esther in on his trip to the community college. He wrapped up with, "So, in the long run, no damage has been done and Axel will act as your chauffeur for a day or two."

She wrinkled her nose.

"Better than it could have been," he said. "Professor Anderson had some curious things to say about Perry Benson and Doug Ryan."

She took a seat. "Lillie Anderson? I don't understand."

"Thacker says Benson and Ryan are buddies. Anderson says they're evil. I have yet to make up my mind. After scaring you today, Ryan led me to Lillie Anderson. It might have been a message for her, but I'm inclined to believe it was to remind me that our professor is a viable suspect in Phoebe's murder."

"Phoebe's murder? I thought this was about James and me being Phoebe's executor and stealing a treasure."

"I'm not convinced there is a treasure."

She jerked back. Thacker, who'd finished his call, gave a low whistle.

"I don't think the prize is loot," Rory continued. "My working theory about this Sheehan treasure was James searching for gold, a manuscript, or some old stock certificates. Any object with considerable value, yet small enough to hide for decades. I think we all had a similar idea. But what if he was searching for an unspecified thing, wanting to find it before someone else discovered it? An unknown object that would do him harm."

"Then wouldn't he have been quieter about the process?" she asked.

Thacker's chair creaked. "The Winterset Library and WCC inherit. How would murder change that?"

Closing his eyes, Rory tipped his head back. "The only way to invalidate Phoebe's will would be to produce a second one dated later than the one we turned over to the lawyer. If James had a second will," he surmised, gazing at the young officer, "and it held up in court, it might change the beneficiaries, the allotments, and invalidate contracts. Keeping it hidden, could certainly provide a motive for murder."

"What about the codicil?" Eshter asked.

"A codicil doesn't hold the same status. The county judge could accept it or throw it out. In any case, James' relationship to the decedent would play in the court's decision. I don't think James had a codicil, or a second will. Not one he could defend." He glanced at Esther. "Have you seen either?"

She looked puzzled. "No."

"Me either. And if he could replace the named beneficiaries with someone closer to home, why didn't he? Not just replaced them but also get himself named executor. What if there is a document in this house proving James isn't Phoebe's next-of-kin?" He paused to let the idea sink in, then added, "I think the murders are about keeping a family secret hidden—a secret that James couldn't let come to light."

"Wait a minute," said Thacker. "Family secret? You think… Are you saying, Nina…"

Suddenly, Esther grabbed Rory. "Oh, you looked at the snapshot."

"What snapshot?"

"The one with Tina in it."

"Who is Tina?"

She shoved him away. "If I didn't know better, I'd say you don't listen to a word I say."

"Honestly, I have no idea what you're talking about."

Her nostrils flared. "Yesterday, I found a letter. Then, because I thought it significant to your investigation, I went through the family pictures and found Tina."

"Again, who is Tina?"

"Where is the snapshot I gave you this morning?"

His turn to be puzzled. "I…" He patted his pockets. "I don't remember—"

"Of course, you don't. It went into your sacred detective book without a glance."

The offending notebook sat on the desk next to his roommate. Rory picked it up and fanned through the pages. "You're sure?"

"Yes, I'm sure." She heaved a heavy sigh and checked for herself. "You must have lost it."

He glanced at Thacker, who began moving items around, searching. After not locating the picture, he stooped to peek under the desk.

While the young officer combed the area, Rory addressed Esther. "Where is this letter?"

"It's in the mud room."

A muffled grunt came from the desk kneehole. Thacker popped up, holding a Polaroid snapshot above his head.

"Thank goodness," said Esther.

"Let's see," said Rory, plucking the picture from Thacker's fingers and studying the subject momentarily before checking the back. "I'll be hanged," he said under his breath.

Although the snap was a color photograph, the sky had turned brownish gray with age, and the clouds a whitish beige. The four teens, however, were easy to identify. "Looks like Gregory Sheehan went into the

Marines."

"Obviously," said Esther, her tone sharp.

"Yup. Parris Island, where marine recruits were trained for the Vietnam War. Nice picture. And you say the girl with the Sheehan kids is..." He flipped it over again. The back was still blank. "Jamison, Phoebe, and the girl Gregory has an arm around is this, Tina? I wonder who took the picture?"

"Probably a classmate," she said with a half-hearted shrug. "I'll get the letter."

While she went to the mud room, the detective scrutinized the shot. "Dang it, Thacker. Professor Anderson has a photograph in her office which documents a Native American ceremony. This same girl took part in it, but at that time, she was known as TiKa."

Thacker, who'd climbed back into the desk chair, gave another low whistle. "Are you saying Tina is Nina's grandmother?"

Rory tapped a finger on the photograph. "I'm saying this woman—err, the girl—is TiKa Mahala."

He purged his lips in thought. "We know that the ever-faithful housekeeper, TiKa, had a baby named Aponi. Likewise, we know that child is Nina's mother. The question is who fathered the baby. It could have been anyone, a boy she met at college or someone from town. But if it was Michael Sheehan, then Aponi is Phoebe's half-sister. Which raises questions, like, why was she left out of Phoebe's will?"

Thacker glanced around as if looking for the answer.

"Furthermore," said Rory, recapturing his attention, "If the child was a Sheehan, James wouldn't have grounds to contest the will because his claim as closest kin evaporates. That would provide a clear motive for

James to employ delay tactics, steal documents, and force a quick solution before anyone made the discovery. All along, a Michael and TiKa dalliance seemed likely." He glanced at the Polaroid. "Now, it looks like Grandma and Greg managed to hook up instead."

The young officer sunk lower into the chair. "Either way, Nina is TiKa's granddaughter?"

"Oh yeah. Not in dispute."

Thacker frowned. "So…Aponi, Nina's mother, is either Phoebe's half-sister—or her niece—or not a Sheehan at all."

"Don't worry, Thacker. Nina doesn't have an obvious motive to murder Phoebe or James. Her mother is still alive, and even if she wasn't, Nina wouldn't profit from the Sheehan estate—unless we had proof that TiKa and a Sheehan were Aponi's parents. We only have circumstantial evidence suggesting such a thing." He took another glance at the snapshot. "However, this girl and Greg look pretty chummy."

Esther came back with a GI airmail envelope. Before she reached him, his phone rang.

—*Esther Mullins*—

"Your fan club," he said, taking the letter from her. He placed the phone to his ear, "Ryan? I wondered when you'd call."

He listened, taking deep breaths, and wanting his expression to remain neutral while the caller outlined an escalating plan to harm him, and threatened to destroy the estate.

"Got it?" Ryan demanded. "I get the list and you turn over the treasure—or else."

"Right," Rory said. "I can do that."

The whole conversation took less than a minute. He

disconnected, took the letter from the envelope, and began reading.

Esther raised one eyebrow and gave him a glassy stare. "Rory. Sometimes I could shoot you and not bat an eye. Tell us what Ryan wanted."

He lifted his chin absently, continuing to read.

The faded, tissue-thin letter was almost indecipherable. He found the reference to Tina. However, he distinctly saw TiKa in the pencil scratches. He refolded it and handed it back. "You're right. This letter mentions a girlfriend. Or a girl who could be much more."

She gave him a terse nod. "Tina."

"TiKa. If you look again, you'll see it plainly, too."

As she impatiently took the letter, he added, "Ryan misplaced what he calls a list. He's given us time to turn it over." He didn't see the need to share Ryan's threats. It would just fuel Esther's anxiety, and he wished to spare her that. "He plans to stop by in the morning to retrieve it."

"Boss?" Thacker said. "Speaking of changed gears, the computer hotshot says changing the light contrast on the surveillance footage will mask a picture's presentation. Plus, he has a procedure that restores any file to its original version."

"Good. Have the computer dude do it. Meanwhile, we have a lot to do before tomorrow. First up is a visit to the reservation. Aponi knows more than she's admitted."

Thacker rubbed his jaw, stalling, but finally gave a hesitant thumbs-up.

"Then," Rory said to Esther, "I'll talk with Petey, while you give a formal statement to the police."

She started to protest, when the front door slammed,

and she froze without uttering a word. Footfalls sounded in the hall and Nina appeared in the library doorway. Rosco yipped and scampered to join the detective. "So, there you are," Rory said with a half-smile.

The girl looked frazzled. Her braid had loosened allowing flyaway hair wisps to dance about her shoulders. The beaded blanket draped over her shoulders hung askew, covering her arms. Wet leaves and debris clung to her moccasins. Naturally, the happenings earlier in the day had bewildered her. "Are you all right, Nina?" he asked.

"I found this at my grandmother's grave," she said, pulling her shawl aside to reveal a shoe-sized metal box. "It wasn't there this morning."

## Chapter Thirty-Three

"On second thought," said Rory. "Thacker, you take Esther to the station. I'll call Petey, and afterward, Nina and I will visit her mother."

"What about the tin?" asked Esther. "How did it get into the graveyard?"

"Could be the box James took into the shed," said Thacker.

Rory jutted his chin at the young officer, who began to type on the computer. Keyboard clicks filled the room. He held his breath until Thacker turned the monitor toward the group, revealing a frozen image—James Sheehan standing in the shed doorway.

"Why does he look back?" asked Esther.

"Boxes match," said the rookie.

Rory pried the lid open. "Hmmm." He scratched his forehead. "When you went through pictures looking for family shots last night, Esther, did you notice this box?"

"Um…uh…" She tilted her head. "I went through the family albums piled on a shelf in Phoebe's bedroom. Why?"

"There are roughly a dozen photographs in here." He prodded them with his finger. "I'd say they rebuke family statements. At the very least, they call for clarification. Who is who, and what is what?"

Nina slumped in a chair, looked up quickly, then turned away without making eye contact.

Esther gasped. "James?" she asked. "He wasn't truly Phoebe's nephew?"

"Hmmm," said Rory. "Nina, you're with me. Thacker, call me when you have the restored surveillance."

Everyone started to speak at once. He signaled for silence. "Esther, Axel is retracing your steps through the woods. He'll switch to his McGruff persona and gather important information, including who visited the grave site. Thacker, continue to work the hardware tapes. Nina, let's go."

They passed a WPD cruiser before they cleared the drive. "Good," he said, "We'll have a secured crime scene and no unwanted visitors." Silently, he chided himself for not arranging for the police to patrol the grounds.

Buckled into the passenger seat, Nina held the metal tin on her lap and stared through the window.

"Go ahead," he said, "look through the pictures." She didn't respond. "You know what's in them?"

She raised one shoulder, eyes still on the horizon.

"Why lie about your relationship with Phoebe?"

"I did not lie."

"As far as I'm concerned, withholding pertinent facts in an investigation is a crime. And failing to admit a relationship is lying."

"You make it sound tawdry and dishonest. We were different people who chose to remain silent because it had no bearing on who we were."

"A Native American dog sitter and an Irish American librarian."

"Yes."

"Yet, both, Sheehan."

"I find more honor in claiming the Thunder Clan."

"And your mother? Who does she claim?"

The girl hugged the box to her chest. "You will need to ask Aponi."

He parked the city car on the street. Mrs. Crouching Bear opened the door to his knock, stepping back to let him enter. She looked surprised to see Nina. "Crouching Bear is here," Aponi said, more to the girl than the detective.

"Great," Rory said. "I need to speak with you both."

Leaning back in the sagging recliner, Crouching Bear still wore his bus driver's uniform. He raised a finger in greeting but didn't rise.

Aponi led them to the sofa, signaling for Rory and Nina to sit. "You have brought a gift?"

"I wish this were a social call, Mrs. Crouching Bear, but unfortunately, I have a few questions for you and your husband."

"I will prepare an herbal tea, and we will discuss these matters."

"No need for tea," Crouching Bear growled. "The girl is not welcome here."

Nina made to rise, but Rory put out an arm to block her from standing.

"She is not of my blood," the big man growled.

"You said that when we first met, but her birth certificate clearly states you are her father."

He grunted. "She is Aponi's child."

Rory turned to Aponi. "My inquiry is about your parentage, Mrs. Crouching Bear."

"We spoke these words on your last visit. Among her people, my mother was known as TiKa. On the Sheehan estate, they called her Nani."

"I recall. Nani, the Ho-chunk word for mother."

She smiled weakly, often glancing at her husband, who sat cross-armed, clenched-fisted, and scowled.

"I have some photographs here," Rory said. "I'd like you to identify the people in them for me."

After another glance at Crouching Bear, she agreed. "If I am able."

Nina had carried the box into the house. Crouching Bear grunted when she passed it to Rory.

Rory cleared his throat. "I want to clarify that I'm not here to accuse anyone. I need to sort out background information pertinent to two murder investigations. I think you can help." He passed a snapshot to Aponi. It showed a young woman holding a baby while two tow-headed men grinned over her shoulders at the camera.

"Nani," she said. "It is the day of the Blanket Ceremony." She identified the younger man as Jamison, the other as Michael Sheehan.

Next, he took Esther's Parris Island picture from his breast pocket. "In this one, I believe your mother is with the Sheehan children."

She squinted at the picture and reluctantly identified each by touching their image. "Yes. Jamison. Phoebe. Gregory. Nani."

"Now, can you say which man is your uncle?"

With her chin held high, she answered. "In our culture, a father's brother is also known as father. Our mothers' brothers are called uncle. There are no uncles in this picture."

Crouching Bear chuckled.

Rory scratched his forehead. Fair enough. Not the epiphany he'd hoped for, but perhaps the admission that Michael Sheehan had fathered her. He withdrew another.

"This picture is Nani with two children. One is you, Aponi, maybe at two years, and an older boy, perhaps seven. Can you tell me the boy's name?"

The recliner snapped. Crouching Bear moving faster than Rory imagined a man with his girth could muster, snatched the photo with sausage fingers, and ripped it into shreds, bellowing, "No more questions."

"I have more," said the detective, unmoved by the threat. "More, which include this boy."

Nina held her ground without flinching. Crouching Bear towered over them. "Take this ungrateful *Wakąja* and leave."

****

On the ride back from the Crouching Bears' apartment, Nina acted pensively, shuffling through the pictures over and over.

"What did he mean when he called you Waka Hay?"

"*Wakaja* is the Ho-Chunk word for Thunderbird."

"Hum," he said. "Crouching Bear resents your heritage."

"Crouching Bear is also Winnebago, but he is Bear Clan, the warriors. He refuses to follow tribal law. He resented TiKa's and the Ho-Chunk teachings' influence on his son."

He flinched, tightening his grip on the steering wheel. *Son?* There was a revelation that shed light on the odd relationships among the Crouching Bears.

"To this day, Aponi is not allowed to participate in ceremonies and pow-wows. She must not repeat our oral history."

"He permits her to work at the casino."

"Keeping her at home would limit their income. On the reservation, he keeps a watchful eye."

"So, living on the estate wasn't just about Mom being the live-in housekeeper."

"No," she said sadly. "To honor our ancestors and continue in our customs, Aponi did not make a home with Crouching Bear."

"But you moved to the reservation after Michael's death…" He knew Phoebe had ended Aponi's employment after her father passed, yet he let the question hang.

She studied a photo, rubbing its surface lovingly, before answering. "We needed a place to sleep."

"And you didn't stay."

"No," she answered, returning the photograph to the box, and securing the lid. "Crouching Bear made that impossible."

Rory could imagine the burly man intimidating his small daughter. Furthermore, he could see Nina refusing to put aside her convictions to gain even minimal comfort. "No roots and berries?" he asked. "No access to carry out your caretaker duties to nature?"

She didn't answer. He let her ride in silence while pondering Crouching Bear's reaction to the boy. Son, she'd said. Nina's brother? Half-brother? Why had the bus driver reacted so violently to the photograph?

Rory pushed the phone icon and said, "Call Rookie."

Shortly, Thacker's deep voice came through the speakers. *"I am downloading the original Hutchinson surveillance as we speak."*

"Good. Is Esther with you?"

*"Affirmative. Axel is back from the woods."*

"Even better. We are fifteen minutes out. Have everyone assemble in the library."

He clicked off. "In those fifteen minutes," he said to his passenger, "you will tell me about Crouching Bear's son without lying and no evasion."

By the time they pulled around to park beside the carriage house, Rory had a clear picture.

Well, he admitted, at least a working theory.

## Chapter Thirty-Four

Esther and Thacker sat at the computer while Axel, in knee-high boots and a camo jacket, perched on the library ladder, leafing through a magazine. Rosco slept in front of the unlit hearth. They all looked up when Rory entered with Nina on his heels. Each wore somber expressions, a family expecting a surgeon's update on a loved one's condition, hoping for good news but prepared to hear bad.

The spell was broken when the beagle woke up, let out a howl and scampered to Nina's side. While she bent to rub his head, everyone started to talk at once.

In the melee, Rory heard, "…twenty-two minutes…", "…in the bushes…", and "…albums down…" Laughing softly, he signaled for a time-out. "I want to hear it all, but one at a time. Esther? More photos?"

Her face glowed. "I brought the family albums down. I'm prepared to go through them if you tell me what to look for."

"Good. Good. In a moment. Axel?"

"I found three sets of prints in the woods. A size-eleven man's work boot, Miss Esther's crepe soles, and a second occurrence made by the same size-elevens. Work Boots came into the woods, roughly from the same spot as Miss Esther, except he went straight through the meadow and onto the grounds. His earliest prints indicate he visited the shed and ended at the carriage house."

"You can tell he was there before Esther?"

"Geez, her prints were on top of his. Doesn't take much imagination to recognize the sequence."

"Go on."

"Also, they're crisscrossed with deer tracks, so he breached the property line before the critters fed this morning." Axel pulled a hip flask from his pocket. "Found this in the bushes and footprints, indicating he holed up for a while. Might belong to Work Boots."

Rory raised one brow. "In the woods, but close enough to keep an eye on the garden shed?"

Axel rubbed his chin, considering the possibility. "Yup. The shed, gazebo, and carriage house."

"And the second trip?"

"Miss Esther must not a known where—"

She jumped up. "I got lost."

Axel grinned. "Ten-four, roger that." A second pocket extraction produced loose pearls. He held them out to her.

As Esther's eyes sparkled, gratitude turned her handsome face lovely.

Rory intercepted the hand-off, slipping the beads into his pocket instead. Then, noticing her smile droop, he muttered, "Evidence," and watched her joy evaporate. *Rats.*

He rolled his shoulders to regain his composure. "I assume the flask doesn't contain whiskey and should find its way to Petey."

Axel saluted. "A third set, boots again, started at the cut-off intersection with County Line Road and made a beeline for the Nani-grave. Work Boots. No doubt they were laid after the first and second trails."

"Good work."

Thacker, with hands poised over the computer keyboard, fidgeted. "Ready, boss?"

Rory moved to stand behind the rookie and Esther. "Fire away."

The rookie clicked an icon, and the restored video began. The first ten seconds showed the overhead exit sign dimly lighting the back door from inside the hardware store. Then a figure crossed to the door and undid the lock. He kept his back to the camera as he propped the door open and stepped out. A trailer could be seen waiting in the alley. A second figure came through the door. Avoiding the camera, he stayed in the shadows as he moved into the store and out of view.

"Geez," whispered Axel, causing Rory to jump and lightly bump into Esther.

"Sorry, I didn't know he…" A glance confirmed Nina stood behind Thacker as well. Sure, why not? They all had a stake in this. He squeezed Esther's shoulders and left his hands resting there.

As the video continued, the two figures moved in and out, each time helping themselves to Hutchinson's merchandise. They alternated trips and never showed their facial features to the lens.

"Only two," stated Thacker, his voice disappointed.

"So far," said the detective. "Concentrate on the clothing. Their movements, does it suggest—"

On the computer monitor, a third man appeared in the alley and blocked the thieves' access to the trailer. "Whoa," Rory said. "What have we here? Hold that picture, Thacker."

The rookie complied, freezing the frame, and

capturing three individuals.

Esther gasped. Nina snorted. Thacker took a deep breath and let it out slowly. Axel, the only one to articulate his thoughts, said, "Holy moly."

"Behold," said Rory. "The butcher, the baker, and the candlestick maker."

"But, Rory," said Esther. "How does this solve the murders?"

"Bear with me. First, did you make a list of book titles, detailing those you intended to donate to the library? And second, did you have it with you this morning when…er… Ryan intercepted you?"

Puzzled, she answered, "Not a list, no. The library can have them all if they like. I planned to see where the estate could round out their collections."

He drummed his fingers against his leg. "I recall you telling me about Phoebe's hidden safe. It, among other things, held personal documents and three folders. One folder was empty?"

"When I discovered it, yes." She glanced at Nina, who had slipped over to the hearth and sat cradling Rosco. "One held poetry, one household receipts, and the third was quite bare."

"Nina?" he said. "Tell me about the third folder behind the wainscot paneling."

The girl tossed her braid and donned a surly expression. "It wasn't my business."

"Perhaps not, but you know what was in it. A list, perhaps."

Her grip tightened on the dog, but Rosco squirmed away. "One page. Notes written in TiKa's hand. That's all."

"Which made it yours?"

"I thought it was a recipe for a natural remedy."

"But it wasn't."

A terse head wag. "When everyone"—she looked pointedly at Esther—"began to sort and destroy, I feared it would be lost."

"Did James Sheehan ask you about TiKa's note? For that matter, did anyone pressure you to hand it over?"

"I took the page to my room for safekeeping before the estate sale."

"Can you get it for me now?"

She studied her feet. Without lifting her chin, she slowly shook her head.

"Okay," he said, "You mislaid the paper."

Her head shot up. "No."

Thacker stood so quickly the desk chair shot straight back and slammed into the wall. Rory signaled for the young officer to remain in place. "Or someone took it from you."

Rory reached under his jacket and withdrew his detective shield. Flipping the leather case open, he removed a page taken from a memo pad and carefully unfolded it. "I found this sheet in Esther's sedan this morning. She says it's not hers."

"TiKa's list." The girl reached for the paper, but he snatched it out of her reach.

Esther crossed the room for a look at the paper. Thacker followed. Axel craned his neck for a better glimpse. Rory held the yellow sheet up for inspection but didn't relinquish his hold.

"Yellow tablets were popular in the sixties," said the rookie. "Not much call for them now."

Axel snorted. "I got a dozen legal pads at my place if you want one."

"While tempted to downplay the significance this list plays in our case," Rory said, "I think it will unlock the Sheehan secret and thus the motive for murder."

All eyes were locked on him. A good crew, he thought, without giving his feelings away.

His cell phone buzzed.

*—Esther Mullins—*

Leaning close, Esther whispered, "The Butcher wants it back."

Chapter Thirty-Five

Rory felt certain Esther was right. Declining the call, he clipped the phone to his belt and straightened his shoulders. "I think we can expect a visitor shortly. Is Officer Hansen still out back?"

"His orders are to remain until you relieve him," said Thacker.

"While we search in here, Axel, I want you down the road. Take any spot where you can see traffic on both the cut-off and County Line Road. Go on foot and give us a heads-up if Ryan shows. We can't discount that he's familiar with the territory and has been inside the mansion numerous times. Do you have a walkie-talkie?" The aging hippie held up his cell phone.

"Good. Thacker, what does this character drive?"

The young officer checked his notebook. "DMV records list a jeep: red, late-model, four-wheel-drive."

"Okay. Yet, there is no guarantee he'll show up in it or on foot. For that matter, we don't know if he'll be alone. The slightest suspicion, Axel, you blow the whistle."

Esther put on her game face, determination edged with tenacity. "What do you want us to do?"

He handed the memo sheet to her. "See what strikes you about this list while I update Officer Hansen."

Esther walked to the doorway, taking the list with her, and glanced down the hall. "Is there any reason to believe Ryan isn't already in the house?"

He didn't know and hadn't considered the possibility. Sure, the call might have come from inside the house or from elsewhere on the grounds. He could take the time to track the call and find the phone. Gone were the days when it took a tech expert to pinpoint a location. These days, anyone with an app… Nope, there was a quicker way.

"Thacker," he said, "secure the rooms and make sure no one is in here with us." When his police radio crackled, Rory added, "Stay off the emergency frequencies. Ryan has a scanner."

Axel accompanied Rory into the back garden, breaking off to enter the woods.

After alerting Hansen, Rory walked the house's perimeter and then returned to the library. Thacker and Esther were waiting. "Where has Nina gotten off to?"

"Preparing tea," Esther said. "She seemed at loose ends, and the task might calm her."

"Everything locked up?" Rory asked. "There isn't a priest hole or a cellar we've overlooked?"

"Rory," she said, "there are no hidden panels except in the dining room, and it's been empty since before the estate sale."

"All right. Let's see the list."

She handed it to him. "I marked several titles."

Thacker wheeled the library ladder to the non-fiction book section between the fifty-year-old Funk & Wagnalls New World Encyclopedias and a collection of self-help books. "We came away with a big goose egg last time," he said, stepping onto the first rung, "James searched these volumes and came away empty-handed."

"He dislodged Nina's leaves," corrected Esther.

"This time," Rory said, taking the chair behind the desk, "we're not looking for a needle in a haystack, and James Sheehan isn't here to distract us."

Nodding, Thacker went up another step. The walkie-talkie function on his radio chirped. Static. He unclipped it from his belt and pressed the talk button. "Hen house, over."

Axel's voice filled the library. *"I say…we've got a four-wheel-drive jeep pulling over to park on the cut-off."* Static. *"Over."*

Rory directed, "Tell him to stand down until he identifies the driver."

After relaying the message, Thacker replaced the radio and scrambled up enough rungs to reach the volumes on the top shelf. "Okay, give me a title."

Rory ran a finger down the list. "Do you see one by Schwartz, *The Magic of Thinking*?"

"What exactly are we looking for?" Thacker asked, reaching for a thin book and passing it to Esther. She opened the front cover, then the back. Finally, she fanned through the pages and shook her head.

"Next?"

Consulting the list, Rory said, "Esther's marked *Healing, The Complete Herbal Guide* by Clapper and *Little Flower Folks*, by Maria Pratt."

"Pratt? Here's one titled *Little Folks* by Sprats." Thacker pulled the book and sneezed. "It's pretty dusty."

"Shouldn't Nina be finished in the kitchen?" Rory asked. "It'd be wiser to stay where we can see one another."

Esther laid the book on the desk. "Honestly, Rory, you sent Axel into the woods alone. The three of us can find the treasure-thing without her. Let the girl have a moment's peace."

Rory scratched his head. What would fit in a hardback book? A document, a message, perhaps a poem? "Look through this magic thinking book again. Look for writing on the pages or underlined words."

The only thing that made sense to the detective was James arriving in Winterset, already knowing a list existed and believing it could alter his future. His father, Jamison, might have mentioned it during an angry rant directed at his sister.

If James needed to figure out where to find the list, it would explain his nighttime break-in. Had he located it then, no one would have recognized its importance. Rory had yet to figure out where the other two men fit into James' scheme.

Esther sighed. "No secrets in this book. The end pages are glued tight. No chance an item is hidden behind the cover either."

"Okay. Check the others." Rory swiveled the chair to face the window and caught Hansen passing through the yew arbor. The policeman went from the front to the back gardens, collar up, hands pocketed against the cold. It couldn't be pleasant out there with the sunlight waning. Rory made a mental note to put in a good word for Hansen with the chief.

He checked the time on his phone. Five-thirty. "No word from Axel? It's been a while."

"If he's all-in incognito, he will be belly-crawling up on the jeep as we speak," Thacker said. "He wouldn't welcome the giveaway."

"True." Rory settled, legs back in the knee hole, chair snug against the desk, nerves ticking. Esther had been through the house thoroughly. If there was a secret to find, why hadn't she turned it up? Tapping fingertips on the desktop, he studied the paper, and came to a decision. "Bring down every book with the word 'family' in the title."

Thacker looked down on him and did a double take. Esther scoffed. "Not very systematic."

"We've wasted enough time. Ryan or his cohorts will be here any moment. We can't expect them to treat us kindly. They've already murdered two people to keep this secret." He glanced at the doorway. "Better get the girl. We need a concerted effort."

The beagle wandered through the door. Weaving a staggered trail to the fireplace, he flopped down on the hearth and seemed to pass out. "If I didn't know better," Esther said, "I'd say Rosco is sleeping off a drunk."

Rory half smiled. At least someone could relax. "I'll get the girl. You two, bring down the books."

He pushed himself up from the desk and discovered he'd sat too long. With a wince, he shook the stiffness from his joints. When he glanced up, Nina stood in the doorway.

Her embroidered shawl hung loose at her waist. The cross-body strap led from her right shoulder to the beaded sack at her left hip. Lips tight, eyes bright, she slumped against the door jamb and took a visual sweep around the room. When she located the dog, she hugged her chest and began to tremble.

"Rosco is fine," he said softly, moving tentatively toward her.

She stared at him with a shocked glaze in her eyes. Behind him, Esther and Thacker were quiet. Too quiet. He heard an evergreen bough rustle in the arbor, a floorboard settled overhead, and Rosco's labored breath.

Nina hung her head.

"Look at me, Nina," Rory said. "I won't let anyone harm your dog."

"Rosco," she whispered.

"Rosco," he said. "Esther will take a look." He pivoted, ready to urge the bookkeeper into nursemaid mode. But Esther, already advancing, was only a step away. "Oh." He turned back, "Now, Nina…" the words drifted off.

Nina looked as limp as a rag. The leather strap pulled tight across her body held her upright. Fearing she'd fainted, he skip-sprinted to her side and slid an arm around her shoulders. The beaded bag, unbelievably bulky, kept him from getting hip-to-hip close, and an obstruction prevented him from sliding his arm low enough to support her at the waist. He glanced over his shoulder, checking it out.

A blue arm—policeman blue.

It could have been Officer Hansen's uniform sleeve. But it wasn't. This man had a dagger on his forehead.

And a bigger dagger in his hand.

## Chapter Thirty-Six

"We're coming into the library," Ryan said. One hand twisted through the strap at Nina's back. In the other hand, he wielded the deadly looking blade. "Do you understand?"

"I'm afraid so," Rory said.

The detective suspected the rookie had scrambled down the ladder. He stood red-faced and winded at the bottom. Esther backed up to stand beside the younger man.

"Stand down, son," Rory warned.

Ryan crab-walked the semi-conscious Nina into the room. "Everyone against the bookcase. Hands where I can see them. You, Detective Rory, put your weapon on the desk."

"Detective Naysmith," he said and made a show, opening his jacket and removing the service revolver from the shoulder holster with one finger and thumb.

"Now, get the weapon from the boy scout."

"So, what are we doing here?" asked the detective, stepping back to join his friends. "The game can't be the same without your buddies. Or was this the plan you intended all along?"

Ryan smirked. "Let's say we had differing agendas. James didn't have the vision."

"So, you found it necessary to do away with him?"

"Unintended consequence." The eye under the

dagger tattoo twitched. "We had a perfect plan which backfired during execution."

"Hmm," said Rory, "you intended to give the flask to Perry Benson?"

A sardonic chuckle. "Benson," he said with disdain and wrestled the girl to the hearth, keeping her body between him and the bookcase where the rest stood. Ryan nudged Rosco with his work boot.

The dog moaned. Esther gasped.

Nina's eyelids popped open. Her body limp and chin down, she locked eyes with the detective.

Man, oh, man. He didn't know how to read her. Desperate or insistent? A toss-up. Thunder Clan, dog sitter, human shield. Then, her focus slid toward the beaded sack. Back to Rory. Down, again. Through it all, her body remained motionless. Was she sending a message?

The pouch bothered him. He couldn't put a finger on why. Odd though. It was different today, not just the extra bulk, which was unusual since it typically held only her slender journal. He'd never seen Nina without the tribute to her Native American heritage and a handy extra pocket.

"Collateral damage," Ryan said. "Benson showed up at the wrong place at the right time." He chuckled and steered Nina to the desk.

As they passed, Nina did the pouch-detective-pouch glance again.

Ryan poked the weapons on the desk with his knife. "This all you got? Not much fire power for a police officer."

"Don't need power, we've got Right and The Law on our side."

Ryan harrumphed, then twisted the leather strap, jerking Nina upright.

"Hey," yelled Thacker.

Ryan slid the dagger tip to just beneath Nina's ear and leered. "The boss man said stand down. Be nice, or you'll end up in the carriage house with Officer Policeman. Where is the list?"

Then it came to Rory. The girl always wore the leather strap over her left shoulder with the sack draped by her right hand. Right to left, not left to right. It was a message. But what did it mean?

"I have the paper," Esther said, stumbling forward.

Ryan turned the knife toward her. "Not so quick."

Stunned, Rory's heart leaped. She didn't have the list. He could see the yellow page on the desk between the phone and the *Magic Thinking* book where he'd left it.

"If you know what's good for you," growled Ryan, "I'll take it and the decipher code."

Decipher? Ryan didn't understand the list or how to use it? Daggerman had intentionally left the page in the sedan for him to find. All along, he'd planned to intimidate someone into explaining it to him—perhaps even when he intercepted Esther that morning. Ryan, the brute, like so many bullies, was lazy and not half as bright as he thought himself to be.

"Better let me translate it for you," Rory said in his manly-man voice. "You don't want to get it wrong."

Esther's eyebrows knit. He cleared his throat. "Miss Mullins can write it down. Esther?"

"Of course," she said, advancing to the desk. She paused and looked at Ryan as if asking his permission. At his grunt, she sat. "You may want to release Nina so you can see that I write it out exactly as the detective dictates."

Squinting with one eye, Ryan gave her a menacing glare. "I'm not a fool."

With his hands held at his sides, Rory grasped the rookie's pant seam in his fingers. "Perhaps, Office Thacker can act as scribe?" he suggested, stepping toward Ryan. The officer came along step by step.

Ryan yanked the strap holding Nina. She flinched and gave a surprised yelp.

Thacker's radio burped. Ryan wheeled on the police pair. "What's that?"

Static "*Come in Hen House, over.*" Static.

Confused by the sudden outburst, Ryan hesitated.

Rory lunged. The rookie acted in tandem, and they didn't have time to blink before reaching the assailant. Nina began to fold. Esther's chair slammed into the wall. Rory overtook Ryan, wrenching his arm from the strap, heaved the leather over Nina's head, and grabbed her around the waist. Thacker snatched the knife from Ryan while Esther plucked the beaded pouch from the floor, swung it lasso-style over her head, and whooped him right in the dagger.

Ryan went down—out cold.

For a moment, time stood still. Then a collective, massive exhale. Rory's heart hammered inside his chest, and he took another deep breath as Thacker pulled handcuffs from his utility belt.

Rory traded the girl for the cuffs. Squatting, he clipped a wrist, then secured the other in one fast, crisp motion. "Better check the bag," he said. "You packed one heck of a wallop."

Esther looked at the detective, emotions he couldn't

assess surfacing in her eyes.

"I believe Nina meant to keep the secret," he said.

She opened the pouch and pulled out a Bible. "I don't understand."

"It seems we had more than The Law on our side."

"But there is no Bible on the book list."

"I suggest you look again."

Uncertain, she perused the list. "*The Magic of Thinking, For Whom the Bell Tolls, Animal Farm, Most Secret*... I don't see..." She looked up, her eyes bright. "It's an acrostic puzzle."

He grinned. "Ignore the first title, and take the first letter from the next six—"

"Why, Rory, you are a genius. Every book with 'family' in the title? I thought you were crazy, but I now see only a cagey old coot would have gotten this."

Back were her tenacity and determination— probably fueled by relief, yet every indication she had weathered the scare.

"The Bible itself isn't important," he said. "See what secrets are tucked inside."

She opened the book and extracted a document.

"Birth certificate or marriage license?" he asked.

"How did you know?" Her face flushed, glowing with pride. "Impressive."

He hadn't been sure how deeply he felt about her until that moment. Her praise was intoxicating. He held out his arms, and she slithered in without hesitation. "Well," he said, "thanks for using the secret to our advantage."

He couldn't see her face, but he felt her nose wrinkle. He wanted to hold her forever, but she wiggled loose. "We should find Axel and Office Hansen," she said.

"Thacker, radio Axel to come in, and have him pick up Hansen on the way."

Esther handed him the document.

Rubbing his chin, Rory said, "So, the housekeeper and the professor. If we hunt hard enough, maybe we'll come across Aponi's birth certificate." He turned to Nina. "You knew all along you were Michael Sheehan's granddaughter?"

She shrugged, returned to the hearth, and checked the dog's condition. She appeared wilted, yet more concerned for the animal than herself. "I thought it was time to hide the Bible when Ryan headed this way. It wasn't hard to pull it from the library shelf when Esther looked the other way." Rosco coming around, laid his chin on her knee.

"Did you know what was in the book, Nina?" asked Esther.

"She's always known. Isn't that correct?" said Rory.

The girl hung her head, and then raised it defiantly. "Yes. Yes, to the Bible, and yes, to the marriage."

From the look on Esther's face, she felt betrayed.

Rory called the station and requested a cruiser to transport the prisoner.

Thacker checked the handcuffs and fashioned a gag using duct tape found in the desk. While Ryan struggled, the young officer asked, "Why murder James and Phoebe? Without the nephew there is no monetary prize."

Rory said, "I'd speculate he poisoned Phoebe because James wanted the inheritance and didn't have the nerve to kill. Yew branches were plentiful. But I doubt Ryan planned to murder James, the goose with the golden eggs."

Esther went to sit with Nina. "If you knew you were her niece, why pretend to be the dog sitter?"

"I did not pretend," she said.

Rory cleared his throat. "Michael and TiKa's marriage wasn't general knowledge. Aponi was raised in the household, and until she married herself, there was no problem with the arrangement. Am I getting this right?"

Nina continued to stroke the dog.

"The marriage license was kept with the other important family papers in the dining room safe. But once your mother married, there was a whole new situation. It was no longer just a white man with a Native American wife, and all the prejudice that would have entailed fifty years ago. It became a Native American man whose wife had status and owned property and you felt the need to hide the truth."

"Is this right, Nina?" Esther asked.

"Crouching Bear wanted the land," the girl said. "She was Thunder Clan, he was Bear Clan."

"And your brother?" Rory asked.

Thacker had dragged Ryan to the stuffed chair, propped him against it, then hobbled him with tie wraps. The scumbag fought against it. The young officer wasn't handling him too gently. "There's a brother?" Thacker said, confused.

"Perry Benson," the detective said brusquely. "You know him as gardener, hardware clerk, and poet."

"My half-brother doesn't care about the land, detective." Nina's eyes slid to the bully boy. "Ryan befriended Perry."

"And from Perry, Ryan found out about the

treasure."

"Ryan has a need to hurt, to steal, to take what isn't his," Nina said with disapproval. "It is not the Native way. Perry knows this; he is Winnebago."

Rory harrumphed. "Ryan found James Sheehan, or visa-versa, James found Ryan." He raised one brow, "Perry went along with them in order to monitor their actions?"

"Only to steer them away from doing harm."

Rosco, fully recovered, leaned into Esther. She patted his head. He sighed.

Rory heard the police siren before Axel and Office Hansen burst into the room. It took another hour to wrap up, and transport the prisoner escorted by Hansen to county lock-up.

Esther insisted on riding home with Axel, much to Rory's disappointment. He left Thacker to secure the house, and Nina.

A long day, Rory thought, but another criminal on his way to justice.

He drummed his thumbs on the steering wheel, his mind ticking on what was left to do. Pick up Benson. Talk to Tom Hutchinson. Interview Lillie Anderson, again. Where was that translation? Some detectives dreaded the wrap up and the paperwork. Not him. Sure, he enjoyed the hunt but seeing it to the end, fitting the pieces into the puzzle left him buzzing.

Crazy.

He wished he'd insisted on taking Esther home.

Epilogue

The sound of the elevator signaled Esther's arrival. Rory looked once more at the table. Wine goblets, placemats, candle sticks, all where Marilyn suggested he place them. He unfolded the list and checked it: mood music, fairy lights, evergreen sprigs, champagne. Commander, lying on the back of the couch, opened one eye and gave him a disapproving look.

"It's for a good cause, boy." He refolded the paper, took a lighter from his pocket, and lit the candles.

Marilyn had delivered the roast chicken and potatoes earlier, transferring them from foil pans into glassware dishes which she placed in the oven to stay warm. The great room smelled savory.

Crossing to the entertainment center, he put the CD in the player and adjusted the volume, so it was just audible. Thacker assured him before he left for his dinner with Nina that the famous jazz singer would set the right mood. Rory wasn't so sure the mood needed adjusting.

The elevator groaned. What had he forgotten? He glanced around fleetingly. A dozen red roses were nestled in the florist box on the coffee table. The champagne chilled in the borrowed ice bucket.

He patted his pocket—gift handy.

Rory straightened his tie when the lift stopped, and the tapestry was pulled aside.

Esther entered, slipping off her coat. She smiled

softly, the kind of smile that made his knees weak. Then she strode confidently into the room. "I hope I'm not too early."

She wore a breathtaking, sleek black dress. Her brunette hair brushed to a glossy shine, matched the sparkle in her eye. He noticed seed pearl earrings when she swept a loose hair behind her ear. Perfect, he thought—she was perfect.

"Not at all. Commander hasn't started to pace the floor."

"Something smells delicious." She glanced around. "Axel wanted to drop me off before he headed to the lodge. Although, I suspect he's lurking somewhere down below." She scratched the tabby under the chin. "You know, keeping dark, nocturnal beasts at bay."

"I can have a word with him?"

Noticing the ice bucket, she said, "Do we have time for a drink?"

"Absolutely." He had no idea if extra time in the oven would ruin their dinner, yet he knew she wouldn't complain. He did the honors, handing her a glass. "Cheers." She lifted one brow playfully. "Not down the hatch?"

His cheeks heated. "I could have offered, 'To crime, punishment, and the men seeing the first ends in the latter.' It's the only other toast I know."

She tapped his flute with hers. "I like that one."

"Thacker and Nina have gone out?" she asked.

"It's poetry night at Kenny's Koffee Shop. That boy wouldn't know romance if it smacked him in the face."

"Hmmm," she said, taking another sip.

The roses. He could have smacked himself. "These are for you," he said as he lifted the box. "Marilyn left a vase."

She followed him into the kitchen area. "The table looks lovely," she said, peeking into the oven. A savory herb aroma escaped.

He managed to get the roses into the water and onto the table. When he turned, she was taking out their dinner. "This looks and smells awesome," she said, placing the ovenware ceramic dishes on the table. "Is there salad, too?"

"In the fridge. I'll get the bottle," he said. After topping off the glasses, he sat and raised his glass. "To you."

"To us," she said, blushing.

They talked about the weather while they ate. Rory admitted his impatience for spring to arrive. Esther said her car would be ready by Friday, and she mentioned her sister, Jesse, would be coming home the following week, having missed all the excitement.

"Oh," he said, "Lillie Anderson called with news on the Ho-Chunk letters. It seems they contain the oral stories passed down from generation to generation among the People of the Big Voice."

"So, possibly written by TiKa?"

"Lillie Anderson says the elders don't believe a woman is among the people proficient in the written language."

Esther's lips pressed together in a grimace.

"That's what she said."

Then, they ate in silence for a moment with Rory wondering when to present the gift and she, he assumed, savoring Marilyn's cooking skills.

Esther said, "I know you don't want to discuss work."

"No, it's okay."

"I have some questions."

"Shoot." He took a bite. It really was an exceptional meal.

"Why did Phoebe name me as executor?"

"She had great trust in her friend, Marilyn Beauregard."

She concentrated on a potato, pushing it around on her plate. "Even so, why didn't she leave the property to Aponi? Wasn't it rightfully hers?"

"While it's true Aponi was Phoebe's sister, Aponi didn't want the burden. I understand they discussed the will beforehand and agreed the library and the college were their best options. Nina was in full agreement. Financially, they couldn't care for the property. Nor could they gift the land to the Ho-Chunk or Winnebago tribes. There are many government laws about ownership, and selling was their only other option."

"I agree, neither Aponi nor Nina would have wanted to lose the land. It's their home and TiKa's resting place."

"I suppose."

"What did Nina mean when she said Crouching Bear wanted the land? And that she was Thunder, and he was Bear?"

He set his fork down and leaned back in the chair. "Thunder Clan are the rulers, the policymakers. Bear Clan are the soldiers, the footmen. I don't understand it, but powerful women threaten many men."

"Aponi seems meek."

"Perhaps, but Crouching Bear doesn't like the respect the tribal members give her."

"And he wanted the land?"

"To better his standing, to be envied among his brethren."

"If they couldn't afford to maintain the mansion, how did Crouching Bear think he could?"

"Maybe he didn't intend to keep it. Money would do the same trick." He picked up the champagne and discovered they'd emptied the bottle. "More wine."

"Sure. One more question. Perry Benson?"

He chuckled. "A great relief for Thacker. Crouching Bear had a son with his first wife. Father and son didn't have the same temperaments. The son was quiet, the father rowdy. Perry is easygoing, while Crouching Bear is easy to anger. Their relationship was tremulous at best. The new wife only amplified the differences between them."

"Perry changed his name?"

"His birth name is Peter Crouching Bear. He changed it when he moved out. I think, at his father's request, who openly dislikes the boy."

"How sad," she said. "But, yes, good news for Thacker."

Rory rubbed his head. "I don't understand the separate dwellings. Obviously, Aponi and Crouching Bear managed to have Nina."

"Many women find it congenial to live apart from their husbands."

"Like I said, I don't understand it."

"This is a lovely dinner. Thank you, and my compliments to Marilyn."

He stood. "Dessert or more wine?"

"I think I'm at my limit," she said. "But this has been a grand way to celebrate Valentine's Day."

Commander wandered over to the table, rubbed his

head on the chair leg where Esther sat. "Oh, Big Boy, we've left you out." She stood and swooped the tabby into her arms. He began to purr. "I can help you with the dishes before I call my chauffeur."

Panic. He still had the gift in his pocket, and Commander was getting all the attention. "Did I tell you how lovely you look tonight?" Naturally, his voice cracked.

"Not in so many words."

"I mean not just tonight, every night."

"It's okay, detective. I think you look swell as well." It made her giggle, and the tabby wriggled free.

He fingered the box. Slowly slipping it from his pocket. "I have a Valentine's Day gift for you."

"Oh, I didn't bring you one. I thought—"

"I don't expect one," he said, gathering his nerve. He held the box out to her.

After opening it, surprise, then pleasure crossed her face. "Why, it's pearls. My pearls."

"I had them restrung. Don't look too closely. I had to add a few, and they're not quite a match."

"They're perfect."

She handed the strand to him so he could work the clasp. She stood back, fingering the beads. "What do you think?"

"They are beautiful. You are beautiful."

Esther gazed at him without speaking. He couldn't read her response but figured he better get on with it before he lost his chance.

"Not only are you great," he said. "No matter how hard the job, how direr the situation, you soldier on with kindness and intelligence. We make a good team."

Her eyes were moist, and he almost lost his nerve.

Should he stop while he was ahead?

"Funny," she said softly, moving into his personal space. "I've had the same thoughts."

He reached for her hand and squeezed. She smiled, that winning, wholesome smile that made him feel all-powerful yet powerless.

"I have another item," he said, pulling it from his inside pocket and slipping it onto her finger. "My grandmother wore this until she gave it to my mother. Who wore it until she gave it to me. I think they'd both approve."

"Rory," she whispered.

"Please, say you'll be my wife?"

Tears pooled on her lower lashes and Esther lifted a hand to her mouth.

*Gawd, he was a big, clumsy oaf.* Too insensitive. Too blunt.

"If you need to think it over…" He searched her face, then quietly added, "I love you," wiping a tear from her cheek.

"I know," she said.

"I know, you know," he said.

She laid her head on his shoulder, and he pulled her into his arms.

"Did you also write a poem?" she whispered when they came up for air.

He had.

But he had no intention of tampering with the mood.

## A word about the author...

Terry Korth Fischer writes mystery and memoir. Her short stories have appeared in numberous anthologies. Transplanted from the Midwest, Terry lives in Houston with her husband and their two guard cats. She enjoys a good mystery, heat and humidity, and long summer days. Visit her website at https://terrykorthfischer.com

http://terrykorthfischer.com